CW00421207

DARK WINTER FATEWEAVER

Volume One Of The Fateweaver Trilogy

By Cameron Lisney

PROLOGUE

~Then~

Sunlight drooped lower and lower under the horizon of trees, their rich green twisted into a hallowed darker shade. The creatures that had been hunting during the day retired to their safe places; under rocks, up branches or inside caves; some satisfied and relieved to have eaten today, others desperate and famished.

Freon reached up to grip the water-sodden rope dangling down for him over the cliff face. Carefully he took hold of the rope in both hands and began the routine climb to his home above the valley. Though he made this journey every day, it was never easy, and tonight was no different. The rainwater soaked into each thread of the rope made it difficult to grip onto and his hands were still bloody from today's catch. As he climbed the white granite stone, higher and higher, the weight of the hunt and his other bundle continued to encumber him.

Sweat fell from his matted hair into his eyes, making it difficult to see where to place his waterlogged boots. The tightly wrapped bundle around his chest began to wriggle. 'Not now,' Freon whispered to himself.

Quickening his pace, he reached up higher for the rope with each stride his muscles whined for a break but he did not relent. Further and further he climbed, the bundle on his chest continuing to wriggle and squirm. For a moment he lost his footing and slammed a knee into the sharp surface of the cliff, the distant ground glaring at him from far below, but he could not slow down now.

Steadying himself, he pushed on to the top of the cliff where he cautiously lifted the hunt onto the cliff edge and hoisted himself up after it. As he did this, the bundle on his chest let out an eye-watering cry; his son had awoken from his nap.

It took quite some time to settle his baby boy, Freon was still becoming accustomed to doing this on his own. Finally, after rocking him back and forth and humming melodically, he managed to settle his son down so that he could start a fire and prepare for another cold night. Tucking the baby tightly into the bed of pelts and furs, he returned to the smouldering fire in the centre of his small cliff cave home.

He thoroughly roasted the day's hunt, his mouth salivating as he did, until he was happy the meal was done and ready to eat. Plucking the charred chunks of meat from the stick he'd used to cook with, he ate hastily but not too quick that he could not savour the meal. Gratuitously he finished the meagre dinner, careful to eat every last morsel of food he had allocated for himself, while lovingly collecting the best parts for his son when he awoke.

As he did this and prepared to settle down for an anticipatedly uneasy night's sleep, he could hear a low rumbling noise, like the sound of an ancient bear growling. Standing up and looking out of the mouth of the cave, he searched for its source.

The sky was charcoaled and the stars were entirely absent, a thick sinister fog drifted across the ground like a nest of snakes. The sound whistled over the top of the cliff and Freon could tell whatever it was, had to be above him. The growling developed so that it sounded like the roar of dragon's breath, when a blazing sphere of bright blue flames blasted into view, tumbling down from the sky towards the earth. Through the cyclone of fire, Freon could make out its elongated and peculiar shape; something quite extraordinary hid within the flames.

Freon stood up in time to see the burning vessel for just a moment more before it crashed into the earth several miles away. It landed way beyond the forest that Freon frequently hunted in, he estimated it would be at least a three-day trek. Impulsively intrigued as he was by this mysterious flying sun, he tried to put it out of his mind.

He turned back to look at his beautiful son, sleeping carelessly in the centre of the cave and thought whatever it was that had just crash landed, would have to go unexplored for now. After all, having to fend for a one-year-old and trying to survive in this dangerous new world wasn't the best time to feed his addictive curiosity. The blazing phenomenon would remain a mystery to Freon and his son, at least for the foreseeable future.

CHAPTER ONE

~Now~

Time was crucial if she were to get this right. It had been on her mind for the entirety of the week, leading to several nights of not being able to sleep properly. The advice from like-minded mums or culinary experts could not help her now; Heather was on her own. The sky outside had dipped to a warm grey colour, the moonlight struggled to pierce the clouds but the neon lights littering the city had no problem leaking through her window as she worked.

Her blade glided through the parsnips like they were warm butter. A chilled hum and buzz emanated from the fridge, and the oven softly purred as the temperature rose. In the next room, Heather's son played with his toys, imagining fantastic worlds and playing with heroes from another planet. His yells of glee and excitement could be heard throughout the apartment.

Heather continued to slice through the vegetables, then scooped the pile into a heavy glass container to put in the oven. Glancing at the clock in the corner of the fridge display, she rushed back to the counter to sort the rest of dinner. Time … twenty minutes left.

Heather had been married for a challenging six years. Her wife Kirsty worked in the consultancy industry. Her role in a large international corporation was recruitment; which in Heather's opinion meant finding people that were good at bullshitting and giving them a job. This led to lots of late nights and early starts, not great for married life or for their son, Henry. Though it wasn't like Heather was around much either, her work kept her quite occupied at the moment too.

Kirsty's mother was coming over for dinner tonight. Not the highlight of the month, as Heather and Kirsty's mum really didn't get along. Judy had disliked Heather since they were first introduced. Quite early on she had openly blamed Heather for, as she put it, 'Turning my daughter into something strange and perverted'; those were her words the day they had met.

Since then, things had never really run smoothly between them and tonight was only going to make things worse. Eighteen minutes before she was due to arrive, a heavy-handed knock at the door sounded through the apartment.

As expected, the carefully prepared dinner did not go to plan. Heather sat at the corner of the dining table, next to her wife and son, opposite sat her mother in law, who was crudely picking at her food like a fussy vulture. Henry happily gobbled up the parsnips, absentmindedly oblivious to any hostilities in the room. Kirsty sat silently hoping they could have a pleasant meal with her mother for once but frivolously not taking sides. After the first few minutes at the table Heather knew the rest of the meal would be unpleasant, so she was just trying to finish her plate as quickly as possible.

The pointed questions and knife-like comments from Judy cut deep - 'When are you going to get a job with normal hours?' - 'It's not fair to expect Kirsty to keep picking up your slack when you come home late.' But Heather would have to deal with that tomorrow morning over breakfast. Before she left for the night shift, she tucked Henry into bed.

'Mum, why do you have to work at night time? Don't you want to go to sleep?' He stared into his mother's dark hazel eyes with curiosity and a hint of sadness.

'Because that's when my work needs me the most,' she replied, lifting the cover of Henry's duvet up to his shoulders, which was covered in superheroes from his favourite comic books. Then she put the cherished copy of Harry Potter down on his bedside table; they had been reading the series together for months, as often as Heather got the chance.

'Can't I just come to work with you? I don't want to go to sleep,' Henry said, pushing the duvet down a bit and rolling onto his side.

'No sweetie. It's not safe at my work,' said Heather, referring to her alleged career as a factory maintenance operative.

'But why, Mum? I'll be careful, you don't need to worry about me.'

He tried to sit up in his bed, pulling a heroic face while sticking out his chest. Heather gently patted his shoulder back down and kissed the top of his head.

'You are very brave, Henry, but even heroes need their sleep.'

Heather stood on the edge of the Trident, one of the tallest buildings in New London. The cold night air whipped through her cape, it flapped behind her like the wings of a demonic creature.

While Kirsty's work kept her away from home, pulling late nights and keeping her a slave to the office; Heather's work kept her away too, a slave to the entire city. She perched sentinel above it all, as she did before every night on patrol. This moment allowed her to drink the lifeblood of the city, see its lights and bright clusters of buildings. It reminded her of why she did this, night after night, year after year. Protecting this damaged place had become more than just a self-appointed calling; it was her obsession, one that she had poured the last ten years of her life into.

Taking a focused and controlled breath she leapt from the edge of the building, diving head first towards the ever-growing concrete below.

Over the last decade, Heather had become one of Europe's most renowned vigilantes. Feared by both criminals and civilians alike, she went by the name of Harrow. For a while, she was New London's sole protector, but over the years others had joined her. This was not to mention New London's police department, who had recruited their own heroes to work for the force.

About seven years ago it had become illegal to act as an independent superhero, a crime that would see you in prison for life. Unless you agreed to work for the government, which often meant law enforcement. You'd have a sizeable paycheck, health insurance, and matching uniform; this had never appealed to Heather. She hated the idea of working for a government, a corruptible entity with hidden agendas. This was a belief shared by many, and thus vigilantes from across the globe had banded together to form the 'Independent Network of Heroes.'

The Network provided many things to its hand-selected members; work, partnerships, technology and collection services for when the criminals captured didn't deserve the mercy of the current justice system. Somewhere off the coast of Spain, the Network controlled one of the most advanced prison facilities in the world. Named 'Terminus', it housed thousands of Europe's most dangerous criminals.

On this particular night, Heather was in hot pursuit of an individual that had attempted to break someone out of Terminus. Having leapt from the roof of the Trident; using her cape like a wingsuit and landing dramatically astride her motorbike; Heather was tearing through the streets of New London and the bullets were flying thick and heavy.

'It's Harrow! Get the bitch!' one of the passengers screeched, leaning out the window wielding an oversized assault rifle.

Harrow, the name that commanded fear and inspired hatred. There were few criminals that didn't know the name and even fewer that didn't flee at the first sign of her. Harrow didn't show the same mercy as other heroes; she'd either kill them or break them so badly they'd be wearing adult sized nappies for the rest of their life. The name didn't come to her in a vision or any special revelation, she had just decided on Harrow in the first few months of her career as a superhero. She was fortunate; a handful of heroes had been too slow to settle on a name and some smug TV presenter had beaten them to it. Golden Newt, The Laughing Rider, and Maskboy were some of the most recent examples, but heroes with shitty names end up in one of two places; dead or early retirement.

'Drive faster, Ty! She's right on top of us!' a second younger passenger yelped, panic oozing from his voice.

He held a small handgun out the window, blindly

firing in Heather's direction. Bullets shattered nearby shop windows and other cars, the sound of horns and wailing tires on tarmac could be heard streets away from them. Swerving through the traffic under fire, Heather raced towards the fleeing car on her custom Harley Davidson. The engine growled and the sound reverberated off the corridors of the city.

Bullet after bullet flew past her, never meeting their mark as though she knew when every shot would be fired and adjusted accordingly. Fiercely narrowing the distance between the car and her bike, with one hand she reached behind her back to draw her sword.

The driver dangled his sweaty arm out his window, flicking something with his thumb and dropping a grenade for his pursuer. Heather noticed it immediately, rolling across the ground towards her and then, as though it hit something invisible, it bounced several feet in the air. Opening the throttle and darting towards the bouncing explosive, Heather lifted her boot from the footrest and kicked the grenade back towards her attackers. Perfectly timed, it tumbled through the air before hitting the car bonnet and obliterating the windscreen. Frantically swerving, the driver caused the car to flip and roll through the flames, shunting another car into a lamppost as they crashed.

From the burning wreckage, the eldest passenger scrambled out, clutching her assault rifle in her sweaty hands. Engaging the autopilot switch on the handle, Heather leapt from her bike, cutting through the air with her sword held high above her head. Crushing down on the fleeing criminal, she sliced through her back, just as easily as the parsnips from dinner. The woman dropped to her knees, red gushed from her shoulders. Moments before hearing rustling from the driver's seat, Heather drew her handgun from its holster and fired a single shot through the driver's glass-littered face. He dropped the gun as his head flopped to the steering wheel horn.

'Please, don't shoot! I surrender, just don't hurt me,' the younger passenger crawled out of the upturned car, his hands and knees swimming through the shattered glass. Blood was already dripping down his face.

Pushing the body of his severed friend away from her, Heather stalked toward him. Skimming the tip of her sword across the road, making bright sparks flicker from the blade. Returning her gun to its holster she grasped her hand tightly around his throat.

'Your friend back there has been trying to get into places he shouldn't,' nodding towards the dead driver, her voice transformed and darkened by the speech modulator in her helmet.

'What did he tell you?' She loosened the grip on his neck slightly.

'About Terminus? He didn't tell me anything. Please don't kill me, I'll come quietly,' he pleaded, warm piss running down his leg.

'If you know that name, he told you enough,' she said, punching through his teeth; a few shards of them stuck to her glove as she retracted.

Sheathing her sword and pressing a discrete button on the side of her helmet she walked towards her awaiting motorcycle, its engine still purring.

'Network, it's Harrow. I need a collection for one, west river bank near the Coleman factory. I'll leave him wrapped up for you.' As she spoke she unravelled a thick steel cable from a compartment at the back of the Harley.

'Copy that, Harrow, we'll send a courier right away,' a voice in her helmet replied.

Heather securely tied the cable around the whining

man's leg, he was clutching his broken mouth until he realised what the other end of the cable was attached to.

'No! Please have mercy,' he begged through a mouthful of blood, scratching his fingers at the cable around his leg trying to untie it. 'You're going to kill me!'

'If you're lucky,' she scoffed, mounting her motorcycle.

'Harrow, it's Andrew,' the voice in her helmet spoke again.

'Yes? Is there something wrong with the site I gave you?' she replied, revving the thunderous engine. Police sirens could be heard nearby.

'No, nothing wrong with it. I just wanted to know if …' the voice awkwardly paused. 'If you were going to the Con next week.'

'Andrew I'm working, get off the comms.' She slowly started pulling away, dragging the squealing man behind her.

At a snail's pace, she pulled alongside the car the driver had smashed into. It was badly damaged but the two passengers inside seemed fine. Ducking down to peer through the crumpled window frame, Heather held up a pointed thumb towards them and they both nodded vigorously with looks of horror in their eyes.

'I know, I know, but are you going? I was hoping you could give me some more guidance. I'm really keen to get out into the field as it were,' Andrew asked, somewhat hopefully.

'Yes, I'm going.' Heather replied shortly.

'Great, that's great. Couriers are en route ...' he responded as she ended the connection.

The police sirens were louder and much closer now, the blue pulsing lights ricocheted across the skyscrapers surrounding them.

'Let's get you to your new home, sweetheart,' she whispered to herself, wrenching at the grip as her motorbike rocketed through the streets, pistons thumping, with the screaming reprobate in tow. A cry that sent Heather's mind wandering through the bowels of her memories.

CHAPTER TWO

~Then~

The cool taste of snow on her tongue was calming and soothing, reminding Heather of walking home from school as a child. The streets were crammed with drunken office workers, students and the blue collars. So close to Christmas, it seemed everyone was out on their work Christmas do.

A middle-aged man with thick curly ginger hair stumbled past Heather and her colleagues, waving at their group as he passed. His shirt was untucked and one of his shoes unlaced.

'You girls want to come back to my place? I can keep you very warm and cosy,' he drunkenly slurred, stood a few feet away.

A few of Heather's friends scoffed and hurled a few obvious comebacks at him, others just giggled.

'You're very kind, thank you, but not tonight,' Heather replied with a chipper smile. 'Have fun out there!'

The unkempt ginger drunk stumbled onwards,

sensibly knowing he would have no luck here.

'Why are you always so nice to nobs like that, Heather?' One of her co-workers asked. 'You shouldn't have even wasted your breath on that pig.'

'Ahhh he's not so bad,' she shrugged. Heather had a good way of seeing the best in people. Had, being the crucial word.

The night carried on with much excitement, gossiping and flirting. Heather's team were all quite young; in their early twenties. This night took place long before Heather had ever met Kirsty or chosen her less than ordinary life. She was nineteen, and the youngest member of this work Christmas do.

She wore a short black dress, far shorter than she should, considering how cold it was tonight. It had been snowing for the last eight hours and the high heels were proving difficult to walk through the snow. The alcohol pulsing around her body both helped and hindered this process. On the one hand, she felt a numb warmth, the unwelcome clumps of snow that had invaded the space between her toes didn't feel as cold as they really were. But the fuzzy view of the white covered street made walking extra hard, and she'd never been very sure-footed in heels.

Heather and the others were making their way to one of the most popular clubs in all of New London's south district, The Cave. Nestled deep below the concrete streets, The Cave was a nightclub totally underground. The only part above ground was the distinctive geological themed entrance. Standing out against high rises and skyscrapers, the entrance stood a mere eighteen feet tall. A grand pair of oil black doors barred entrance to the club beneath. The queue snaked outwards for at least a hundred meters. Men and women with chattering teeth bounced up and down on the balls of their feet and pressed their bodies close each other to keep warm.

As Heather turned the familiar street corner it was hard to ignore the length of this queue. Leading her colleagues past it, the group merrily skipped towards the doors and their protectors. Two metallic X fifty-two sentries stood guard, slowly letting in new patrons as horny and inebriated ones left. Approaching the robotic bouncers, one of the co-workers, Tiff, reached into her thin shiny black purse and retrieved a burgundy slip of paper, then held it out for the sentry to read.

'I see you have a fast track admission pass for you and five other guests. Please indicate who will be accompanying you this evening,' the sentry stated in the monotone robotic voice they were starting to become accustomed to. It had a slight American accent too, Heather thought that maybe the Americans did that on purpose when manufacturing the X fifty-two's.

'Just these bitches,' Tiff replied in a cocky and confident tone, pointing over her shoulder with her thumb at Heather and the others.

Amongst their group there was: Heather; Tiff, Heather's closest friend at the time; Callum, a lanky basketball player with a gruff look and patchy beard; Sara, very nosey and even more chatty (not the kind of girl to tell your secrets to); Georgie, a voluptuous gamer from Ireland who excelled at beer pong; and Steve, fairly quiet but very hardworking and generous with sugar on the tea and coffee runs. Heather had grown quite fond of them all in the few months she had worked for the company. There were others from the office that had been with them earlier, but they had flaked out in the pub they'd just left; made excuses about getting home for the babysitter, dog or to catch up on "Young Billionaires." In truth, they'd probably just struck out and gone home for a final drink and a quick wank. But for "these bitches" the night was still young.

'Thank you, ma'am, enjoy your night in The Cave,' the sentry stated, ignoring the profanity.

'Oh, we will,' Tiff said, giving Heather a not-so-subtle wink.

The six of them pounced towards the opening doors revealing a beautiful glass lift which looked like it was made of hundreds of fat gemstones. To the left and right of this, stood two deep-set spiral staircases carved into the rock itself. Though they couldn't see where the staircases or lift went to, it was clear they just went down.

Muffled sounds of club music vibrated through the walls as the group entered the lift. There were only two buttons on the lift panel; "The Cave" and above it, "Everywhere else." Reaching out her neatly manicured fingers, Tiff tapped the glowing pink button and they descended to the party beneath them.

Heather had not been to many clubs before, let alone The Cave. She'd turned nineteen just a few months ago and wasn't hugely outgoing, but Tiff had encouraged her to stay out later tonight. There was another reason she had agreed to come along, fighting the usual introverted desire to stay at home and watch her favourite yoga videos on the web.

A week ago, they had had a delivery at work, just stationery supplies and general bits for the office. Heather had been procrastinating at reception, milling about talking to Georgie, when the delivery arrived. Hair like a stallion and arms like a gorilla would be perfectly reasonable ways to describe the delivery guy. Heather couldn't help but stare at his defined physique. Georgie gave her a sharp nudge in the ribs, lacking subtlety. As the receptionist, Georgie had signed for the large parcel and as the gorilla-man waited, he turned to talk to Heather.

'Love your necklace by the way,' he said in a bright bold voice, pointing at her old Game of Thrones merchandise. His voice had a distant tinge of an Australian accent, Heather couldn't quite place it.

'Oh, thank you, winter's coming, right?' she joked, fondly stroking the silver wolf's head hanging from her neck.

'You know it! Hey, speaking of winter, what are you guys doing for your Christmas party? Ours got cancelled 'cause not enough people wanted to do anything. Trying to think of something else me and some of the boys can do.'

'Well we're going for a meal in town but then we're going to The Cave!' Georgie jumped in with rather too much excitement.

Heather, quickly realising what she was trying to do, kept her mouth shut and tried to act cool. Her skill at flirting had never really been a strength of hers.

'Nice, been there a bunch of times this year, great atmosphere. Already got tickets?' he asked, pretending to busy himself with his tablet but looking at Heather.

'Yes, booked for the eighteenth, there's a bunch of us going!' Georgie butted in again.

He transferred the receipt from his tablet and passed it to Georgie with a small grin on his face but not small enough to hide. He glanced at Georgie but his attention swung straight back to Heather.

'Will you be going ...?' he paused, trying to get her name.

'Heather,' she finally piped up, wanting to swim through his jungle-like locks. 'And yes, I will be.'

'Awesome, well maybe I'll see girls you there.' He tapped his fist on the reception counter twice and gave

Heather a charming and severely obvious smile. 'My number is on the receipt, send me an IM and we can meet up if you want.'

Smiling one more time and giving a polite nod to Georgie, he turned away and strode towards the exit. The two girls waited until the handsome delivery guy had closed the door before swiping the receipt open to see a phone number glowing at the bottom of the page next to a very heavy set 'Kyle'. From the other side of the office floor, some co-workers may just have been able to hear two poorly disguised squeals of glee.

Heather had messaged Kyle a day later and they'd been talking daily ever since, exchanging funny stories and playing twenty questions. He spoke about his cousin visiting India, and his love of motorbikes but he was also keen to find out more about Heather. She told him about her love of hockey, how much she adored spaghetti and why she couldn't help but sing when it rained.

The night before the work Christmas party she took a photo of herself; wearing new Christmas pyjamas from her secret Santa, they were tight and fitted her well. She sent it to Kyle with some cheesy phrase as the caption. The following day, hours before she left on the night of the party, she sent another photo; in the dark black dress she was wearing, it hugged her skin and curved smoothly with her body.

'What do you think?' she wrote.

'I think you know what I'm thinking,' he responded moments later.

Heather had planned to meet Kyle at the club tonight and had dressed accordingly. She'd never had much luck with men and her last relationship at college had just fizzled out. No massive break up or penultimate fight, just a decay into mediocrity and boredom. Heather hoped she'd have a bit more luck with Kyle.

As the lift descended through the club's spine, the music became louder and less muffled. After a few more moments the flashing white lights and luminescent neon glow bled into the lift, and the excited group of colleagues beheld The Cave in all its glory.

Strobes flashed and flickered in time with the heavy house music. Electric bolts of blue energy danced across the rocky ceiling, colliding with hanging glass orbs. The orbs generated more lightning-like energy, of which, the audible whip-like cracks could faintly be heard amongst the music. The sparks of blue lightning illuminated everything below them. Beautiful male and female dancers gyrating on raised platforms with eager and lascivious onlookers. Wearing very little, the dancers twisted and pulled their bodies in time with the music. Punters filled the busy bars encircling the room, pressing themselves forward to order a much-needed drink; the heat was fierce.

Exiting the glass lift, Heather looked down the sloped decline out onto the dancing crowd. A DJ wearing a loosely fitting vest top and a shark-like helmet, leapt into the air as the beat dropped. The crowd on the centre dance floor jumped up and down in time with the pounding of the bass, drinks spilling, fat jiggling and tits bouncing.

'Heather!' Kyle's voice cried out from behind her. 'You made it.'

Kyle was sporting an expensive black shirt, some well-known logo resting on his puffed-out chest, smooth grey jeans and well-polished shoes with several beer droplets ruining the finish. His chestnut hair was tied back and his beard neatly trimmed. Heather had been drinking, but even without the alcohol, Kyle looked gorgeous.

Walking up to the group, he went straight to Heather and gave her a warm kiss on the cheek, his beard gently brushing her jaw.

'It's so good to see you, how's your night been?' he asked her, paying no attention to the five friends around her.

'Yeah pretty good so far,' she replied, feeling a lot more nervous now they were face to face again.

'Well it's about to get a whole lot better, the DJ is on fire. Come on, I'll get you a drink.' He turned his shoulder towards the nearest bar. It was clear to see he'd already been to the bar a few times tonight, his pupils were like black holes and his stance wonky.

Heather turned to look over her shoulder for the approval of her friends.

'Go, you nob,' Tiff half yelled with a smirk. 'We'll catch you in a sec.'

But that was the last time that they ever saw Heather.

At nineteen, amaretto was Heather's drink of choice. Often, she mixed it with lemonade or something else fizzy, she'd always had an overpowering sweet tooth. Alcohol slows people down and alters their sense of reality, but for Heather, alcohol had a much greater disabling effect.

Since she was old enough to spell her own name, Heather had been able to do extraordinary things. Things that other little boys and girls could not do. Her first clear memory of using her abilities was at a very young age.

Standing at the top of the stairs in her childhood home, her mother screaming at her for a long-forgotten act of mischief, Heather cried and shouted back. In one fist Heather's mum held a half-empty wine bottle and in the other, a cheaply made trainer, the laces tangled up together like knotted hair. In her drunken frustration, Heather's mother hurled the shoe towards her daughter.

As the shoe tumbled through the air, soaring straight towards her, it was as though Heather could see what was about to happen, before it happened. The shoe crushed into her cheek ... tangled laces whipped across her nose ... Heather stumbled as she yelled out in pain and fell towards the mountain of stairs … and then, she blinked.

Her mum was yelling, wine in one fist, shoe in the other, rewound as though she'd never thrown it. She pulled her arm back and threw the shoe again, but this time Heather instinctively stepped to the side. The trainer slammed into the wall behind her. Completely bewildered, Heather stopped crying and stared at the shoe and then her mum, who drunkenly stomped up the stairs; apparently oblivious to this change of event. Imagining her mother misjudging a step and slipping, Heather blinked again. As though Heather had forced her mother's foot to miss the step, her mum dropped the wine bottle, giving Heather enough time to run to the bathroom and to lock the door behind her.

The discovery of these two unique and strange abilities didn't save Heather from the smacks she received later that night, but it was still an incredible revelation.

Over the following years, Heather continued to learn more about her power to control fate, how she could see events happen a few seconds before they did and how she could alter minor things around her. This made her teen years considerably more difficult for her than most girls her age, but her powers had come in handy numerous times and were the reason she had shelves full of sporting awards and other personal triumphs. However, with all the benefits that came with being able to manipulate fate, she did feel quite isolated growing up.

There was another element to her powers she discovered as she got older. When drinking alcohol, she was utterly powerless. She couldn't explain why it had that effect on her but it simply did. It wasn't just alcohol though, it was anything that inhibited her ability to concentrate. Severe dehydration, lack of sleep, un-bridled rage and right there in The Cave, on that snow painted December morning, it was the alcohol.

Kyle had just brought her another drink, she'd lost count of which number this one was. Having the abilities Heather had was quite incredible, but it was also exhausting, so occasionally she would drink ludicrous amounts just to give her a break from spoiling fate.

Grasping the slightly sticky glass, Heather eagerly took a mouthful and then reached out to take Kyles hand. They'd had a really fun night so far, or at least Heather felt that way. He had reminisced about previous visits to The Cave with his mates, complimented her dress and hair several times over and done some rather questionable dancing to some house tracks from the twenties. Heather was completely infatuated with him though; it was his charm and the dark chocolate eyes, that made her bashful and shy every time she looked into them.

'Let's get out of here, babe,' he said after they'd both knocked back another shot. 'I'm staying at the Phoenix Hotel.'

'I should really go see how the others are doing, I haven't seen them all night,' she replied, feeling quite guilty for abandoning Tiff and the others.

Kyle firmly held onto her bare arm, shifting closer to her in his seat.

'I'm sure they're having fun, now maybe it's time

we go have some fun of our own.' And with that, he stood her up and gently guided her towards the bright glass lift.

Taxis were uncomfortable at the best of times and tonight was no different. Heather's stomach had started to twist and strain deep within because of the alcohol, and now that niggling pain had started to writhe up her stomach and past her chest. Kyle sat close beside her, his hip pressed close to hers, hand gently resting above her knee.

The driver was friendlier than most, even at such a ridiculous hour he was chatty and light-hearted. He spoke about his son's degree and the plans he had after university, there was a lot of pride in his voice, the way he spoke was like he was talking about his own achievements. Kyle politely responded with some nods and 'mm's' but wasn't really paying much attention. His hand was gliding further up Heather's leg, sometimes dipping down to her inner thigh. She didn't know how she felt about this.

Arriving at Kyle's hotel he got out and paid the driver, as Heather stumbled out of the car, nearly falling over completely.

'She okay?' the taxi driver called out, as Kyle went around the front of the car to help steady her.

'Yeah, she's fine, no worries mate,' Kyle replied, pressing the two of them onwards up the steps to the hotel.

It was a cheap and stale place. Rubbish bags were piled up on the road outside and a couple of forgotten beer bottles lay dried up in the gutter. A flaky looking orange phoenix glowed half-heartedly on the sign outside the hotel. As they walked through the lobby, Heather stared at the grossly coloured salmon pink carpet and could see a few bits of chewing gum woven into the fabric.

'Kyle, I'm not feeling so good. Maybe I should just go home,' she said to him, glancing at his face but then back to the sticky carpet. She really wasn't feeling very sexy at all.

'Don't be silly, a little bit of food down you and some water and you'll be back to normal. Come on, I'm already checked in.'

He had one arm wrapped around Heather's waist, the other holding his phone as he messaged someone.

Stood at the door fumbling with his wallet for a second, Kyle forcefully pushed the room card into its slot. Holding an outstretched hand towards the dim room he ushered Heather in.

'Kyle, I'm really not in the mood for-' but he cut her off and pushed her body forward with his.

'Wow, she really is a looker. Nice work mate.'

The voice was coming from another man sat in the corner on an armchair. He wore faded jogging bottoms and a navy puffer jacket. Greasy hair slicked back with flecks of grey amongst the black.

'Who the fuck are you?' Heather glared in his direction, trying to sound more threatening than she felt, and quickly trying to sober up. 'Kyle I'm going, get out of the way please,' she said attempting to push past him.

'The fuck you are, darlin',' he laughed as he closed the door and locked it.

'Bring her over here, so I can get a better look at her,' the other man said, getting up from his chair.

'HELP!' Heather screamed, hoping to get the attention of staff or guests nearby.

Cool steel licked her neck, Kyle was holding a knife to her throat, gently pushing it and his body against her. She could feel his arousal already.

'Every room around this one has been booked by us, but just in case …' Kyle paused as he whispered into her ear. He slowly lifted the bottom of her dress up, revealing her jet-black lace underwear. 'Keep it down.'

The nauseating and soul tearing hours that followed felt never-ending. Heather felt pain throughout her body but mostly in her stomach. It felt as though it was being pulled into an abyss. The stench and putrid smells were overwhelmingly foul.

Morning finally came, and after a sleepless night of torture, the two men spoke to her once more. Heather lay broken and defiled on the ruined mattress, spots of blood and semen surrounding her.

'In case you're planning on going to the police this morning just know there are people watching you, your house and your office,' Kyle said flatly in a rehearsed tone, pulling his trousers up.

Moments after, the pair walked out the door without another dirty comment or filthy stare, their lust sedated for now. Heather lay on that hideous mattress for hours until one of the hotel cleaning robots knocked on the door to reset the room, oblivious to the depravity that had clearly taken place. A depravity would haunt Heather for the rest of her life.

CHAPTER THREE

~Now~

'Can I just say, your Harrow costume is freaking amazing.' An adolescent photographer was ogling Heather in the fast track queue to the San Diego Comic-Con. She wore an offensive yellow t-shirt with some electric looking tiny monster on the front, camera hanging from around her neck.

'Thanks, it's my first time cosplaying as her,' Heather lied to her young admirer.

'And you've done her voice modulator, holy shit it's spot on!' She'd started flapping her hands like two large hummingbirds.

'Big fan?' Heather casually asked. This wasn't the first time this had happened at a Con.

'How could you not be, the chick is a total badass! She defeated the Reaper gang, rescued half the royal family during Buckingham, and last year captured Professor Vantonder before he could slaughter all those politicians. Just last week there was a story on the web about her saving a six-year-old from being abducted, she's a fucking hero!'

Underneath the helmet, Heather could feel herself blushing very slightly. The queue began to move, she and the photographer shuffled forwards with the crowd.

'Not everyone shares your opinion of Harrow you know. Most just say she's a heartless bitch who kills for money,' Heather replied, a small bit of her hoping to get the contrary response.

'Yeah well, those people are morons, what she does is for the good of the people. Sure, she's pretty drastic at times, I mean, did you see what happened to the smugglers train four years ago? But she gets the job done. So how do you reckon she does it?' she said all this without taking a breath.

'Does what?' Heather asked but knew exactly what the girl was referring to.

'The super stuff. I mean, there's no denying she's got powers. Everything just seems to work out for her. She never gets hurt, she's always a step ahead of the bad guys and just the weird unexplainable shit that happens around her. I think she's got telekinesis or has some sort of energy manipulation ability.'

'Maybe she's an alien from another universe,' Heather jokingly theorised.

'Nah, she's way too hot to be an Alien. I know she's wearing armour, but those legs are the real deal.'

Heather had definitely gone a shade of pink now. The queue was starting to split, so people showed their tickets to stewards, and with a tinge of disappointment, she and the photographer were separated. It was not often Heather got to speak to people when she was Harrow, and most of the ones she did, either tried to kill her or run away. Though she didn't want to admit it to herself, she was having fun talking to this excitable nerd.

'See you in there?' the girl said as she was herded to a different steward, the hope quite transparent in her voice.

'Sure thing,' Heather replied, feeling as though the girl was gazing at her legs as she walked away.

'Ticket please,' an elderly man asked, his voice crisp and clean like it had just been valeted.

Heather held out her phone, the bold black and yellow light from the screen reflected off the steward's glasses. Scanning the code, his registration device buzzed twice. Then handing her a wristband and leaflet with the day's events on, he ushered her forward. 'Next!'

Heather walked past him and took an immediate left, obscuring herself from the queue behind. The energy and passion for all things nerd radiated from the crowd in front of her. Thousands of people squeezing past each other to explore all the stalls and exhibitions. Huge posters hung like tapestries from the ceiling, advertising the latest games and movies. All manner of costumed cosplayers posed for one another, the camera flashes bounced from one shield to another. Among the warriors, villains, and obscure Japanese animated characters, there were even a couple of Harrows.

Even from the entrance, movement and action were abundant. Graphic novels were exchanged for cash, many still eager to have a physical collection rather than going digital. Two teenagers were performing a choreographed fight routine, their hair span wildly as they dodged each other's blows and strikes. A boy of a similar age to Henry ran past a transformer, wearing a Batman mask, his joy and pure glee at his first Comic-Con was contagious, as he leapt into the air; but he didn't land back on the ground.

Stuck floating mid-air, the boy posed frozen in time, apparently completely unaware of the phenomenon. Beside him, the teenagers were also frozen in dodges and high legged kicks like statues from some of the stalls. A comic book vendor that had enunciated too forcefully stared at his droplet of spit flying towards a customer.

Heather turned around to face the entrance behind her, the grey-haired ticket steward with the crisp voice stood smiling at her.

'Harrow, great to see you! It's been years, I didn't think you'd come,' he said walking towards her, frozen geeks surrounded them.

'Nice to see you too, Otto. Yeah, Nahmar requested to see me. I see you haven't lost your touch,' she gestured to the paused convention hall.

'Ahh it gets harder every year, I keep getting older and there's just more and more of them,' his perfectly clear voice echoed across the silent hall.

Heather gave a polite nod to try and show kindness but her helmet covered her entire face, so communicating without facial expressions had never been easy.

'Anyway, terrible news about Captain Mega-stone. What a nasty way to go,' he said, respectfully shaking his head.

'Hmm,' the voice modulator in her helmet hiding the distinct lack of shits Heather gave for the death of this fellow vigilante.

Captain Mega-stone, (who in Heather's opinion was a cocky, egotistical ass), could control rocks telepathically. He couldn't talk to them or anything as ludicrous as that but could move and manipulate rock with his mind. Six weeks ago, he was killed in a showdown with a nemesis of his, Blackbrooke. On the bright side, he managed to bury Blackbrooke in the process but their bodies were trapped under the crushing weight of rubble for days.

'So why does Nahmar want to see you?' Otto asked, changing the subject.

'Can you let me in now, Otto?' Heather asked, feeling quite finished with the conversation.

'Of course, of course, Harrow.' Otto nodded apologetically.

Reaching into his pocket, he retrieved a small silver device with a single smooth button on it, like a light switch. Otto flicked the switch and a huge electric zap sounded below them, like the cracking of a whip. The noise then altered to a deeper lower pitched buzzing, it had a magnetic rhythm to it. A few feet away from them, beneath a group of steampunks and one of the duelling teenagers, the floor began to tilt up. Rising like a giant trap door, the people stood on top, frozen in place with some temporal gravity field. The moving floor revealed a grand dimly lit staircase, leading down to the Network below.

Heather handed back her Comic-Con leaflet to Otto and turned towards the secret passageway but as she placed her foot on the first step she turned back to him.

'How's your brother, Otto? I heard what happened. I'm sorry.' Even with the helmet on, she couldn't quite look him in the eye.

'Ahhh it's shit what happened to him. I told him these powers were too dangerous but he never listened to me, stupid fuck. I haven't been able to get a word out of him for months and I think it's getting worse. I think he's frozen time in his mind or something, not even Nahmar knows what to do.'

'He was better off just focusing on the small stuff, not everyone with powers needs to be a superhero. Sometimes it's better to just help your neighbour rather than the whole god-damn world. Even if it does mean you're a glorified doorman twice a year,' he smiled.

Heather felt quite guilty about being so short with him now, but not knowing what to say she awkwardly stood there; like one of paused thousands surrounding her.

'You best get down there, Harrow, I think you're one of the last ones.'

'Thanks, Otto. See you around,' said Heather, turning back to descend the stairs.

Pushing the remote's singular button, the trapdoor slowly lowered itself back into position, the people glued to it were carefully lowered with it. Otto wandered back to his table and on his way there, his eyes caught a beautiful woman dressed as a princess, with thick almond coloured hair and large boulder-like breasts. She was leaning forward to collect a dropped trinket, nearly spilling out of her corset, the oceanic blue of her dress matching a thin streak of blue in her hair.

'Now old boy, we've been down this road,' he mumbled to himself, shaking his head and trying to look somewhere else. Time unfroze and the young masked boy landed spectacularly, the choreographed teens introduced a spin kick and the busty princess stuffed herself back in.

Reaching the bottom of the stairs the noise of the crowd and themed music above began again, muffled and suffocated. The stairway opened out to a wider passage with clean white walls and shiny grey concrete floor. A young woman stood resting her back against the wall, talking softly into her phone. Illuminated by gentle pale light, the passage had no decoration or theming like the halls upstairs. It was plain and bare, all except a bronze plaque mounted on the door at the end of the passage. Engraved in the centre of the plaque were three impactful letters sitting on top one another ... INH. Below that, in a thin rigid font read; International Network of Heroes.

On approaching the door, the plaque began to glow white slightly, a dusty ethereal ring appeared and hovered a few inches in front. It was cloudy and on closer examination strange glyphs faded around the cream coloured fog, the ring of fog spoke.

'Who seeks entrance through this door?' The fog rippled with waves as it spoke.

'A hero,' Heather recited.

It dissipated, and the glow receded after hearing Heather's voice. Several clicks and pings went off at once and the door retracted into the side of the wall, allowing Heather to pass through the frame. This extra security measure was one that had become very familiar to her. The location of the Network was a very closely guarded secret by its members, of which there were relatively few. However, it was entirely possible that one of the three hundred or so selected members could betray the Network and reveal its location. Front doors enchanted with magic-like technology was just one of many ways the Network kept its members safe. Detecting if you were an unwanted visitor or a would-be attacker was the function of this ring.

The first thing that caught Heather's eye as she entered, was a young man barely taller than five feet. He paced across a small stage erected in the centre of the white-walled room. His hair was a brilliant white and his skin a soft caramel, he wore simple robes with sparse embroidered patterns. Surrounding the man were a hundred or so occupied chairs, spread around the stage in a deep semi-circle. Another man dressed in pale kevlar and a mask the shape of a bear's head, raised a hand amongst the chairs.

'Nahmar, what of the body? Has it been recovered

from the aftermath?' he asked the man stood on stage.

Nahmar's head was bowed as he gripped onto to the lectern in front of him, and as he lifted his gaze to address the question, he spotted Heather taking a seat in the back row. They looked at each other for a split second and then he looked back at the man wearing the bear mask.

'We have recovered Captain Mega-stone's body and our top medical professionals attempted to revive him but with no success, I am afraid he is lost to us.'

'However, with this sadness for a fellow fallen hero, we can find joy, as we honour all that he did and accomplished. I urge you all to share your fondest memories of Captain Mega-stone with others throughout the day, I know some of you worked quite closely with him over the years ...'

'Such a shit name,' Heather whispered to herself as Nahmar continued his eulogy. 'And where do shit names get you?'

'Dead or in early retirement,' a voice in front of her finished her sentence, just loud enough for Heather to hear.

The man who the voice belonged to stood up and clumsily stepped over his row to sit next to her. Unlike most of the people in the room, he wore no mask or disguise. Flicking his dusty blonde hair away from his glasses, he held a hand out to Heather.

'Zack Hemant,' he said keeping his voice soft and low so not to disrupt the others around them.

'Harrow,' they both said simultaneously as Heather firmly grasped his hand and shook it.

'I'm a big fan of yours, seen the stuff you can do on the news and to be honest, it's breath-taking. Sorry, I'm being too forward, aren't I? The last thing you need is another fanboy pestering you.'

Heather quite agreed, however, he had a soft smile,

so she refrained from telling him to move back to his seat. The two of them sat quietly for about a minute until Heather asked him a question.

'When Nahmar mentioned people that had worked closely with Mega-stone over the years he looked right at you, did you know the guy?' she asked him, still looking ahead to Nahmar as he addressed the audience.

'Yeah, I was his partner,' Zack replied, straight-faced.

Heather spun round to look at him with surprise.

'I'm sorry,' she said, feeling awkward and uncomfortable again.

'Ahh don't be, I told him it was a shit name that would get him killed.'

He turned to her with a grin on his face, showing perfect straight white teeth. A little chuckle burst out from Heather and a couple of heroes looked over their shoulders at them, one mumbling his annoyance in Portuguese.

The pair looked at each other properly, Heather looking into his crystal blue eyes and Zack stared back at his own reflection in her helmet. He had a very strong face, but it wasn't overbearing, his jaw was well defined and clean shaven. The glasses he wore looked customised, with an augmented reality lens unit clipped on the top.

'He was a great guy though and what happened really sucks. I'm gonna miss that old nut.' He finally looked away from Heather.

'Did you work together for long?' she asked. As she did, Nahmar came to the end of his introduction.

'For a handful of you, this is a first-time visit. We welcome you. There are free refreshments and lunch will be served at one if you'd like to stay. All courtesy of the bad guy's wallets,' he chortled at his little joke and the audience made a forced laugh of politeness.

It was common practice amongst vigilantes to keep the money confiscated at various gang or villain busts. They'd either donate it to charities, give to individuals in need, spend it on tech research, or just keep it. The common thread among the Network's members was that they'd never hand it over to the police; Heather did a mix of all these. Over her ten years of crime fighting, she had taken millions from criminals, and the suit she wore was just one of many things she'd done with that money.

When Nahmar finished speaking a schoolyard of activity began, with vigilantes from across the world sharing stories and experiences from over the last six months. The stage had now been cleared and a handful of tables were dotted about the room with food and drinks on. Beside one of the tables, a sultry looking inventor showcased his latest grapnel hook model. It used a gravity displacement field similar to the Comic-Con trap door; allowing the user to grapple up buildings, sticking to any desired surface without damaging the city's architecture.

Computers had also been set up, demonstrating the latest citywide surveillance technology; several men dressed as samurai were exploring the tool. Zack and Heather were stood in a corner near the Terminus exhibit, joking about a villain she'd beat called Grizmor who dressed up as a fluffy forest bear; the vigilante in the bear mask did not look amused when he overheard.

'Why don't you wear a mask,' Heather blurted out. 'Don't you have a secret identity to hide?'

'Not really, I've got nothing worth hiding,' he replied with a shrug. 'Besides I never really get out much; I'm more of a behind the scenes kind of guy.'

'You mean computers?' she said.

'Yeah, way to dumb it down!' he snarled jokingly.

'I handled all of Mega-stone's technology, finances, security, contracts, research; even did the bloke's laundry from time to time.'

'Don't you want some of the action?' Heather asked.

'Are you kidding? Get all of these golden locks ripped out by some off-his-face junkie,' he said, flicking his long blonde hair.

'No thanks. I prefer being on the other end of the phone to the loser taking the beating, or in your case dishing the beating. Never really been much of a fighter myself.'

They spoke for several minutes more until a woman carrying a thin glass tablet approached and interrupted them.

'Harrow, Nahmar would like to see you now,' the woman beckoned, then turned her shoulder to escort Heather to him.

'I've got to go, nice talking to you, Zack.' She meant it, as she stepped to follow the woman.

'Harrow, wait. I wanted to ask you something,' he darted in.

'I've been thinking about it for a long time, even before Mega-stone died,' Zack paused, acting a bit less confident now; like he was a nervous child about to ask a parent for something where they didn't expect to get a yes. He continued.

'I know you don't really work with other people and you've never really had any partners or sidekicks ...'

'I've got to go, Zack, just spit it out,' she said with some frustration, already having seen several seconds into fate and seeing what he was going to ask her.

'Will you be my partner? I need a new one and you don't have one. I'm really good at what I do, and I think I could be a real asset to you for what you've got going on in New London. I'm based there myself! I've got a ton of experience, not as much as you of course but I've got so much to offer you …' he spurted out. The assistant waiting for Harrow looked at the pair of them with her eyebrows raised.

'Let me stop you there, Zack. I appreciate the gesture, but I prefer to work alone.'

Heather turned away and nodded to the assistant, who sighed impatiently and led her towards one of the doors leaving the room.

'Wait, at least take my card.' He held out a thin black card; its corners were frayed and a bit bent. A cartoon character of himself with big curly hair posed on the front with a toothy smile and his thumbs up. Zack stuttered forward and handed Heather the card.

'Just have a look what I can do and think about it,' he said. 'I promise you won't regret calling me.'

The assistant led Heather down a side corridor to a thin oak door among a series of others like it. Heather reached out a hand to open the door but as she did, it was opened from the other side. Stood in front of her was the man who had just been speaking in front of everyone, Nahmar. He nodded to her and walked past, saying her name as he did. Another voice came from behind him.

Sat on the floor, legs crossed and in a meditative-like pose was another white-haired man. His skin was a similar warm colour to the first man's and his robes identical, although he was clearly a different man as their faces looked nothing alike, this man was also known as Nahmar.

'Harrow, how are you? Please take a seat,' he gestured to the floor in front of him.

Unlike the rest of the facility, this room had minor decoration; a couple of mismatched trinkets sat on shelves and there was a bespoke wooden desk with a beautiful birch chair tucked into it, the legs looked like the branches of trees. Nahmar sat on a thick woollen rug and incense burned around him. Covering a couple of the walls were paintings, all in different art styles, and in the corner was an art easel and paints.

'Thank you for your work on the Terminus leak, I was worried about the security of our prison for some time until you tracked that man down.'

He spoke very slowly, as though deliberately savouring each word. Heather didn't say anything, she just stood looking down at him, her eyes were sharp and unfaltering.

'I can tell you're frustrated to see me,' he said, looking up at her.

'Seven years, I must have met twelve Nahmars!' Heather yelled, towering above the small man. 'And now I meet a new one? What is your problem, don't you trust me?'

'You are one of my most trusted heroes, Harrow. For now, it is just better this way, safer for us all. Now, you want to know why I have summoned you here,' he said in the same calm tone as Heather grudgingly slumped to the floor in front of him.

Nahmar had over a dozen proxies that each dressed and behaved in the same way. They all seemed to know the same information and recall conversations that were had with them, even if it was a different Nahmar that was spoken to. Their ages varied and Heather was convinced some them used makeup to look older or younger. It was no secret either that Nahmar had many versions of himself, but which one was the real Nahmar still remained unknown to all, perhaps even the other Nahmars. The Nahmar she spoke to this afternoon was quite young and well postured, sitting upright and regarding her tranquilly.

'Harrow, I have another assignment for you. However, it is quite unlike anything I have asked you to do before. It will be more perilous than anything you have attempted in your career and there are men and women who have died trying to do what I am about to ask of you,' he said in his calm relaxed voice, but his eyes were stern and serious.

'I've been to hell and back before, Nahmar, what is it?' Heather asked, trying to mask her intrigue. It wasn't often he personally asked for anyone's help on specific cases.

'Tell me what you know about the seven deadly sins?' he asked.

'Christian monks used the doctrine as a tool to deter followers from giving into primal and base urges, like lust, greed and pride. The modern concept of the sins is linked back to a fourth-century monk called Ponticus,' recited Heather monotonically.

'And what an interesting fellow he was, where did you hear that name?'

'My mother was a Christian,' Heather replied, shifting awkwardly on the floor. Heather thought back to the countless Sundays her mother had dragged her to church.

Nahmar smiled politely, took a meaningful breath in, then continued.

'For the last four thousand years, our planet has been an unknowing habitat to seven incredibly powerful beings. Ponticus called them the seven deadly sins but their true names are the Pandarians,' he began, fear and hatred now visible in his dark maple eyes.

'Everything I'm about to tell you is going to sound irrational and quite insane but everything I say is true. The Pandarians are real and have been a very real threat to mankind for millennia. Their claws are sinking deeper into our world and soon it will be too much. I have been trying to find a way to destroy them for very long time. Fortunately, the weapon of our salvation has finally been recovered.'

From beneath his robes, he extracted a small silver cube. It was dark, rough in its texture and covered with strange markings and symbols. Protruding from the sides and lid of the box were indentations of the bodies of people contorted into weird and seemingly uncomfortable positions. Nahmar held the little box in the palm of his hand for Heather to see.

'You know what this is?' he asked, holding it out for her to take.

Nahmar couldn't see Heather's face under the helmet, which she was glad of as she wore an un-maskable expression of scepticism.

'Pandora's box?' she forced herself to say, perhaps coming across more mocking than she had intended.

'That is one of its names, yes. The important thing is that this box is the one and only way to stop the Pandarians and contain them.'

Nahmar returned the cube to a pocket tucked away inside his robe, the whole while looking into the one-way glass of Heather's helmet.

'Since they arrived on earth, the Pandarians have been a blight on our race. Residing inside human hosts, they have worked their way to positions of great power, controlling our societies. The Pandarians not only control what we watch, eat and say but they also influence how we feel. Injecting feelings of lust, greed, wrath and envy into our hearts, they feed on these behaviours. Our "sins" as religions call them are literally a food, a fuel to these beings and they are insatiably hungry. They feed off our darkest emotions and they're doing everything they can to encourage more from us.'

'I have spent my entire life seeking the identity of each of these beings and looking for the means to destroy them. They must have a human host to control and manipulate, without one they are powerless. However, there are millions of powerful people in this world that are available to them to invade and use, thus destroying the host was meaningless without a way to capture the Pandarian inside. Until now.' He patted his robe where the cube sat.

Before Nahmar could catch his breath, Heather got a question in, wanting to establish more of what this farcical quest would involve.

'Who are the hosts?' she asked.

'In the past, they have been conquerors, kings, inventors and explorers. Now they are in more modern seats of power; politicians, celebrities, artists and CEOs. Seven powerful men and women across the globe, that need to meet someone with your talents.' He stared into the glass of Heather's helmet, as though he could see right through.

'Why ask me? There's plenty in the Network who are just as capable, probably more so. For what you're asking, you need an experienced assassin, not me,' she said in a dismissive tone.

'I've asked you, Harrow, because I know what you are capable of. And though you might not like to admit it, you're a Fateweaver.'

Heather sat back a bit, startled that the small white-haired man had figured it out. Anger began to boil up inside her, wondering what else he knew that he was keeping to himself.

'I know how you can see glimpses of what is about to come and how you can alter reality in the subtlest of ways. Not many Fateweavers exist anymore but I know one when I see one. Most of all Harrow, I asked you because I trust you,' he sighed, sounding somewhat exasperated.

'Well I don't trust you!' Heather burst out. 'First, you show up, a new Nahmar that I've never met before. Then you give me this bollocks story about evil beings that are taking over the planet, hiding in the bodies of the world's leaders. Finally, you claim to know what I am, in what? … an attempt to relate to me? You have no idea what it's like to have these powers, how utterly exhausting it is to constantly see what's about to happen, especially when it's something you don't even want to experience once! What were you hoping to gain by telling me this?'

He remained in the same calm cross-legged position on the floor as Heather rose to her feet.

'No, don't say anything. As you've pointed out, I already know what you're going to say before you know it.'

'Find someone else to be your trigger puller, I've got real work to do back home.' Heather turned to walk out, her fists clenched with rage.

'Harrow, whatever your opinion of me is, it must be put aside for the sake of humanity's protection. The Pandarians are real, soon you will see that for yourself. They will corrupt and poison even the greatest among us. They will not stop until this world consumes itself and there is nothing left. Their hunger knows no self-restraint and the human race will be destroyed because of it. I will be right here when you decide to let go of your pride and stop acting like a child,' said Nahmar with un-maskable frustration.

And with that she was out the door, slamming it behind her.

CHAPTER FOUR

Luke York had been an inmate at Graywick prison for six months; six lethargic, painful months. The morning began the same way it usually did, with roll call. Fifteen sleepy minutes stood by your cell waiting for a human guard to make sure you hadn't escaped during your sleep. A few years back they used androids for these sort of tasks but smarter inmates had figured out how to tamper with the facial recognition programming, so the warden reverted back to a more human orientated staff system. Luke, or Yorkie as the other inmates called him, was particularly sleepy today.

The others had decided to nickname him Yorkie, after the chocolate bar. His name was the obvious reason, however, it was actually because of the old snack's slogan - "it's not for girls." Luke had never hidden his sexuality outside of prison; what was there to hide? The problem was that any experimenters on the inside assumed Luke would give them a free pass just because he was gay. Six months of straight guys dying to get their cock into something other than their own hand meant they all came knocking at his door. Sometimes politely, other times less so.

'YORK!!! Get your head out of your ass!' the guard on roll call bellowed towards Luke, as his head nodded down about to fall back asleep.

'Though we all know you love things being up there,' the guard sniggered, loudly enough for most of the men around to hear.

This kind of snide commentary was just part of the daily homophobic abuse that Luke had been forced to deal with in the last six months of his life.

Breakfast was grisly as usual, you could always count on the Graywick kitchen staff to disappoint. As he ate, he stirred the porridge round with his spoon, trying to mix in the cold bits with the hot. Surrounding him, other inmates picked at their food, the sound of plastic spoons scraping across the bottom of the bowl were drowned out by the chatter and talk. Luke didn't speak to his table much, as his old cellmate and friend, Harry, had been taken to the infirmary. A shiv to the ribs had landed Harry in there last week and after breakfast, Luke was going to visit.

A smuggled chocolate bar tucked into his trouser waistband, he made his way to the infirmary; breakfast still sitting uncomfortably at the bottom of his stomach. Most inmates couldn't just walk into medical but seeing as he'd been there himself so many times recently, Luke had a good relationship with the doctors.

Walking through the maze of sick or injured inmates, Luke found Harry's bed.

'You know, I expected more of Dickins, really I did. An author that has survived centuries of competing literature and I was not impressed. What does that tell us about the things our society holds dear?' Harry said as

Luke approached his bedside.

'What would you know about impressive literature, you hadn't ever heard of Dickins until I told you about him yesterday,' Luke said, grinning at his pompous friend.

'Hello, my dove, how are you?' Harry softly replied, placing the book down next to his waist. Luke put his own hand on top.

'Ahh same old, bored and tired. You missed a great breakfast,' Luke joked.

'Is that right? Well you shouldn't have been such a terrible criminal on the outside and you wouldn't have gotten yourself landed in here with me now, would you?' Harry smiled sarcastically, brushing his finger back and forth across Luke's wrist.

'Doc says I can't stay long, but I brought you something.'

Checking over his shoulder that the room was quiet, Luke dipped his hand into his trouser waistband and pulled out the warm chocolate bar he'd smuggled in. Handing it to Harry he couldn't help but let out a laugh as he did so.

'What on earth did you bring me? Is that … a Yorkie!?'

The pair burst into fits of laughter and didn't stop until one of the Doctors asked Luke to take his hilarious act somewhere else.

The warm plastic of the communal phone rested against Luke's face as he spoke to his mum. They had always had a strained relationship, but prison had surprisingly helped the pair come closer together. She visited whenever possible and took his calls every Sunday night. For the first time in a while there was no queue of thugs behind him; eager to call their girlfriends or dealers, so Luke was able to take his time.

'She should get a dog or something, it might help,' Luke said into the scratched mouthpiece.

'I don't know if it will, sweet. Your sister is quite traumatised by the whole ordeal,' his mother replied on the other end of the phone.

'Yeah well, he was a twat, she's better off without him. Honestly, mum, I'm surprised it's taken this long to get rid of him.'

Luke stood with his back to the wall, resting his Graywick issued brogans on the badly painted skirting boards.

'Oh Luke. Let's talk about you, how did your counselling session go with Fran?'

'Mum you know how it goes, it's the same every time. I mean, she's great and she's given me some really helpful techniques to use, it's just ... difficult.'

'I know sweetie, I can't imagine what you must be going through. Listen, your lawyer came by the house yesterday to speak to Dad and me. He explained what was going to happen at the hearing. We're going to get you out of there, Luke.' The desperation and hope were both transparent in her voice.

Six months prior, Luke had been driving home from work; racing down familiar country lanes to get home for his favourite meal. Music was pouring from the speakers; Zoey Web was his favourite pop star, and he'd been in love with her music since hearing the first notes.

As he drove, belting out the lyrics word for word, he approached the familiar bend adjacent to a rustic pub house. He gently pressed his foot to the brake but it wasn't enough, and as he passed through the blind corner he collided with a college student, blind drunk and skipping across the road. Her body had hurtled through the air, while her intoxicated friends looked on helplessly.

Later that month, Luke was found guilty of manslaughter and sentenced to eight years in prison, by a jury and a judge that took pity on a young girl's grieving family. The girl had consumed enough alcohol to subdue a fully-grown man and walked out into the road foolishly but that wasn't how the jury saw it; with at least six eyewitnesses testifying that Luke had been speeding and driving recklessly. His lawyers were hard at work trying to build him a stronger case or find a way to reduce his sentence and Luke was hopeful, but it didn't make it easier to be in there.

'Thanks, Mum. Hey listen, I start my shift in a couple of minutes. See you on Wednesday?'

'Indeed you will, my son. I love you loads.'

'Love you too, Mum.'

Luke placed the grubby phone back on the receiver, wiping his hands on his trousers and face on his shirt collar. Then he made his way to the canteen to start his shift.

Work assignments were common in Graywick, and the better your relationship with the COs, the better your job. Luke didn't have a good relationship with COs, nor did he have the money to bribe his way to a better work assignment. Gardening was always the most attractive job to him, mowing the lawns, pruning the trees and just getting to spend an extra few hours outside each day. Graywick was just on the outskirts of New London and despite its name, the weather was mostly good around here. However, instead of being out in the delicious sunlight, Luke was glued to a sticky tiled floor, mopping the empty canteen after dinner. The multicoloured strands of the mop head were frayed and battered, and though he'd asked the CO in charge of work assignments for a new one weeks ago, nothing had been done about it.

He splashed a big dollop of steaming hot water on the tiles, forcefully spreading it across the filthy floor. Erasing muddy footprints and removing grisly food evidence was another daily punishment Luke endured, he had never enjoyed mopping, even on the outside. However, on the plus side, it kept him out of trouble; he had the entire canteen to himself, and having personal space was not something he had in abundance right now.

Hot water poured down Luke's face, with soap running down his chin and neck. After finally completing the canteen he had made his way to the showers to de-grease and cleanse, which was very much needed after the sweat-inducing hours it took to scrub the floors.

Showering was once an extremely therapeutic part of Luke's routine; however, in Graywick it was something he could not wait to get over and done with. It was in these showers he had been approached for sex countless times, drastically impacting his desire to be clean; these days his showers were efficient and short.

He'd just finished washing his face when two older men stepped into the showers, grey towels dangling around their lumpy hips.

'Yorkie, glad we pinned you. Derek and I were hoping to find you in here and borrow you for a few minutes.'

The two men in their late fifties stood side by side in front of Luke, blocking his escape.

'Thanks for the offer chaps but I'm all done in here,' Luke said, turning off the shower and attempting to step around them.

The lumpier of the two men slammed a damp fist

into Luke's ribs, the sound of them cracking against his knuckles was just about audible. Old and lumpy number two, thrust a hand against Luke's still soapy neck, trapping him against the cold, wet shower wall.

'We don't care if you're done here, you piece of shit, you're going to suck Derek off and then you're going to do me.' With that, he pushed him down to the floor; Luke's naked knees smashed onto the sodden rough tiles.

Balding Derek removed the towel from around his waist and stepped towards the kneeling inmate, clasping his limp pecker in his hairy hand.

Before anything else could be done, the unmistakable sound of an explosion rumbled through the prison. The walls of the bathrooms shook a little and a tiny spurt of water trickled out the shower head.

'What the fuck was that?' the inmate still wearing a towel grumbled in confusion.

The pair backed away from Luke to listen at the bathroom entrance. They could hear distant yells and shouts of terror. In a rushed panic they ran to the dressing rooms to collect their clothing. Seeing his opportunity, Luke grabbed the discarded towel and made straight for the exit. Wrapping it around his waist, soap and water still dripping down his face he looked down the corridor. A young inmate, similar age to Luke sprinted towards him.

'What's going on?' Luke quickly asked him as he ran past.

'Infirmary, shit's going down!' the sprinter yelled behind him, as he ran in the opposite direction.

Luke hesitated for a moment, his body still wet and dripping onto the floor and his naked feet. In the moment of hesitation, the prison alarm sounded, white hot and blinding. The few times it had gone off during his time here, it had felt like his ears would bleed from the volume.

Without wasting another second, he grabbed hold of his towel tightly and raced towards the infirmary. Whatever was going on, he had to help Harry.

As he ran, he wanted to retract his head into his neck like a turtle; the sound of the alarm was practically unbearable. Twice he ran into men fleeing in the opposite direction, one of whom was a CO. He paid no attention to Luke at all, he simply bolted straight past him looking dishevelled and petrified.

Luke could smell it first, burning and a strange chemical-like smoke. The further through the prison he ran, the more smoke he had to charge through, making it much more difficult to see where he was going, his eyes stung painfully. Skidding around the final corner he could feel the extraordinary heat of a blazing fire enveloping the infirmary, the flames licked the corridor and completely encased the twin door frame. He stopped running as the heat from the fire became too overpowering. He tried to shield himself from the fire, but it was useless; the water from his naked body had evaporated entirely. Squinting at the flame-covered doorway he tried to figure out what to do. But before he could come up with any scrap of a plan, a tall figure encased in flame, emerged from the infirmary.

'Harry!?' Luke called out hopefully.

'I'm afraid he's busy cooking, maybe I can help you,' the figure crackled, projecting his voice forcefully down the melting corridor.

A hanging light fixture behind him fell from the structural damage and shattered on the ground, sending shards of glass spinning across the floor and past the approaching figure. Through the clumps of dense black smoke, Luke could just distinguish fire from body and recognised the man stood a few feet before him.

'H-helix!? Wh-what are you doing?' Luke shouted

through the smoke.

Menacingly pacing towards Luke, was the well-known superhero, Helix; whose suit glimmered and shined with the heat of the fire.

'Scum like you don't deserve second chances and free passes, the only punishment suitable for your kind is death,' Helix raised his hand while he said this, aiming it directly at Luke.

'No wait, please I'm not like …' but before he could finish his plea, a compact sphere of white-hot energy erupted from Helix's outstretched palm, hurtling towards Luke.

As the ball hit his chest, parts of it spread across his body incinerating the skin beneath. The rest of the ball bombarded its way through his chest and burst through his back, leaving a crispy hole the size of a large melon. Luke's charred and bare body fell to the ground, his back slapped sickeningly against the hot floor, his final thought evaporating.

CHAPTER FIVE

Half of the prison was still alight when Heather arrived. She nimbly dismounted her bike and scaled the prison wall using her newly commissioned grapnel gun, which she had collected at the Network. Slumped on the battlements of the outer wall was another dead prison guard, she'd seen three already. His face had been completely obliterated, a melted rifle still clasped in his hands. Smoke was drooling out of a large cavity in the main building, rubble scattered all around the opening; it was this that she ran towards. The neatly kept grass was dead and ashy like an infernal beast had slithered across it, killing everything it touched.

Leaping through the gaping hole in the wall, Heather landed in what was left of the Infirmary. Beds and medical equipment had been melted and destroyed, bodies lay frying in the heat. Using her powers as she navigated through the thick smoke, she willed the fire to simmer and die down, imagining it losing its speed and ferocity. It didn't help greatly but she made a small dent and was able to charge through the infirmary, protected by her armour.

She felt as though she was melting inside of it, but the suit had cost over two million pounds to create, so the flames mindlessly attacking were not too much of an issue. Dodging the naked body of a young man, the hole in his chest filling with ash and bits of crumbled ceiling, she briefly wondered who he was and what he might have done to end up here, before hastily continuing down a corridor deeper into Graywick.

Moments before it happened, Heather could see in her mind a large section of the roof collapsing, crushing her beneath the immense weight. She blinked and put on an incredible spurt of speed, charging beneath the groaning ceiling. The massive heap collapsed and came crashing down, narrowly missing the fleet-footed vigilante. Heather pushed herself to keep sprinting, taking short sharp breaths as the collapsing roof chased her. Diving through the air, Heather managed to avoid the last of it. Rolling back to her feet she immediately continued running towards the hottest point on her scanners.

Heather tore through the building until she found her way blocked by a large iron gate. It was unscorched; perhaps the arsonist had taken a different route, she thought to herself.

'Suit, deploy hydrofluoric acid,' she commanded.

A small compartment in her suit sprung open, revealing several vials of clear liquid. Without wasting any time, she hurled two simultaneously at the hinges of the gate and taking a few steps back for a run-up, she rushed towards the melting iron. Springing into the air for a flying kick, she hit the upper hinge, ripping it from the wall. Smoothly landing away from the fallen gate she continued through the prison. Moments afterwards, however, she was stopped again by another obstacle blocking her path.

'Did you see what that freak did to the block?!

Come on let's get out …' an ogre-like inmate paused as he noticed Heather. 'Holy shit boys, look who it is.'

The ogre and several other rather gruff looking criminals stood a few feet in front of Heather, who had now stopped running. One had a deep bloody cut across his face and another had been burnt along his right arm, but the rest all looked healthy, just scared.

'Are you going to tell me what is going on, or just stare with your dicks hanging out?' Heather said coolly.

'It's your fault I'm in this fucking shithole!' one yelled at her frantically.

'There's a bounty on your head, Harrow, dead or alive. Taking you down would set us up for life,' another jeered, looking around at the others to check they were thinking the same as him.

'Dicks hanging out it is then. Come on then fuckwits,' she withdrew her glistening black sword from its sheath and skilfully spun it round in her hand, 'give us your best.'

At the thought of being dismembered, the group deflated their puffed-up chests and stood down, trepidly pressing themselves against the wall to allow her to pass. Heather walked alongside the gang, religiously peeking into a potential future as she did.

'Do not leave the prison walls, if I catch you on the outside you'll wish I had finished you off in here.' She turned to continue the search.

'And if you try and throw that thing in your pocket at me, it will miss, and you'll be pissing blood for the rest of your miserable life.'

Darting in the other direction Heather could just make out the distinct sound of a poorly made shiv hitting the floor and one of them whispering.

'How the fuck did she know?'

Heather would usually slaughter scum like that without a second thought, but in here it felt cold-blooded and unnecessary. After all, she had come here to rescue inmates, not kill them herself and until they posed a real threat to her or others around her, they could keep their lives.

Having the prison layout and blueprints on her visor's heads-up display, she knew the quickest way to the cell block. This was where her scanners showed the largest heat signature, on the other side of the imposing nine-inch thick wall before her.

Speaking to her suit again she withdrew a small sticky grenade from a utility compartment. Heather squeezed the device against the wall and activated the timer, before taking a few well-paced steps backwards. Seconds later the device exploded, sending jets of blue and purple plasma waving across the wall. Rubble and debris blasted through the other side, scattering across the cell block floor.

Instantly Heather could hear the screams of terror coming from the inmates trapped in their cages. Helix stood centrally, launching balls of white fiery energy at each cell. Heather could see the wrath and anger in his eyes, the whites of them as bright as his projectiles.

'Helix, stop this!' Heather shouted out. She blinked and stepped calmly to the side, having seen the fireball he was about to hurl at her. It missed by several feet and blasted against the wall behind.

'Why are you doing this?' she shouted across to him.

His body burst into the same face melting white fire and he rose high into the air, the force of the fire allowing him to hover a dozen feet from the ground.

Helix was a well-known and much-loved hero,

especially here in England. His powers lent themselves to firefighting, as he could tolerate any level of heat he came up against. But firefighting felt small time compared to what other heroes were accomplishing, so he had expanded his offerings and dealt with all manner of situations. As with most heroes he had taken up the government's offer of being employed as a super. Not only was it a legal requirement if you wanted to participate in hero work, but it was also a hell of a lot easier. It seemed now however, Helix had decided to quit the day job.

'Harrow, I should ask you the same question,' he said with judgment in his voice, gently hovering in the air.

'Come down, let's talk,' Heather requested.

'I have nothing to talk to you about, now are you going to help me? Or should I eliminate the untouchable Harrow too?' said Helix.

'This isn't you, you're not a murderer. You save lives, you're a hero!'

'And I spent many years wasting my time and energy as one. Fixing the problems but not removing the cancer at its source. I spent so much energy putting out fires but never thinking to give the arsonists a taste of their own medicine. These killers, paedophiles and thieves … they don't deserve second chances, I thought someone like you would understand that.'

He stared at Heather, hoping for approval or some form of acceptance for the bloodshed he was committing.

'These men are scum, and maybe they don't deserve a second chance,' said Heather. For a moment she thought about the numerous men and women's lives she had taken or ruined over the last decade, feeling a sharp pang of guilt in her stomach. 'But this is not how we deal with it. Slaughtering them in cold blood is … wrong,' she said, staring back at him.

'Whether it's out on the street or here in prison, these men deserve death and I'm going to give it to them,' said Helix.

He rose up higher, building a white fireball in his fist. 'And if you are going to defend them, then you deserve death too,' as Helix said this, he ferociously hurled the scalding ball at Heather.

Elegantly flipping backwards in the air, she dodged the ball of lightning hot energy; even through the suit, she could feel its radiating heat. Landing cat-like she dropped a small canister on the ground. It spurted out thick clouds of black smoke, quickly concealing her movements as the plumes spread. Glancing at the ventilation ports in the ceiling, she blinked and envisioned a small component malfunctioning. Through her grip on fate, the fans immediately stopped spinning; a small clicking could be heard coming from each of them like the sound of a cog stuck in clockwork.

Helix continued his assault, blindly firing into the black, hoping to hit her but of course Heather knew when and where he was going to strike, even if he didn't. Reaching into her apparently never-ending suit of gadgets, she extracted a singular ammo clip of thick cryo shells. Slotting them into the blaster extruding from the gauntlet of her suit, she took aim and fired; doing all of this in a single breath.

The first bullet whistled through the air and hit the ex-hero hard in the chest. A patch of bright blue ice-like crystals burst across the point of impact, making Helix stop and falter for a moment. His white-hot fingers brushed the icy layer and it melted to his touch. Before he could look at his assailant, she fired again, this time shooting him in the neck. He shouted out in pain, grabbing hold of his neck to melt the spreading cold and with his other hand wildly hurling fire towards Heather.

Seizing the opportunity, Heather all but unloaded the clip of cryo bullets into him, every single one making its mark through her control over fate. As Heather attacked, she skirted along the edge of the block to take cover and catch her breath in one of the unoccupied cells.

Helix twisted and writhed in pain, thrashing mid-air, frantically trying to pat out the ice covering his body. Heather withdrew her sword and flicked a discrete switch on the hilt, instantaneously igniting the blade with thin wire-like beams of electricity. Sparks of the lighting jumped and sprang from the sword but most of the power flowed up and down the sharpest edges, the crisp blue of the sword's lightning reflected onto her suit.

Advancing out of cover to move in with her sword, she pre-emptively realised she had underestimated her foe, diving out of harm's way just in time as dozens of fireballs were launched in every direction, several very narrowly missing Heather.

Regardless of her foresight, it was extremely draining, darting out of the way of a continuous hailstorm of fire. Any inmates still in the block at this point were either dead or cowering under their beds, whimpering like mutts. Launching herself off the ground and just managing to avoid a wildly flung missile, she charged towards Helix once more, but having got rid of the ice patches covering his body, he turned and focused his attention entirely on the now exposed vigilante. As he threw blast after blast at her, she ducked and span out of the way, but the continuous onslaught had worn her down and even with her extraordinary gifts, she was too slow to dodge one final fireball.

Knowing she would not be quick enough to dodge this one, she dropped her last smoke canister as the painfully hot ball crashed into her breastplate. She soared across the ground, the armour protecting most of her body from the impact, but Heather still felt as though she had been hit by a bus, the wind completely knocked out of her. Trying to land on her feet, she ended up in an awkward sprawl against the edge of the room, her lightning infused sword spinning away from her.

With her hand pressed against her burning chest, she coughed, 'Suit - extinguish,' and high-powered foam pumped out of her suit's wrist, extinguishing the white fire licking her armour. However, the sound was loud and clearly identified Heather's position in the room. As she tried to stand up through the pain of several fractured ribs, Helix forcefully landed a few feet away from her, chuckling as he did so.

'Wow, they always said you were un-killable. The greatest Hero this country had ever seen!' Helix mocked, walking towards her.

'Well it seems that was all rumours and lies, you are nothing more than an angry little woman who will quickly be forgotten.' He grabbed her around the throat, his boiling hot hands melting into the material protecting her neck.

She could feel the flexible carbon fibre melting, small droplets of it dripping down her neck on the inside of the suit. Clawing at his hands she tried to pull them away but he was too strong and the heat of his arms too excruciating to touch. The glass mask plate on her helmet cracked like the beginning of an earthquake and she envisioned her armour giving way and her head being torn from her body. But before this could become a reality she lifted up her wrist-mounted gun, holding it inches away from Helix's ear, and squeezed the trigger.

Helix's grip around her neck instantly faltered and

his heat was suffocated. His bright eyes seemed to shrivel slightly as the light and life left them. Cool air puffed out of his nose and gaping mouth; which had begun to fill with the icy blue crystals, his skin also blending to the same shade of cobalt. Pushing his warm body away from her onto its back, Heather looked at the devastated head of her attacker. It had been subsumed by blue ice, his now cold eyes had a look of lifeless shock as the crystalline substance spread down his neck and across his collar bones. She stood up in agony, staring at the destruction around her and back to the now silent ex-hero. She wondered what had happened for him to so drastically turn like this, yet regrettably, she felt she already knew the answer.

Lifting one of her giant thick boots high above him, she brought it stomping down onto the frozen head, shattering it into millions of tiny pieces. In synchronicity with this, another loud crashing noise came from above her, as more chunks of ceiling rubble fell all around her. This time, however, it was not caused by the fire.

A tank of a man floated above Heather, shrouded in the remnants of her cannister smoke and the smoke from the fire. Foreseeing who the man was even before he arrived, Heather calmly walked the length of the room to collect her discarded sword and expended canisters.

Like a great beast inhaling, the floating man took a single giant breath in, the smoke and patches of fire littering the room were all sucked up into his vortex of air. Then, taking another similarly epic exhale, he lifted his head to the hole he had created in the ceiling and spat it back outside into the cool night sky. Picking up the sword and flicking the hilt switch again, Heather calmly sheathed the weapon and turned to look at the human vacuum.

He wore a bright blue and white uniform, like the

superheroes of old, but modernised and conforming. Instead of a large traditional emblem across his chest, a small badge sat pinned to the right; and across his back, in a bold black font, the word "police". He wore no cape and no mask; had short tidy hair and clean-shaven face, his eyes were a gentle brown; and though he was in his late forties, his skin was smooth and wrinkle-free.

'Job's all done here, you can tell your masters that you were too late and I took care of it,' said Heather.

'What happened here?' he asked.

Heather gestured behind him towards the decapitated mess that was Helix.

'You can still put him in handcuffs, though I don't imagine that will be necessary,' she said dryly.

Effortlessly, he glided over to the body to examine what was left.

'Helix? You're telling me Helix did this?' he exclaimed, pointing to the destruction around them.

'Does this look the sort of thing in my repertoire?'

'No,' he thoughtfully paused for a moment. 'But Harrow, what the hell happened here? Why did Helix do this?'

'I have a couple of ideas, one in particular,' she said, thinking about her recent conversation with Nahmar. 'But maybe he just got sick of working with you and your friends.'

The towering superhero before her was called Paladin. He, like many others, had taken up government contracts when it became illegal to practice unregistered hero work. Heather had known and worked with Paladin in the past; but since he began working for the government their professional relationship had been in a very bad place, for many reasons, but mainly because he had been ordered to detain her and any other vigilantes on sight.

'Harrow, don't be like that. Look they're still willing to grant you immunity in exchange for your registration and contracted work for the units. Please reconsider, it's not what you thought it would be like,' Paladin pleaded.

Heather glared at him, the crack in her mask barely holding the glass intact. A few of the prisoners still alive and in the block emerged from the cover of their cells, now sensing the battle had concluded, but on seeing Harrow and Paladin instantly retreated backwards.

'I have no interest in becoming a government pet. Now are you going to let me go, for old times' sake, or am I going to have to kill you too?' She said this with confidence but knew that even with her powers and all her tools and weaponry, there was no way she would be able to defeat Paladin in a fair fight. But this response was just what he needed to hear to show her clemency and Heather knew that before she had said it.

'The rest of the unit is converging on the south bank as we speak, several officers have already entered the prison, heavily armed. The Eastern side has a very limited police presence, though fire crews are swarming across the exterior,' said Paladin. 'Just ... promise me one thing?'

Pulling out her grapnel gun and signalling her motorcycle for a pickup, she aimed up at the large hole in the ceiling.

'I'll find out why Helix did this,' said Heather before she pulled the trigger on her gun; releasing the cable that pulled her high into the air, past the flying super cop and propelling her out onto the roof of the prison.

Paladin was left feeling as he always did after encountering Harrow, concerned that she was going to get herself killed; worried that he'd finally get caught for letting her escape; and pissed off that she always finished his sentences.

Tired and fractured, Heather drove her bike into one of the dozen discrete safe houses she has set up throughout the city. Ten years of hero work and a great deal of confiscated money meant Heather could afford these highly advanced and well-protected bases; all strategically placed so she could hide her armour and tools each night before going back home to her family. This particular safehouse was one of the closest to her apartment, so she could easily cycle home tonight.

The safe house itself was very simple in its layout, it was well organised and clean. A few shelves floated across the smooth concrete walls, with tools and devices resting on top. An empty mannequin stood in the corner and as Heather started to undress, she adorned it with her battered and melted bits of armour. Removing the helmet proved quite difficult and after several minutes trying to get it off and foreseeing that she would not manage like this, she picked up one of the tools from the shelf to cut it off. Gently curving a thin plasma blade like a scalpel across the layers of the helmet; she laboriously cut away the material, finally cracking it open allowing her to breath fresh, unfiltered air. She applied some soothing and rejuvenating gel to her neck that she had stored in one of the few drawers in the room. Heather had never really been one for having more than you need; within her safe houses were the bare essentials, the things she couldn't do without, and rejuvenating burn cream was one of them.

Sitting in an armchair wearing nothing more than a thin, skin-tight lycra suit, she gently rubbed the gel across the blistering burns on her neck, thinking about this evening's events. Helix had once been a selfless and kind hero who would sooner die than hurt someone, but he had just brutally murdered hundreds of men in cold blood. Even Heather thought what he did was an atrocity and it was a slow week for her if she only killed one person. She kept thinking back to the wrath in his eyes, it had burnt so fiercely.

As she applied the last of the gel to her burns she reached out to pick up her battered helmet. Moments later the built-in earpiece rang for an incoming call.

'Suit, receive call,' she said, un-surprised about who she was going to speak to.

'Nahmar, what an ... unexpected pleasure. What do you want?' She still felt irritable with him for what he had said at Comic-Con.

'Harrow, how are you?' His voice had the same slow gentle tone as always, but it was clearly a different Nahmar than the two she had seen at the Con.

Heather didn't reply.

'Well, you already know what I'm going to ask you,' he said.

'So, ask me,' said Heather, nursing her busted ribs whilst speaking to him.

There was a paused moment of uncomfortable silence until Nahmar spoke again.

'I saw what happened at Graywick, do you want to talk about it?' said Nahmar.

Heather didn't really want to talk about anything, it had been a very long night and she was ready to return home and get some much-needed sleep.

'What is there to say? A good man went bad, killed a load of degenerates in cold blood and now he's dead too.' Heather cursed herself for letting her rage getting the better of her back in the block, killing Helix like that was ... unnecessary. 'Did he deserve to die, Nahmar?'

Slightly taken aback by this question Nahmar let

out a slow 'um,' something he never really did. His speech was so direct and purposeful usually.

'I am afraid I don't have the answer to a question like that, Harrow. Perhaps he did deserve to die but are we the most qualified judges of who should live and who shouldn't?' he asked.

'This isn't why you called me tonight, Nahmar. You want to know if I will reconsider and stop the Pandarians.'

The rejuvenating gel was acting quickly on Heather's damaged skin and for a few moments, there was a clear silence between them while Nahmar carefully considered his response.

'Every day you see the hold they possess over humanity, whether you realise it or not; and tonight, you saw how they can make even the purest and most selfless amongst us, turn to hate and anarchy. They must be stopped and we must not delay any longer. If I were as skilled a fighter as yourself, then I could deal with them alone. But for all my years, I have never been one to get into a physical conflict,' said Nahmar.

Heather pensively looked around the small softly lit safe house, deeply considering the request. She had nothing from her personal life here or any of the other locations across the city. It would be too dangerous in case anyone ever managed to get inside one of them; even the smallest clue could be disastrous for her family. But in this moment her thoughts were off with Kirsty and Henry. If the Pandarians were real, then they were a threat to her family that she couldn't allow to continue.

In the silence Heather played a number of scenarios through her head, imagining other heroes becoming corrupted by these things. Helix was a symbol of goodness and sacrifice, at least he had been until this evening. If he could be twisted and disfigured into the monster he became, there was no knowing who else these Pandarians could get to. What if they were somehow able to influence Paladin and turn him, Heather shivered at the thought.

'I'll do it,' she said slowly, following the three words with a heavy uneasy sigh.

Even with her extraordinary powers, Heather had little notion of what the next year of her life would entail. If she had, then there would be no doubt she would have destroyed her safe houses that night, incinerated all traces of Harrow and taken her family and the first possible flight out of England.

After cycling home on one of her many safehouse push bikes, Heather arrived at the towering apartment block where she lived. It was early, robins were singing and the blocks of traffic had already emerged from their beds; the bitter air was harsh and sharp.

Sharing the lift with the other residents on a night shift, Heather silently got out on the thirty-first floor. Her apartment was stylish and well decorated. Kirsty was a lot more materialistic than she was but even Heather couldn't deny, it was nice to come home to this. Beautiful illustrations hung from the neatly painted walls, a bold iron statue of a hawk rested on a table in the corner of the hallway.

Heather walked into the kitchen and went straight to the well-stocked alcohol cupboard. Pouring herself a large glass of brandy, she slumped against the countertop.

Alcohol was one of the only ways she could sleep these days, the control over fate and her powers of foresight made quite the terrible concoction for a good night's rest. Her nightmares were only getting worse as the years went by, but the alcohol numbed her powers enough to have a moderately good sleep.

Pouring the brandy down her throat like it was water, Heather washed the glass and went to bed. Kirsty and Henry would be up for school soon and normally she'd wait until they were gone to go to bed, but tonight she needed that extra few hours' sleep. Even superheroes have their long nights at the office.

CHAPTER SIX

~Then~

Freon and his son had been foraging for hours, but with very little success. It had been a challenging few weeks for them both and food had been scarce. This troubled Freon as he'd never really experienced a shortage like this before. They were forced to explore new areas of the land, so Freon had taken them to a large forest far to the south of their hidden cliff-home.

Trudging through the damp woods with his son trailing behind him, Freon listened intently for any sound of life. The wind wilfully hummed, rustling the small branches of the trees above them as they moved through the grass below. Freon thought he heard something to his left but before he could focus on the sound, his son interrupted speaking in a language long forgotten.

'Papa, when are we going home? I am tired and in need of rest,' he asked in a soft, yet complacent voice.

'Do you want to eat today, my son?' Freon replied, not taking his eyes off the point the sound came from.

'Yes, but it is nearly nightfall,' he whined.

Freon did not respond to his son this time, whatever that noise was it was getting louder. Like a distant storm, it thundered, but its repetitive beating made it clear that this was no storm.

'Papa, what is that-'

'Shhh!' Freon hissed at his son.

Chanting and shouting joined in with the rhythmic beat, men and women yelled in unison with it. This was both a comfort and a worry to Freon; the noise was clearly coming from other humans but what was it? His curiosity getting the better of him, Freon snuck towards it wondering if the people responsible for the noise, were the same ones responsible for the shortage of food.

Creeping closer to the music, Freon and his young son hid amongst the numerous thick trees. Through the green sea, nestled in a worn-down clearing, was a large tribe.

'Son, keep very quiet,' Freon whispered, and his son obediently pressed his fingers to his mouth.

The tribe was lively and full of men, women and children. Their bodies were mostly bare except for fur loincloths taken from the skin of wolves, and their torsos were covered in deep red patterns painted onto their flesh. Many of them jumped and danced around a roaring fire in the centre of the camp. The heat was incredible and Freon had never seen a fire this grand before, nor had he ever witnessed people dancing around one. The tribe shook sticks in their hands with small animal bones dangling from them; they rattled and jingled the sticks to compliment the sound of the beating drums. Freon now recognised the drums as the origin of the thunderous sound, men thudded the stretched hide with their palms and fingers. Throughout the tribe people feasted; it was now clear to Freon where all the food had gone. There were piles of boars ready to be roasted on one of the many smaller fires throughout the clearing, a rope fastened between poles with rabbits hanging by their paws, woven baskets full of fruit and berries. It was an astonishing sight for the father and son to behold. Freon's son's mouth had dropped to the floor in awe.

'Papa, can we-' he started to ask but Freon cut him off again.

'No son, this is not right. We must go,' he said, staring at the sheer size of the people in the tribe, most looked like they weighed at least twice what Freon did. Their faces were full and their bodies well curved. None of them were obese, but unlike Freon, you couldn't see their ribs.

Reaching to his side with his free hand, Freon took hold of his son's scrawny arm. But as he turned his back on the gluttonous tribe he knew he'd lingered too long. Foreseeing half a dozen men silently approaching them, wielding strange bendy wooden weapons, he dropped his spear and instructed his son to do the same. The two of them stood with their hands raised in the air as a gesture of surrender, hoping they didn't end up on a pile too.

Six ox-like men silently escorted Freon and his son through the camp, a few dancers stopped as they walked past but quickly lost interest and returned to the fireside drumming. Two young girls whispered and giggled as the son walked by, pointing at his different skin and snow coloured hair. The pair did stand out amongst the dark complexion of the tribe.

Their captors said nothing as they walked until they were next to a mammoth of a man teaching a handful of boys how to use the curved wooden weapons. He was huge, his arms were the size of tree trunks and he towered above the boys. He was at least a foot taller than Freon who wasn't exactly short himself. The man held a curved, strung weapon in one hand and in the other, a sharp narrow stick, the end of it had a pointed rock tightly fastened to it. Pulling back the stick, the tension in the string pulled tautly. Then he released it. Soaring through the air, faster than anything Freon had ever seen, it impacted into a small target many feet away from where he stood. Freon's son couldn't help but let out a gasp of awe.

'Impressed?' the huge man said, now turning to face the two intruders and speaking the same ancient language. 'It's called a bow, and it will redefine the way that we hunt, and the way we kill.' He tossed the bow and an arrow to Freon who skilfully caught them without hesitation.

'Quite the creation. I've never seen anything quite like it,' said Freon, hoping he could talk his way out of this situation. There was no way he could fight his way out, he thought to himself.

'You wouldn't have, I invented it,' the chief laughed in a deep maniacal voice. 'So, what can I do for you, are you here to steal our food or our women? Perhaps both, eh boy?' he chortled, winking at Freon's son.

'No, we are not looking for any trouble, we just heard your thunder and strayed too far. We mean you and your tribe no harm.'

The man looked back and forth between them thoughtfully, Freon stared back at him but his son just stared at his own feet. The boys that were being trained with the bow all looked on in anticipation, wondering if their chief was going to kill the two white-haired strangers.

'I'm glad you enjoyed our music,' he smiled, but then looking at the Freon's son again, it disappeared as quickly as one of his numerous arrows. 'Before I let you go, and I am going to let you go, so you can stop shaking like a mutt, boy ...' the man barked.

Freon's son looked up sheepishly and tried to stop shaking.

'You think I'm some kind of monster?' he grinned.

'No, I do not,' mumbled the son.

'Well, perhaps you should trust your instinct a bit more boy,' he laughed again. 'What is your name child?'

'His name is-' but before Freon could finish answering for his son, the huge man swung a heavy arm across Freon's face. Knocking him to the weathered dirt and sending the bow flying through the clearing.

'I was talking to your boy,' he said, calmly looking back to the boy as though they were good friends.

'Nahmar, my name is Nahmar,' the boy winced.

'Well Nahmar, it is very nice to meet you. I have an offer I would like to make to you, and I promise you it will be unlike any other offer you have ever received.'

Freon fumbled around on the ground for a moment and slowly got to his feet. He held a hand across the red mark on his face, drawing the huge man's attention to the wound.

'Nahmar, you've seen how much food we have here. Yes?'

'Yes,' Nahmar mumbled back.

'More than you have probably seen in your young life?'

'Yes.'

'Well Nahmar, are you hungry?' he held out a giant hand to press on his shoulder.

Nahmar looked up at the chief with a mixture of fear, disbelief and confusion. Freon remained silent and rigid.

'Because my offer to you, and your unruly father if he wants to too, is to stay here. Become part of my tribe! You will have as much food as you desire, the tribe will keep you both safe and we will find you both suitable mates,' he said, pressing his palm into Nahmar's bony shoulders.

Nahmar shuddered slightly when the chief's hand touched him and turned to look pleadingly at his father.

'Thank you for your kind offer but I'm afraid we must decline, we do not belong here,' Freon said firmly.

'Perhaps you do not belong here, but Nahmar was born to live the life of luxury, weren't you son?' He reached his whole tree trunk arm around Nahmar's shoulder, squeezing him tightly. 'Why don't you stay here with me boy and we'll send your father back to whatever hole he crawled out of.'

'Get your hands off my son,' Freon said boldly, his voice was strong and steady.

The man released Nahmar and strode towards Freon, puffing his chest out and tensing his fists.

'You really must learn your place!' He launched an enormous fist towards Freon who had prepared himself for the second attack. Withdrawing the arrow he had stealthily retrieved after the first hit, he plunged it into his attacker's shoulder. The arrow bit deeply, sinking at least a foot into the giant man.

Freon ducked underneath the outstretched arms that were trying to crush him and darted to his son. Grabbing hold of Nahmar's arm and the discarded bow, the pair sprinted away from the chief and through the camp.

'Do exactly what I tell you, my son,' Freon commanded.

Behind them, the roar of anger and pain resonated through the maze of tents. Other men in the village pursued them, firing arrows at the escaping father and son.

'Down!' Freon bellowed. Nahmar ducked in time to dodge the arrow that would have pierced his neck.

Fleeing through the camp, Freon spotted a large barrel of salted meats. Running by, he shoved it onto one of the smaller campfires and continued bellowing instructions to his son. At least half of their pursuers stopped in a panic to salvage the barrel full of their precious food, the rest continued charging after the boy and his father. More arrows flew past them, each one Freon smoothly avoided and instructed his son how to do the same. The attackers yelled in anger every time this happened.

They reached the edge of the camp, villagers had abandoned whatever they were doing to see what the commotion was. Groups emerged from their tents and stared, as the two ran back into the woods they had come from. A few of the men continued chasing them, but their speed was no match for Freon and Nahmar's agility, they quickly outran them and found a hiding place to catch their breath underneath the exposed roots of an old willow tree.

For what felt like hours neither of them spoke, the sounds of their pursuers died down and the forest around them went quiet again, save for the rippling of a nearby stream.

'Are you okay, my son?' Freon asked.

'That was pretty scary, Papa.'

'Yes son, it was. You were excellent back there,' he spotted Nahmar fiddling with his satchel. 'What have you got there, Nahmar?'

Nahmar reached into the sheepskin bag and slowly pulled out a large rabbit, freshly killed and untarnished. Freon laughed, deep and jolly.

'My boy, you truly are one of a kind. When on

earth did you get a chance to take that?' he asked with prideful surprise.

'On our way into the camp.'

'You had it the whole time?!' Freon laughed warmly again. 'I'm impressed, son. We'll eat well tonight.'

The two stayed under the old willow until all traces of sunlight had vanished and they could move through the cover of darkness; then they quietly made their way out of the wood and towards their discrete cliffside home.

Deep purple flickered through the sky, stars billions of miles away twinkled and glittered on the cloudless night. The pair walked side by side, Freon still holding the stolen bow and Nahmar carrying tonight's dinner, joking as they walked. Nahmar went quiet for a moment; his father sensed his son had a burning question.

'Go on son, speak your mind.'

'Papa, how did you know where their weapons would fly? Every time you moved us out of harm's way, even though their attempts to kill us were without number. How did you know where they would aim?' Nahmar asked curiously.

A small smile appeared on Freon's face, impressed with his son's observation and attention to detail.

'Nahmar, I have never told you this before but we have not always lived in that cave within the cliff. For most of my life and the beginning of yours, we lived beneath the earth.'

'With my mother?' asked Nahmar.

'Yes, with your mother.'

There was pain and resentment in Freon's voice like it hurt to say the word.

'Perhaps we should save this story for another day, it is late and we still need to get home and prepare our dinner,' said Freon.

'Please Papa, I just want to know how you do it,' he begged.

'Very well ... In truth my son, I do not know how it works; nor why I was chosen for this power but I will tell you what I do know.'

'Since I was a boy I have been able to see things before they happen and by glimpsing what has not yet come to pass I can change it, alter what happens next.'

Nahmar's mouth had fallen wide with awe and astonishment.

'I can also alter minor things around us, like the balance of a creature or the speed at which a stone will fall or the height I can leap through the air.'

'Do you think I will be able to do the things you can, Papa?'

Freon paused for a moment, and after a deep sigh replied.

'I hope not, my boy.'

The two had reached the base of the cliff that safely hid their home, its jagged rocky surface jutting out at every angle.

'Why not, Papa? Your powers would make me unstoppable, like the mighty rivers or undying storms.'

Nahmar gripped hold of the weathered rope, dangling down from rocks above. He began climbing as he yelled over his shoulder to his Father, telling him all the things and creatures he would be stronger than. Freon scaled the rope beneath his son, poised ready to catch him should he lose his footing as he himself had done in the past.

'Son, you see the benefits so clearly but you do not consider the curse that comes with this power.'

'What do you mean, Papa?' said Nahmar, pulling himself higher and higher, lapping up the familiar luscious view.

'I see everything around me, moments before it happens. I see death, pain and misery. Often, I can do something to change it, but this is still after I have witnessed it. I saw you die four times today, Nahmar, and even though you did not, the paintings in my mind never fade. There are sometimes where no amount of foresight or visions of what is yet to come, are any help at all. Sometimes people die and there is nothing I or you will ever be able to do about it.'

The two of them went quiet as they clambered the last few meters to their cave, Freon pulled up the rope behind him.

'Is that what happened to Mother?' whispered Nahmar.

'That is enough questions for today, Nahmar, get that rabbit skinned and prepared now.'

His son sheepishly wandered into the cave and gathered some dry logs from their reserve, leaving Freon to stare, blurry-eyed into the distance. His foot twitched as his thoughts drifted back to a powerless and unforgettable morning many years ago, clasping his dying wife's sweaty hand, wishing more than anything it was him in her place.

CHAPTER SEVEN

~Now~

Blistering sunlight lashed against Heather's exposed skin. She wasn't used to this kind of heat back in New London but here, along the west coast of America, she didn't have much of a choice. The sun was unforgiving and she had definitely not packed enough sun cream. Heather's pale skin had never stood up well against hot summer days; she burnt and then she peeled without fail. Hastily making her way up the hotel ramp with her heavy suitcase in tow, she was reminded why she loved her broken city so much. Its gloom and drizzle would be very welcome right about now.

Heather had returned to California that morning on an expensive private jet; it made getting her suit and gear through customs a lot easier. She told Kirsty she was going on a training course for her work and would be gone for the week. It wasn't an uncommon lie to tell her but it was never pleasant to do. The reality was that she'd been lying to Kirsty for the last seven years of their relationship, so although it wasn't pleasant, it had become easy to do. Heather had never revealed her identity to anyone before; no one else knew that Harrow and Heather were the same person. Trust wasn't something that came naturally to Heather anymore and although she trusted her wife, she had made the decision early on to never tell her who she really was. As much as she loved Kirsty, some secrets are simply too burdening to share.

As she stood in the busy hotel lobby queuing to check in, her thoughts were interrupted by a couple of kids a few years younger than Henry, aimlessly running between the guests. They were sprinting without fear, judgment or prejudice as their parents were busy hauling in the bags from the taxi. Their small flip flops pattered on the recently polished marble floor and the sound bounced across the lobby over the noise of the chattering grown-ups.

'Ma'am?' the tall receptionist called to her again, having already tried several times.

'Oh. Sorry, my head was in the clouds.' Dragging her case forward, Heather approached the pristine desk.

'Name, please,' the receptionist asked politely.

'Helen Peters.'

Heather had many alternative identities when working away, each one with accompanying passports, billing addresses and national insurance. Handing over her passport to the man, he glanced at it and quickly started punching the keys on the keyboard with his fingertips.

'Can I take your bags, Ma'am?' a young overly eager bellboy had appeared next to her, his tie scruffily misplaced around his neck.

'No, I've got them, thank you,' she said, giving him a false smile.

'Are you sure? They look heavy,' he chuckled,

eyeing up the large case and the smaller one stacked on top.

Heather felt like retorting with a sharp and sarcastic comment but managed to dial it back to - 'I managed to get them this far, I think I'll be okay.'

The bellboy awkwardly nodded and walked towards the next guest.

'That all seems to be in order, Mrs Peters. Are you staying with us for business or pleasure?' the receptionist asked, handing over her shiny room card.

'Oh pleasure, definitely.'

Upstairs in a quiet and serene hotel room, Heather unpacked some of her gear and her custom-built laptop. Booting it up she laid it on the pine-smelling bedsheets and got dressed into something more comfortable.

Rooting through her bag she pulled out her pyjamas, along with the small silver cube Nahmar had given her before leaving for California.

'This box is how you will defeat them, Harrow,' he had said. Heather thought back to their last conversation.

Meeting at a homely cafe in the heart of New London, the two of them had sat down together in an empty corner for about an hour, discussing the task ahead. Nahmar was wearing a thick and sagging raincoat, his cap was folded on the table between them. Heather had worn a wig, sunglasses and several exaggerated prosthetic features, precisely glued to her face. Nahmar sipped a piping hot cup of hot chocolate, small droplets had licked his scruffy white facial hair.

'Once the host is dead they'll just be drawn to it?' Heather had asked.

'Yes, the box was designed to trap the Pandarians in their corporeal forms.'

'And who designed the box?'

Nahmar had remained silent, taking another long sip of his drink.

'Still don't want to tell me the full story? If we're going to work together you'll have to learn to trust me.' Heather had said, with annoyance etched into her voice.

'All that I can tell you right now is that that box is irreplaceable. The fate of our world rests with you, Harrow.'

'Don't worry about your precious box, I can handle this.'

'I believe that you will. Harrow, there is something else you really must understand about the Pandarians. Not only do they feed on our darkest desires and behaviours but they also draw it from us. They are temptation itself; they force humanity to behave in these sinful ways and they feed on the results. Never forget that just being near them will be like wanting to breathe while drowning; you just won't be able to help yourself.'

The two of them had then discussed Heather's first target that Nahmar had identified: a world-famous pop star called Ria. Loved and idolised by hundreds of millions of people across the globe, Ria was number one in twenty-seven countries, had just released her fourth bestselling album and starred in three award-winning, box office smashing films. She was the face of the world's largest and most well-recognised leukemia charity and had donated millions of her wealth to that and other charities. It was Ria who had brought Heather to California. Heather was going to kill her.

Fluttering his tiny wings, the spotted red ladybird took off from the perch he'd been using for the last minute. Heather's high-powered binoculars, now insect free, were pointed directly into the truly astonishing mansion that belonged to Ria; her address provided by Network Intelligence. Heather lay still as stone, on a warm concrete roof several hundred meters up the hill away from the house. Staking it out for several hours, watching who went in and utilising her hyperspectral imaging technology, allowed Heather to see exactly what was going on inside.

Silently lying on some other millionaire's roof for hours she watched a number of different people approach and enter the house: a delivery man, a boyfriend, some sort of talent agent and a couple of friends. Four of them were lounging about the living room drinking prosecco, the lenses of the binoculars easily spying the label of the bottle through the living room window.

Heather had done this for two days and an evening, recording all the comings and goings to build a picture of the Pandarian's movements. Ria had not left the house much and when she did, it was only for a couple of hours. Evenings were spent alone; such a huge home for just one person felt ludicrous to Heather. Thinking about it more, she supposed that was part of the point of why she was lying on this roof in the first place.

Peering through the exuberant floor-to-ceiling windows, she watched Ria pour herself a drink, filling her crystal glass. Her soft perfectly manicured fingers held the glass gently as she poured.

Ria was a truly stunning woman; her skin was flawless and glittered in the sunlight that peeked through the window, her thick blonde hair was curly and bounced with excitement whenever she walked. Heather couldn't help but imagine what she might smell like and what it would feel like to touch the body that half the world wanted to touch.

Heather planned to sneak into the house tonight. She would return to the hotel, collect her armour and weapons; and return on the off-road motorbike she had hired upon her arrival to California. It felt strange to be working away from New London. She had done it in the past but over the last few years, she had completely devoted her skills to her hometown. California was mostly uncharted territory for her and she didn't like it.

Adorning herself in the nightmarish armour, she stocked it with her gear and devices, placing the final ion laser cartridge into her utility belt.

Sliding open the hotel room window she envisioned what lay below her, looking for a clear landing. Activating her cape's glide mode, Heather charged towards the open window and launched herself into the cool Californian sky. Soaring down from the forty-first floor of her hotel she whizzed by several oblivious guests, spreading her arms angelically, her cape springing to her hands and lifting her high into the air. Gliding in between buildings like an owl on its hunt, she flew towards the multi-storey where she'd parked her bike. The sky was dark like dusty coal, the moon wrapped up in a blanket of clouds.

Blasting through the streets of Orange County astride her hired motorbike, she raced towards Pelican Hill; her cape whistling and whipping in the jet stream. When possible, Heather avoided main roads, she didn't need the world knowing that Harrow was visiting the States. As she approached the familiar cluster of mansions, Heather dismounted the rented bike and stashed it between the thresholds of two oversized gardens.

Sneaking low between the religiously trimmed hedges she advanced towards Ria's home. The white brick of her house glowed with a gentle blue hue from the garden lamps. Heather's intimidating silhouette dipped between the shadows as she traced the outside of the building. Effortlessly she disabled the six external security cameras, subdued the two guard dogs with tranquillizer darts and vaulted the eight-foot garden wall, skirting round to the back of the house. It was late, Heather assumed the Pandarian to be sound asleep in some overly expensive king-sized bed, she assumed wrong.

Planting a small controlled EMP mine on the external window ledge she backed away and flicked the switch. A small invisible pulse rippled across the window, disabling any installed alarms that may have been on the other side. Pulling the handheld ion laser from her belt she carefully cut through the window latch and, slowly lifting the window up, she gently stepped inside.

Pristine and beautifully designed, the study was full of unloved and unread books. They were organised and alphabetised neatly on glistening white shelves. A grand wooden desk sat in the corner of the room, an expensive branded computer on top of it. Heather spotted a handful of awards as she activated her helmet's hyperspectral imaging, mapping out a view of the house, creating a sonar-like vision of her environment. Perched in the study, she silently searched for her target.

The house was enormous and after several minutes of using her scanners she came up short. Deciding she had come too far to turn back now, she stood up and gently approached the study door.

Carefully pushing it ajar she peaked into the wide, cream carpeted hallway. Expensive canvases and paintings hung from the walls. She passed by one of an ox standing mightily atop a crumbled building. Wasting no time to decipher its symbology she pushed on and activated the parabolic microphone built into her helmet, recently replaced after her scarring battle with Helix.

Facing forward she listened for any sound of her target, carefully peeling her ears for signs of noise. She crept through the house, pointing the microphone in her helmet all around her. But Heather couldn't hear anything other than the hum of the fridge, a couple of clocks ticking and the neighbour's TV as they watched some late-night show about the extinction of polar bears.

Just as she was about to give up and leave, figuring that Ria must be sleeping at a friend's or partying somewhere, she dropped her head slightly to switch off the mic and a muffled moan played through the helmet speakers.

Finger hovering over the microphone's off switch, she paused. There it was again. A deep moan of pleasure coming from a woman, the sound came from directly beneath her. Moving through the kitchen she hunted for any other sounds from below, but her microphone couldn't pierce through the floor. Heather assumed there was something thick across the ground physically blocking her audio feed, she deduced the sound had come up through a ventilation shaft.

Feeling that her opportunities were limited and not wanting to waste any more time second-guessing, Heather began searching for the door that would lead her to the moaning.

Back through the hallway, adjacent to the marble staircase, was a tall black door. Opening it revealed a long utility cupboard with a collection of appliances including a state of the art robotic cleaner. There was a bunch of umbrellas, lent on a shelf stacked with household supplies; everything from toilet paper to air fresheners. Other than that, it was quite bare, not packed with the junk most people store in their cupboard under the stairs.

Heather pressed the tiny switch on the temple of her suit, retracting the visor up a few inches so she could smell the room. One quick sniff was the only clue she needed; the room had the very faint aroma of beer. Perusing the room for just a few moments more, she instinctively took hold of one of the umbrellas that seemed new and unused and by doing so, pulled a lever to the hidden entrance she was looking for.

Rolls of toilet paper and boxes of air fresheners sunk into the floor on the moving shelf, slowly revealing a steep staircase with another tall door at the foot. Returning the visor to its closed position she cautiously stepped over the entirely lowered shelf and descended.

Her heavy boots thudded on the steps like the gentle rhythm of a bass drum as she walked. Reaching over her shoulder she grasped the familiar hilt of her sword, unsheathed it which made an awe-inspiring metal on metal chime. Her left hand reached for the pistol holstered to her thigh, the silver cube from Nahmar patiently waiting in a utility belt pouch.

Just as she reached the bottom of the stairs she could start to hear the moaning again, but this time there wasn't just one voice. Frantically estimating, Heather could hear at least fifteen separate voices all grunting or moaning in some way. Slapping and pounding noises dribbled out of the door, a young woman cried out, begging for more in a desperate and pleading voice.

'Fuck,' Heather whispered to herself. She had not been expecting this and certainly hadn't prepared for it. Assassinating Ria with that many eyewitnesses would be unwise, but she was still torn on what to do now she'd made it this far. In her mind's eye she envisioned opening the warm door and the sticky sweaty people it would reveal.

Concentrating she glanced into this potential future she was creating, seeing several seconds into what could happen. Hot steaming bodies writhed up against each other. Mouth-watering supermodels were having their hair pulled on as rich and powerful men pleasured them from behind. 'YES!' one of them screamed in bliss. A gorgeous man, whose muscles dripped with sweat and oil, knelt on the floor, lifting a supple young woman's curvy leg up over his shoulder, while another muscular man around his age lay beneath him. A twister of ample redheads entwined their naked bodies together, delighting in one another. The trio were being watched by many others while engaging in their own sexual exploits, including Ria who lay seductively on one of many beds dotted about the room. Ria was surrounded by men and women, all of whom wanted a taste of her.

Returning to the present moment Heather forced herself not to open the door, which doing so would play out all that she just saw. Perhaps patience was the best approach tonight she thought. But as she began to return up the stairs, back to the house she could hear another noise. This time coming from upstairs.

'Ria! I'm back, and I brought those guys you wanted to see. Boys, put your phones in here, they're not allowed downstairs.'

The voice belonged to one of the boyfriends Heather had spotted during her earlier surveillance and by the sounds of it, he was extremely drunk.

'Sorry we're late, baby, but we are totally going to make it up to you,' he laughed.

The group of drunken horny men were rapidly approaching the utility cupboard. Heather had waited too long. Deciding there was nothing else for it, she cursed her own carelessness and rammed the door.

Crashing to the heated linoleum floor, the sound of the door shocked the two dozen or so celebrities engaged in the lustful orgy. Pulling apart or unmounting, several hazy eyes spun round to look at the intruder. The dark metal covering Heather's suit reflected the blurry shapes of their nudity, like a smudged watercolour painting. Powerfully stepping over the splintered door Heather moved to the centre of the room staring at Ria, whose exposed body could just be seen past a wall of eager and erect admirers.

'I just want Ria, everyone else … get out,' Heather's voice was strong and commanding, yet the sensual crowd remained frozen with shock or fear.

'NOW!' she yelled, flashing her sword menacingly.

Most of the room fled towards the fractured door frame, fake breasts and shrinking cocks bouncing as they ran. A handful tried to grab a blanket or pillow but most valued their lives more than their modesty.

A burly man built like a rhinoceros blundered towards Heather, his hands curled up into heavy fists. He swung a wild jab towards her face but she ducked effortlessly and nicked his waist with her sword, lightly slicing his skin.

Two more huge men lunged towards her, their naked bodies swinging as they attacked. Their punches were weighty and strong, she timed her dodges and counter-attacks with precision, focusing on every strike before they even thought to make it. Flexing forward and ducking between feral punches, she brutally kicked one of them in the throat and swung her sword down with finesse, severing the other's hanging manhood. It fell with an audible slop as it slapped the floor. Screaming in agony he fell backwards, clutching the blood gushing stump between his hairy legs, revealing Ria, who had got up from the bed and was making a break for the exit.

Glancing into fate Heather could see a minor consequence to stopping her escape. With that in mind, she drew her pistol and blindly fired in Ria's direction. Heather heard the bullet impact just as the naked rhinoceros dove on top of her, as she knew he would. His overweight body pinning Heather to the ground, she thrashed and kicked, trying to push him off; her weapons were knocked out of her hands in the struggle.

The other man still with his genitals attached, ran over to another bed to retrieve a set of thick iron chains, then gripping onto the leather wrist straps, he wrapped them around Heather's neck. Writhing on the floor trying to shift the weight of this hulk of a man, she pulled both arms up to try and drag the chain from her neck. It was one of the few areas of her suit that wasn't as heavily armoured, after all, she needed to be able to turn her head. In her peripheral vision, she spotted a wounded Ria, weakly crawling towards the stairs while gripping the gunshot wound in her leg. With a burst of strength, Heather thrust her hips up and stretched her hands past the chain to grab the hands of the strangler. She spoke in a single choked breath ... 'Suit, Shock.'

Sharp white lightning poured from the plates in her suit, licking the exposed skin of her attackers. It danced up and down their bodies as they spasmed in pain. For several moments the incredible charge of electricity convulsed from her armour and through the two men. Heather rolled the fried rhino man from her body and un-looped the chain around her neck. The two men lay motionless and steaming.

Stumbling towards the stairs catching her breath, Heather picked up her weapons and watched the wounded woman attempt to crawl away. Tugging on her smooth ankle, Heather yanked her down the few stairs back to the floor. Somewhere far above them, shouting and screaming could be heard. The police sirens wouldn't be audible for several more minutes.

Grabbing hold of her hip, Heather twisted Ria onto her back, exposing everything. Her body was unquestionably exquisite and Heather couldn't help but feel a great amount of desire towards this woman. Her eyes traced down Ria's body to her navel, down her smooth legs to the bloody wound in her calf. A tiny bit of Heather felt regret for ruining something so perfect.

Heather's eyes wandered, absorbing every inch of Ria's delicious body. Her skin was smooth and flawless. Her face was beautiful and features unimaginably designed. Lips red and full, Heather imagined pressing hers against them. Her mind flustered through what this woman might feel like, what she might taste like. Ria's eyes were striking and bright, the sky-blue tint shone even in the low lighting. Beginning to recognise the arousal within herself, Heather tried to focus but kneeling straddled over Ria's naked body, she couldn't shake the aching desire to do something about her hunger. Heather's hand glided across Ria's face like she was no longer in control of her body.

'What are you waiting for bitch, get on with it,' Ria spat. Her face was fearless and defiant.

Breaking Heather out of her guilty dream-like fantasy, the insult ripped her mind back to the present. Heather grimaced beneath her helmet, the mask concealing her tormented expression. She traced a finger from Ria's love bite covered neck, all the way past her breasts to the centre of her chest, resting it on her sternum. Hiding something in the same hand.

'You'd like that, wouldn't you? If I just killed you now. You see the thing is ... I know what you are,' whispered Heather.

Heather placed the small silver cube where her finger had just been. The cool metal against her warm skin made Ria lift her head up a little, looking down her chest to see the infamous Pandora's box. Her face flooded with terror and she had just enough time to look into Heather's blank visor and see her own terrified reflection before Heather stabbed her in the heart. The thin black blade easily sliced through her body and into the floor beneath.

A dying breath later, a powerful fountain of bright red energy burst from Ria's body like lust being drawn from her pores. In the corner of the room, the cockless man stared in astonishment with blurry eyes, moments before passing out. The red mist whirled above Heather as though about to form a twister, the speed and force pushing Heather back a distance. Then the cube began to glow.

The bodies decorating the box, all posed in grotesque and awkward positions appeared to move and change but Heather couldn't tell for sure. Like a black hole, the crimson energy spun violently and was entirely consumed by the glowing cube. The air became still again, as though nothing had happened.

Extending a hand to pick up the device, Heather noticed the bodies now looked a tiny bit less grotesque than they did before. It also felt considerably heavier in her hand. Striding over Ria's lifeless body and taking the stairs two at a time, she could hear the bedlam above.

Tearing across the tarmac on the hired bike, Heather fled from the pursuing sirens. They rang wildly across the suspended freeway, piercing the ears of all who heard them. Several police cars wailed as they closed the gap on her, now just a few meters away. The hired bike was pathetic compared to her custom Harley, the engine whined and complained as she demanded more and more speed. Mere inches away now, the leader of the pack pulled alongside Heather but was forced to break off as they caught up with other drivers. Heather used the chance to blast between traffic, narrowly avoiding the car wing mirrors. But even with a couple of late night drivers to use as blockers, the police caught up quickly and cars were starting to pull out of the way ahead of the high-speed chase.

'Stop now, or we will fire upon you!' a senior officer bellowed through the car's inbuilt megaphone.

Three of the fastest pursuit vehicles led the chase and were now tightly ganged up on Heather's bike. Her mind raced with countless possibilities and potential futures, but her time for decision making was rapidly shrinking.

Further down the spot lit highway, the police had pre-emptively set up a roadblock: no spikes, just heavy SUVs forming a barricade across the freeway. Squeezing the brake and swinging the rear wheel around a hundred and eighty degrees, Heather rocketed towards the three approaching cars and oncoming traffic; smoke billowing from the tyres as they screamed across the road.

Weaving around the cars with ease, knowing where they would turn before they did, she soared back the way she had come. However, she rapidly met another roadblock of police vehicles. With very few options left to her, Heather plucked a small sticky mine from her suit and slammed it onto the ragged engine below her. With a loud beeping, it began counting down.

Bombing towards the line of cars she prepared to do something completely reckless; even for her. Hopping up so she stood on the seat, Heather poised herself to leap from the bike. She felt a boiling anger within herself as she did so; how could she have been so careless? Her fury was only increased as a news helicopter flew overhead, capturing every moment for live television. Heather knew this was the biggest fuck up in her career, what she didn't know was that in the near, but unforeseeable future, it was going to get a whole lot worse.

Moments from colliding headfirst into the roadblock she launched herself off the bike and over the edge of the suspended freeway. The mine detonated a second later and the bike was entirely incinerated, leaving nothing but dust for some persistent crime lab officer to hopelessly search through. Windows rushed past her as she soared through the air like an arrow. Tyres above her screeched to avoid crashing into the roadblock. As Heather fell to the wide well-lit road beneath, she quickly pulled out her grapnel gun. Aiming it at the tallest building in her vicinity, she fired the cable towards the upper windows. Making its mark the cable went taught and Heather swung through the air like a monkey with a vine.

It took her about ten minutes of running through quieter back alleys before she finally managed to lose the persistent news chopper. With no sign of the police either she scrambled back to her hotel feeling as though, regardless of killing Ria, the mission had been a complete and unquestionable disaster.

CHAPTER EIGHT

'And this is when our camera team lost sight of the vigilante known as Harrow, the prime suspect in the murder of billionaire pop star, Ria Loretta. Harrow was seen leaving the superstar's house at twenty past one last night and several eyewitnesses are claiming to have watched the brutal attack take place. The President of the United States had this to say on the matter ...'

The news channel cut to a scene of the American President in some lavish White House press conference room. She wore a smooth velvet forest green jacket and a dull grey sash around her neck.

'This despicable misuse of power will not be tolerated. Harrow will be stopped and will be made to pay for her crimes. The United States of America is collaborating with the United Kingdom's government and police force on this matter. Rest assured that this illegal vigilante and all others practising unregistered hero work will succumb to justice.'

Cutting back to the news channel station the

reporter continued.

'Security in the UK has rapidly increased since the attack on Graywick prison. Many are speculating as to who the next superhero to turn against us will be ...'

Kirsty turned off the TV and continued getting dressed for work. The sun was peaking through the gap in the drawn curtains, painting a thin line of the bedroom with an orange glow. Zipping up her skirt, Kirsty thought about the report. She had never been a fan of supers in general but she really mistrusted the vigilante lot and this Harrow seemed to be the worst of them all.

Kirsty had never seen her in person before but had a friend that frequently sang praises about the night she'd been saved by Harrow. The colleague had nearly been involved in a train accident, some dire malfunction with the tracks, but Harrow had been there to save her and the lives of over two hundred passengers. Regardless, Kirsty had never been sold on the idea of an especially powerful individual working outside the law. She herself had never broken a single law in her life and prided herself on having a glimmering and spotless record. Even in school, she had never received so much as a break-time detention. This Harrow character was a rogue and, regardless of what others claimed her to be, Kirsty saw an out of control sociopath.

'Henry, get your bag and coat, please. Shoes on!' Kirsty called from the bathroom.

Brushing her teeth, she stared at the empty side of the bed where Heather usually lay at this time of day. The constant night shifts did put a strain on their relationship, with them only getting a couple of hours together when Kirsty got home from work but before Heather started. It was something Kirsty frequently brought up in their arguments, demanding to know why she insisted on working such unsociable hours. But Heather would always reel off a list of reasons why she needed this job and why Kirsty should just be grateful they both had full-time work. Her excuses were becoming tired and repetitive, and now she was away on business; Kirsty was sick of it. As she brushed her teeth that morning she decided that when Heather returned, she would ask her to reconsider looking for a new job. Spitting the gloopy white foam into the sink, she rinsed her mouth and toothbrush then hurried Henry and herself out the front door.

Heather left California on the first flight available. She spent the entire flight home thinking about her next six targets but struggling to put the first out of her mind. The whole world knew where she had been but worse than that; if the other Pandarians knew that Ria was one of them, they'd now be on their guard. Her thoughts wandered to the strange silver box sat at the bottom of her carry on luggage and the spirit captured within it. Mind racing, she considered what her next steps were. She would need further preparation and more detailed analysis of her targets. Doubting she would be as lucky to escape as easily next time, she spent the rest of the journey considering her options.

It wasn't until she arrived in England and got back to a safe house, did she see the news report on Harrow. Some well-known blogger from Scotland had called her the Star Killer and it seemed to be sticking.

Heather stood in the underground safe house, staring at the large computer monitors now covered in web stories, videos, blogs, social media posts and news reports all saying the same thing. Harrow: the Star Killer, now a supervillain?

Screaming with primal rage, Heather wrenched

one of the monitors from the wall bracket and hurled it across the room into a glass cabinet. Glass and shards of TV components shattered across the floor, spreading like a box of Lego being tipped over. Turning back to face the other two TV monitors she slammed her fists into them repetitively. The displays cracked and crunched beneath her bloody knuckles. Broken twisted fragments of pixels still showed the images of her racing across the Orange County freeway, fleeing from police.

Slumping down against the wall she began to silently cry. She could feel the pulse in her temple throbbing with anger and rage, her knuckles gently weeping with blood. Wiping her eyes with her forearm, she then began to pluck out tiny chunks of the screen from her fists. Everything she had spent the last ten years trying to achieve, ruined in one night.

Perhaps this was a mistake, she thought to herself. Ten years was a long time to fight crime, but this was different; maybe she wasn't cut out for this. However as she sat there pulling out the glass from her knuckles she thought back to Henry and Kirsty, the reason she had accepted Nahmar's quest in the first place. Why hadn't she just left Ria's house when she had the chance; there had obviously been other people there before she even went downstairs. She could have just left and returned when Ria was asleep in her bed alone. But in truth, Heather knew why she had stayed.

If she was entirely honest with herself, and she didn't find it easy to do, she had wanted to see. The curiosity that night was overpowering, knowing that just on the other side of that door was a couple dozens of beautiful, young and sexy men and women. She hated herself for wanting it but what Heather had really wanted to do was stay there and fuck them all. The women, the men, every last one of them, but most of all, Ria. Unlike any person she had ever met, Heather had just wanted to break down that door to see her wet, glistening naked body.

Nahmar said these beings fed on sin and desire but that they also inspired it within those around them. Had Heather been forced to behave the way she did or was it her own sinister desires? Confusion and regret festered in her mind as she questioned how much control she truly had over her actions that night; then her thoughts drifted to Ria's body again.

'Stop!' she yelled at herself and bumped her bleeding fist against the cool stone floor. If Heather was going to take on another six Pandarians and keep her life and sanity intact, she knew she would need help.

In this moment she stood up and noticed the discarded thin black business card she had been given at the Comic-Con, laying on top of her desk. She had completely forgotten about the square faced, blonde computer guy she met at the Con but, thinking about it now, perhaps he was exactly the help she needed. Someone to handle the intel and carry out the extensive research that Heather didn't excel at. Perhaps if she had known what Ria was involved in beforehand it would have been the discreet operation it was intended to be.

She picked up her helmet from the still packed suitcase and voiced in the number. Not that there were windows in here but Heather knew the sun was just beginning to stick its nose up to smell the day.

The phone rang for a few seconds and then a soft and melodic voice answered.

'Zack speaking, how may I help?'

'Zack, It's Harrow,' the voice modulator in her helmet disguised her voice with Harrow's formidable tone.

'I was hoping to discuss your offer.'

'You called! I didn't think you would, how are you? Oh damn it, what a stupid question. Terrible I imagine, I've seen the news. Did you actually kill that woman? Oh god, that was such a stupid thing to say, I'm so sorry. Erm … h-how are you?' His blundering voice faltered at the end. His fanboy attitude to Harrow couldn't be more obvious.

'Zack, I need your help. Are you still looking for a partner?' said Heather, pushing aside his flustered introduction.

'Are you shitting me?! Er yes! I mean, yeah I'm definitely available,' Zack spewed.

'Right, well I'm looking for someone to handle intelligence, research and tech for me if you think you're up for it?' Heather tried to sound off hand but felt quite awkward asking for help, especially when she was supposedly the greatest vigilante in the country.

'Say no more, when and where do you want to meet?'

'Really? You're still interested?' Heather asked, a glimmer of surprise in her voice.

'Indisputably. I'm dying to get back in the game.'

Heather felt a confused mixture of relief and hesitation.

'Well look, I'm just looking at all my options but if you're still interested in working together then let's get together for a proper chat.'

'Amazing. Hey, I know just the place we can meet!' said Zack with so much excitement in his voice, Heather had to turn the volume down.

'What the hell do you call this?' Heather asked in amazement.

The two of them were stood in a softly lit and completely deserted underground station. Zack in a grey woolly jumper and jeans, Heather in her armour. A couple of tube carriages sat parked alongside the platform; their paintwork faded and peeling in places. Most of the windows had been knocked out but a couple of grubby panes remained. Handfuls of ceiling tiles had fallen from their places and lay shattered somewhere on the tracks beneath the carriage. In the corner of the platform lay a heap of torn out plastic seats and handrails, gutted from the carriage. It was quiet and peaceful, all except for the gentle warble from the power generators and Zack's computer equipment on the train. It was a ghost station.

'It was Knightsbridge, but after Buckingham and once the dust settled, they forgot to clear this station. It was so badly blocked off that the government just decided to leave it and save some money. I suppose with everything else the country had going on at the time, one little station was the least of our worries. I discovered it wasn't as badly destroyed as they thought, a couple of cave-ins along the track and hardly anything left of the upper levels but nothing too bad,' smiled Zack.

Heather thought back to Buckingham, the event that had shattered the country barely five years ago. Heather had been one of many involved in the rescue efforts, it was one of the most traumatic days of her life. The country had come a long way since that day but there was still a lot of anger amongst New London's people. Even with the "New" part in the name, many people here found it almost impossible to move on.

'I moved my kit down here about a year after the attack and I've been here since, I call it The Catacombs,' he said with pride.

'Bit of a creepy name don't you think?' said

Heather.

'Nah, I thought it was pretty cool. Every hero's lair needs a cool name,' he said this as though it was part of a superhero code. It made Heather think about Zack's age for a moment. He had to be around her age, perhaps a few years younger. His face was soft and wrinkle free; his thick blonde hair showed no signs that it was going to recede anytime soon.

'How old were you when you moved here?' Heather said, trying as hard as she could to sound coy.

'Why, are you trying to figure out how old I am?' he laughed.

Heather shifted on the spot awkwardly. But Zack jumped in to rescue her.

'It's fine, I'm twenty-six,' he chuckled. 'And how about you? It's pretty hard to tell with that helmet covering your face.'

He was becoming much more confident the more time they spent together and the cocky attitude beneath the surface was shining through again.

'Do you always ask women their age? I thought that was something you were supposed to avoid,' asked Heather.

'Not always but I thought it would be fair,' his eyes were warm and benign.

After the train wreck of a week Heather had just had, talking to Zack on the chilled derelict platform was actually quite comforting. He was much easier to talk to than most people Heather encountered, both as herself and as Harrow.

'Older than you and let's leave it at that,' she smiled beneath the helmet.

For the next half an hour or so Zack gave her a tour

of his fondly named Catacombs, showing off the infrastructure and advanced tech he was using down here. Most of which he'd built and commissioned himself. His computers were like nothing she had ever seen before and it was not like she knew a lot about them herself, but she could tell it was high-end kit. Zack explained how he could hack into most CCTV feeds across New London, he could have eyes on every foot of the city. He also gave a few demonstrations of his capability, hacking into the webcams of several famous football players, watching one doing his morning make-up routine. Next, he showed her his favourite family of sparrows nesting by a camera on London Bridge. After showing her how he could change bank balances and delete police files, he swivelled around in his chair to face Heather.

'So, what do you think?' he asked, eagerly awaiting a reaction as she'd been silent for some time now.

Heather stared into his sweet sapphire eyes, desperately hoping she could count on this man. His talents were extraordinary and with his help, she felt far more confident about tackling the remaining Pandarians.

'Why did you join the Network?' Heather asked.

He looked a little disappointed it was a question rather than a clear answer.

'Well the thing about being able to do all this stuff … believe it or not, but after a while, it can get kind of boring.'

'You became a vigilante because you were bored?' asked Heather.

'No, no. I mean it can get kind of boring if it doesn't have any purpose, and it started to feel like a waste of time, then I lost a couple of friends in Buckingham. All this … and I couldn't do a thing to save them,' he gestured to the towers of expensive equipment and tech around him.

'But then I saw you guys on TV. Heroes from all over the country pulling together to save as many people as possible. I mean what you and the other heroes did was just incredible, I knew I needed to be a part of that; and it was easily the best decision I've ever made. I joined the Network for the same reason everyone does, I never wanted to be bound up in red tape and bureaucracy. Plus being able to spy on an entire city isn't exactly something employers like seeing on a CV.'

Heather leant against the carriage wall while he spoke, staring out at the forgotten platform. She had also been looking around the carriage and noticed a clearly cherished bobblehead collection in the old luggage racks. When Zack finished talking she stood up straight and walked over to him.

'One night. Let's try out a night, Zack. You help me on patrol; feed me intel, provide the required resources and we can go from there. What do you think?'

She was genuinely impressed by his work and could feel the passion and honesty in his story.

'Seriously?' Zack asked gleefully.

'Yes, and if it goes smoothly and we're working well together, I have an important assignment from Nahmar that I want to bring you in on.' She could see his eyes widen with awe as she said his name.

'Do you have a night in mind?' Zack asked.

CHAPTER NINE

Zack and Heather briefly discussed details and responsibilities and agreed on Friday night. Heather shared that she was working on bringing down a prominent group that had been infecting New London for months; Neuro and the Dukes. Neuro Calvins, (sometimes known as The Vanquisher) and the Duke brothers, Warren and Neil, had been operating out of New London for years but their activities had dramatically spiked recently. They dealt in military grade weapons, drugs and human trafficking. Over four hundred missing person cases were reported this year and the largest chunk of that were girls between the ages of fifteen and twenty-five. Heather had been looking for clues and signs of their operations but so far with little success. For Heather, this was Zack's trial run.

Returning home after a relatively quiet night, she rested her push bike in the large closet off the hallway. It was about seven o'clock in the morning and Henry was already up playing with his action figures in the hallway. Unlike most ten-year-olds, he was willing to voice over the action still and shamelessly loved playing make-believe. Normally this was something Heather encouraged but today was the first time she wished he would play a different game.

'New London Police! Put your hands in the air, scum! We have you completely surrounded, put your weapons down!' Henry's voice was coming from the living room, putting on an awkward and forced accent, as children sometimes do.

Heather silently moved through the hallway, using her powers to ensure not a single step made a sound and disturbed Henry. From the edge of the room, she listened intently to the story he was playing out on the coffee table.

'You'll never catch me, losers!' This voice that he was putting on was more sharp and harsh than the other; clearly, today's bad guy.

He began making dramatic slow-motion noises and booms like the overused effects on a Hollywood trailer. Heather had to admit he was getting a lot better at them. After a few gunshot noises and a couple of explosions, Henry spoke again in the bad guy voice.

'Haha! New London will be mine, then the world! And there's nothing you can do to stop me, muahahaha.' His maniacal laugh was fantastic, Heather wished she was recording this.

'Enough, Harrow. Your reign of terror will end … tonight!' Henry yelled in a new and dramatic voice.

Heather whipped her head around the corner in shock, her heart in her mouth. Henry kneeled over the large glass coffee table, the bodies and cars of tiny police officers littered the table and floor. Makeshift cardboard buildings and houses were upturned leaving just two toys remaining. In his right hand was a Paladin action figure; the white and blue of his costume bold and exaggerated, his torso was large and considerably more muscular than the real Paladin's. In Henry's left hand, was a Harrow toy. The helmet had the same reflective silver-tinted glass on the front and the same deep midnight blue across the rest of the armour, the design of the suit was wrong but it was quite obviously Harrow.

'Come to die as well, hero? Very well!' Henry launched the Harrow toy through the air, its plastic fist collided with Paladin's jaw.

With his back facing the doorway, Henry played completely oblivious to his broken-hearted mother's reaction. Heather stood there with a thin blur of tears resting in her eyes as he played. The two toys traded punches and kicks while Henry jumped them around the table, continuing the cinematic sound effects. Paladin flew high up in the air then came crashing back down towards Harrow, fists extended. On impact, Henry threw his Harrow toy across the room; sending her smashing into the window. Running over to it he held Paladin high above the beaten Harrow.

'Surrender or suffer the consequences,' Henry's voice cried out as Paladin.

'Never,' he answered for Harrow, in the darkest most twisted tone he could muster. Then he brought the toys crashing together again.

'Stop!' cried a completely different voice. Henry span round to see who had yelled at him, but it wasn't Heather. It was his mother, Kirsty.

Kirsty bustled through the living room wearing her crisp pressed work suit jacket and a tight black skirt, her hair was forcefully tied back but her curls were still out of control.

'Why aren't you ready for school young man? Get your bag together now. Your homework is still all over the kitchen table. And could you help out instead of just standing there,' she directed her pre-coffee rage at Heather now.

Heather stood there for a moment, staring at the toy of herself now lying face down on the carpet. Kirsty turned to look at her unresponsive wife.

'What's the matter with …' but before she finished her sentence she rounded on Henry again.

'Henry, what is this?!' she yelled through to the Kitchen as she picked up the Harrow toy. 'Did you get him this?' she turned back to Heather, who simply shook her head.

'Where did you get this toy from, Henry?'

'Just from one of the boys at school, they gave it to me,' Henry said timidly, gripping onto the pockets of his trousers.

'Well you can give it back, I don't want you playing with this toy. Do you realise what this person is?' She shook the figure aggressively as she spoke, the head of which wobbled madly as she did.

'No, Mum,' said Henry.

'She is a monster. A monster that kills people and now apparently kills good people, I don't want to see you playing with toys like this again.'

After she finished reprimanding her son and told him to go finish getting ready, she walked over to Heather and passed the toy to her.

'Can you make sure this gets back to whatever kid's parents it was that gave it to Henry? Did you see her on the news this week?'

'Mmm,' Heather responded, barely meeting Kirsty's eyes as she tried to hide her the thin line of tears in her own.

'Horrifying, bet you're not her biggest fan now. I

always told you she was nuts, running around the city killing criminals for all these years. I never understood why you liked her, and now she's bored of just killing the bad guys.' Kirsty tried to tame her hair in the mirror as she spoke. Heather just made the same acknowledging 'Mmm.'

'What's up?' Kirsty said, now trying to face her.

'Yeah, yeah fine. Just a slow night.'

Kirsty didn't look convinced that this was the full extent of what was up, but she knew if she didn't leave now she'd be late. Whatever it was that was bothering Heather, would have to wait until later.

'Henry's lunch for today is in the fridge, there are a couple bags of the crisps he likes in the top cupboard. Thanks for taking him in; see you tonight!' Kirsty grabbed her satchel and slipped on her heels as she shot towards the door.

'Oh, and good morning,' she popped back to exchange a fleeting peck on the lips and rushed out the door; leaving Heather stood alone in the hallway clutching a sweaty, scratched, best-selling action figure of herself.

Rainwater dripped down the steel roofing, the last few beads of water raced each other to the edges as the rain let up. Heather crouched cat-like in her armour, peering down through the roof of the neighbouring warehouse using her scanners.

She was in an old industrial estate just on the outskirts of eastern New London. Rain which had been relentless for the last day was just starting to die down. The night was late into the grim unsociable hours of the morning and the estate was deserted, except for a single warehouse tucked away between a custom car garage and a packaging factory. It was the factory roof that Heather hid on. The last few droplets of rain bounced off her suit as she continued to patiently wait for the signal from Zack.

Before their first mission together, Heather had conducted her own research on Zack. Twenty-six-year-old Zack Hemant, born and raised in the city by a beige and almost unextraordinary family. Zack, however, had an arsenal of impressive qualifications and had published several insightful papers, including: "The future of the web", "The seventh flavour of quarks" and "Collecting a multiverse"; each of which Heather had scanned through. Throughout the trial night, Zack had done nothing but prove his great worth and value.

Right off the starting line, he had sent her extensive, documented research, all meticulously organised on Neuro, the Dukes and all known associates. His findings offered Heather several leads to follow up that would supposedly bring her to the crime lords. The pair began the night with Zack's first recommended lead, an ex-convict with connections to Neil Duke, and he'd recently skipped parole.

Earlier in the night, staking out the man's crummy and beaten up apartment, Heather didn't have to wait long before he left and got into a Ford Fiesta with blacked out windows. Astride her trusty Harley Davidson, she followed him out of the city and towards the outer ring. It was around this time in the evening she intercepted a report of an armed robbery on her filtered police scanners.

'Ahh crap,' she mumbled.

'What's the matter?' Zack's cool voice asked from within Heather's Helmet. She told him what came in on the scanner.

'Go get them,' he had said confidently.

'What? No, we'll lose the trail. It's been cold for months and I've got to find these guys.'

Zack Laughed. Not in a mocking way but it was the sort of laugh people make when they think they know best.

'We're not going to lose them, I'm monitoring traffic cams and I'm intercepting dash cam feeds every mile or so. Don't worry I've got them, you deal with this robbery.'

And that is exactly what Heather did. Taking the first exit she plummeted down quiet night-soaked roads until she reached the fuel station that was being robbed.

Wiping her fists of blood and pulling out a small shard of shrapnel that stuck out of her chest plate, she soared back to the motorway to pick up the trail; on her way there, Zack guided her to avoid four separate police patrols. The force had now been instructed to shoot Harrow on sight so avoiding them was necessary; now more than ever.

Twenty-two minutes after answering the armed robbery call she had the fiesta in her sights again. Zack had not lost the car for a moment. Tailing it for a few more miles and one more police avoiding detour, they arrived at the warehouse.

From her rooftop lookout, Heather had just activated a complicated looking device that Zack had given her to test out. It was thin and circular, similar size and shape to a pizza; six plum sized silver balls sat within the device. Heather pushed the sleek green button in the centre of the surrounding balls, which sent them silently launching in several different directions. They flew out to circle the particular warehouse, hovering in the air, completely invisible now because of their built-in cloaking devices.

Even Heather couldn't pick them up on her scanners. She wondered how much each of these tiny floating drones cost and how Zack had ever managed to afford this tech; he did, after all, appear to live in a derelict underground station. It was from there, back in the heart of New London, that he had complete control over the drones and everything they could see.

'Okay, Harrow, I'm picking up eleven guys on the inside, three on the outside. One is in the van parked out-front and the other two are around the back having a cigarette.'

Heather could see a few of them with her own scanner but her tech didn't have the same capacity and range that the drones had. She was impressed and a little bit covetous.

'What's going on in there, Zack?' she whispered, trying to see if she could spot any of the drones against the canvas of black sky.

'Well, it's as we expected. Huge shipments of guns, crates nearly spilling over with ammo; how does that suit of yours hold up against gunfire?'

'I can handle it,' Heather said. Her suit was built to take a beating.

'Well, can you handle rockets? They look like they're gearing up for an all-out war,' said Zack. Heather could hear the fear in Zack's voice as he said this.

'Then let's take away their toys. Where's my entrance?'

'Roof is too thick to cut through quick enough without attracting attention, they'll open fire before you can cut a hole big enough with your ion laser. Windows are non-existent and there's a large number of hostiles at the back of the building. You need to take out the van driver before deploying the signal blocker I gave you. My advice ... knock on the front door.'

Heather ran to the edge of the roof and leapt from

it, swooping to the ground silently.

Inside the large van, a gruff looking man with bronze piercings covering his eyebrows and ears was sat comfortably reading a magazine. Just as he was moving onto the article about the best exercises to do to gain mass, there was a forceful knocking on the driver side door.

'Bloody hell, I'm coming,' he rolled up the magazine and flung it onto the passenger seat. Opening the door and popping his head out he didn't see the messenger he expected, in fact, he didn't see anyone. Looking the other way, all he could see was the quiet grubby road of the industrial estate.

Out of nowhere something small and jagged bounced off the steering wheel and struck him in the chin. Caught off guard he flustered while a collection of furious insults tumbled around his mind. Before he could realise what had happened or who had thrown the rock, Heather launched herself at him from the open door. After a quick silent struggle, she choked him to unconsciousness. Then taking the keys from the van she dropped them through the slits between a large drain grate, partially covered by the vans fat balding tires.

Heather then pulled another device Zack had given her from her utility belt, a powerful signal jammer which would block all incoming and outgoing communications that weren't on Zack's protected frequency. Meaning that Heather and Zack could still communicate once the device activated. Usually, she would use one of her own EMP grenades, but they were hoping to find some useful information and potential leads from any of the men's phones, which an EMP would crudely fry. The device had a finite lifespan due to its impressive range and small size, Heather would have ninety seconds before their phones would return to normal and they could potentially call their bosses.

'Start the clock, Zack,' Heather said, smashing down the front door with a single heavy kick.

Two men lifting a cumbersome wooden lid onto a crate full of ammunition were the first to die, one well-placed bullet each. A wisp of smoke spat from Heather's gun after the second shot. She charged to cover behind the crate; nobody had seen her yet.

'You've got four pointing assault rifles on your position, they're on the balcony,' Zack's voice was calm and clear through her helmet.

Tucking into another gadget in her belt, she pulled out a fist-sized grenade and hurled it towards the hanging ceiling lights. Another perfectly placed bullet from her gun cracked through the air and into the grenade. Exploding as it reached the highest point, it blasted across the thick steel roof, decimating the warehouse lights and plunging everything into total darkness.

'Suit, night vision,' she said, leaping out from behind cover and shooting at the four arms dealers blindly firing into the black. Each shot met its mark with unforgiving precession. More men poured into the main expanse of the warehouse, a few of them using guns with attached flashlights. The laser sights on each of their guns danced around the room searching for their elusive target.

In her mind, she knew what the consequences of each step was, which directions and moves would keep her alive and which would not. Heather fired with such speed and ferocity it was like watching a cheetah hunt. She had little worry for the echoing volume of the gunshots. It was loud but there were no residential areas for at least a mile and this industrial estate was completely deserted at this hour.

Another wave of men dashed out of some side

room, ineffectively wielding high calibre pistols and shining torches in Heather's direction. Using her grapnel gun, she repelled to the upper levels while shooting at the men on the ground. Another two down.

'You've got six remaining, one of them ... no, two are running to the back exit. Want me to tell you when they're by the cars?' Zack said inside her helmet.

'If it's not too much trouble,' she replied, a small smile flickered across her mouth.

Working so closely with someone was quite new to her, and Zack wasn't like the others. She found him very easy to work with and talk to, even the way he spoke to her was pleasing. Heather shot another two while sprinting across the top balcony towards a stocky man aiming a thick stubby shotgun right at her.

'Harrow, they're by the cars.'

'Thank you, Zack,' she replied. 'Suit, detonate E charges one to six.'

A blink later Heather could hear the faint ripple of intense energy blasting across the cars outside, destroying the fleeing thug's means of escape and probably all traces of their inner ear balance.

The shotgun-wielding man; barely visible to most, only illuminated by fleeting beams of light or the flashes of gunfire; dragged the pump action back and forth for another shot. Seeing everything moments before it happened Heather fluidly dived through the air, her hydraulic enhanced boots giving her astonishing height as she flew over the cloud of shrapnel. Before he could reload, she was on him. Wrapping her sharp glove around his neck she ripped the gun from his hand with the other. Slamming her helmet into his nose she saw the splatter of blood across her visor as she broke it. He howled out in agony but the crying was quickly silenced after she hurled him from the balcony. He fell for a brief moment, then crumbled into another crate of weapons.

In her mind Heather saw a thin rocket head crash into her from somewhere and explode on impact, completely obliterating her. Snapping back to reality she dived from the balcony herself and rolled across the grimy floor on landing. Not a moment too soon, as the section of the roof she had just been directly beneath, burst into fire and smoke in the blast. Huge chunks of the roof came crashing down and the balcony caved under the mass of damage. Several large panels fell and crushed the man she'd just headbutted.

Holstering her gun, she turned to the final three men, each of them with terror and panic etched across their faces. The bright flames that had begun covering the roof illuminated them like an oversized candle. Even the man holding the weighty rocket launcher looked as though he'd just pissed himself.

Heather stood up and switched off the night vision, the remaining grunts opened fire on her one final time. She charged towards them like a bull seeing red, avoiding some of the bullets with her foresight but most simply missed. The fear within them had drastically thrown off their accuracy. A couple of shots hit Heather's armour but it was built to take this kind of onslaught, they harmlessly pinged off and hit the floor.

Driving her fist through the teeth of the closest assailant she turned his body to face the remaining two, who carelessly filled him with lead. Grabbing his wrist, she spun his lifeless body towards the next man, knocking him to the floor, his finger still wrapped around the trigger sent the rest of the magazine round splattering across the room and remaining sections of roof.

The final man tried to put up a struggle but was so

many leagues below Heather, she nearly felt bad for him. He swung the butt of the rifle towards her head which she anticipated and dodged, sharply jabbing him in the ribs. Striking his knee upwards, he tried to catch her off guard but she sidestepped and shattered the knee of his balancing leg with her boot. He fell to the ground in blinding agony for a moment before she put him out of his misery.

A stillness swept the warehouse floor, the only sounds were the gentle sizzling roof and the whimpered cries of a still living arms dealer trapped beneath a deadweight colleague. Heather approached him slowly, the noise of her heavy metallic boots bouncing off the empty walls as she walked.

Lifting a boot onto his neck, the sharp studs of it tickled his throat uncomfortably.

'Talk,' she said, staring at him with the reflective visor that gave nothing away.

'I'm just a packing guy, they don't tell me anything really, just what I've got to pack,' he whined. The man was easily younger than Heather, he can't have been much older than twenty-one.

She applied a small bit of pressure to his neck. Not that she could see it, but she assumed it was drawing blood.

He cried out in pain and his hands scrambled around her boot, just trying to lift it a few centimeters.

'Tell me something worth letting you live for,' said Heather.

'The shipment was supposed to go to Kensington …' his eyes flickered to the right, where a meter away his gun lay abandoned.

'Where in Kensington?' she shouted, applying more pressure.

'Ahhhh, to some museum. The … AHHHH … NATURAL HISTORY ONE. Please let me-'

'Is that where I can find your employers?'

He was trying to scrape a breath in between her talking.

'I don't know, I've never even met them. They're elusive as fuck. Most of the guys here had met them but you went ahead and killed them ... AHHHH!'

Heather was pressing hard into his neck, trying to decide what to do next.

'Harrow, can you get one of their phones? They may have a number I can trace,' Zack said, the young guy with Heather's spiked boot on his neck unable to hear.

'Phone. You ever called Neuro or the brothers?'

'No, but ... the guy in the crate does, he was in charge ... of tonight's shipment,' he spluttered.

'There we go, and that's something worth letting you live for.' Before he could complain or say anything else, Heather lifted the boot up and brought her knee crashing down against the side of his head.

'Zack, call the Network and get me a collection. Thirteen dead, possibly eleven. One alive, Terminus can have him.'

'Already done, Harrow, they're twenty minutes out.'

'Great work, tell them I want my usual cut of the shipment's value wired to my account. There's several millions worth of guns and ammunition here, Zack. You'll be able to retire on your cut if you wanted?'

'Hmmm I always imagined retirement would be really boring, maybe I'll stick this hero business out a little longer,' he joked, sat in his comfortable reclined office chair, buried many meters beneath the streets of New London.

'I thought you might say that,' she chuckled. 'Thank you, now get me out of here. Police must have been scrambled. How much attention did that last blast cause?'

'None, I placed about thirty fake calls saying there was a hit and run several miles from here. So, any local units have been dispatched to that. You've got a clear road, Harrow.'

She was in awe of his technical know-how; this man really wasn't messing around. As she collected the phone and signal jamming device from earlier, Heather couldn't help but feel she had lucked out when she met Zack.

Over the following months, it would be her responsibility to rid the world of six more powerful and extremely influential beings that had infiltrated the highest members of society. With what she'd seen from Zack on that night, the feeling of dread and anxiety that had been building up inside her, started to drain out; like an overflowing bath having its plug pulled.

CHAPTER TEN

The month following that night flew by. Firstly, Heather met with Nahmar to discuss her elimination of the first Pandarian. He wasn't pleased with how the first mission went and his frustration was apparent, however he was glad to hear that Heather had decided to take on a partner. Yet again it was a different Nahmar but at least Heather had spoken to this one before.

Nahmar gave her the name of her next target and she flew to Paris, leaving Zack behind in the affectionately named Catacombs.

Paris was warm and welcoming; the large preserved patches of grass had been cooking in the sun all day. Tourists and locals alike lounged out on it hoping to turn their skin a shade darker. Heather was wearing a simple peaked cap, keeping her hair neatly out of her face. She'd been in town for a couple of days, working with Zack to stake out her target.

On this blisteringly bright afternoon, she sat pretending to read a French novel she had picked up in the airport, sipping on a tall cold glass of orange juice. Tiny droplets of condensation were dripping down the glass and onto the small round table where she sat.

Heather had visited this café half a dozen time since arriving, as it had an excellent view of the building opposite where her next target worked.

Renėe Chamberlin, the chief editor for Bloom - the world's hottest fashion and lifestyle magazine. Where every month, five hundred million copies were shipped around the globe, ending up in bedrooms, schools and office desk drawers. Renėe was obviously a busy woman and pinpointing her during the day was extraordinarily tough, but by intently watching the Bloom offices for the last few days, Heather had built up a clear idea of her movements.

Infiltrating through an upper window, Heather slithered passed security. With Zack's technological help she disabled camera feeds and got to the closed office door undetected.

Neither of them said a word but as Renėe looked up from her desk to see Heather stood there, fully suited in her death coloured armour, she had this look on her face; as though she had expected this visit. Renėe's hand whipped beneath her desk, withdrawing a high-powered plasma pistol, the likes of which Heather had only heard about and went to open fire on the intruder.

As ever, Heather's reactions were lightning quick and she circumvented the smouldering blasts that Renėe would have fired, ramming into the woman with her shoulder. Heather slammed her into the glass, pounding her skull against the cracking window again and again. Renėe stared at her defiantly, barely struggling as she knew she was no match for Heather's strength. But just as Ria had, her face lost its confidence on seeing the small silver cube Heather pulled from her belt. The beating continued, large cracks were rippling across the surface of the thick glass. It distorted the breath-taking view outside, like a broken mirror.

Another heavy slam into the window and it was enough. Renèe fell to her knees, breathing heavily and spitting blood. The whole right side of her face was swollen, badly cut and her eye had begun to bulge.

'My friends are going to find you,' the Pandarian spat, looking up at Heather's blank helmet.

'They know you're coming and they're going to kill you. Your family too, everyone you have ever loved. Regret will devour every inch of your being …'

But Heather had heard enough, grabbing the side of Renèe's head and underside of her sharp jaw, she snapped her neck and let the body fall back against the fractured windowpane.

Pulling out the silver cube from her suit, Heather held it firmly as the life left the woman's body. Bright thick energy zoomed out of Renèe's chest, just as it had Ria's. Swirling around the room, helplessly trying to escape, but inevitably being dragged back towards the cube with every cycle.

Heather did this three more times before returning to New London. After telling Nahmar what Renèe had said, he instructed her to hasten her efforts or else the Pandarians may change their hosts and the years of research and time to track them down will have been for nothing. Taking discrete private flights, Heather travelled to Denmark, Egypt and Istanbul where she killed three more of the world's most influential faces. Each of them more difficult than the last, they were clearly preparing for the potential assassination attempts. However, with Zack's assistance and meticulous attention to detail, it made it manageable.

The first, a portly man who owned over two-thirds of the meat and dairy farms in Denmark and was a key stakeholder in a vast empire of farms across Europe. With Zack's help, Heather managed to discover and prevent an entire plot this man was about to set in motion; one that Heather knew could single-handedly destroy all life on earth.

From the second, an extraordinarily rich businessman living in Alexandria, Heather wired millions from his account to her own ghost accounts. This was something she often did when taking down the more affluent criminals. Before she killed him, she tortured all of the necessary details out of him, limb by limb. The money she stole would fund her expensive career choice but also be used to help those in desperate need back home. In this case, the fifteen women's shelters that she had hand-selected across the south of England.

The third was a bloodthirsty warlord that had taken control of Istanbul, the crossroads of the world. He and his forces were well prepared for the potential assassination attempt; not that any of the warlord's soldiers knew why some vigilante from England was coming all this way for their fearless leader.

The battle was brutal and bloody. Heather lost count of the number of men she had to kill to get to the Pandarian. Their weapons were advanced and tailored to rip through tank armour, which certainly gave Heather a challenge.

Stumbling out of the decimated hideout covered in bullet scores and explosion scars, Heather clutched onto the shattered armour below her breastplate. She could feel several ribs had broken in the fight and blood was drooling out onto her hand. Her faceplate was cracked and made it difficult to see where she was going. The suit servos in her right leg had also been severed in a particularly bad shotgun blast, making it incredibly difficult to walk. It would take months to repair her suit in the field and she just didn't have that sort of time. She needed to make a return visit home before completing her quest.

Walking a mile out from the warlord's hideout, (that Zack had managed to find in a single weekend) Heather began removing pieces of her armour one by one. The terrain was harsh and difficult to traverse, even more so with three broken ribs and internal bleeding, but she pressed on. Hot sunlight pushed down on her like a playground bully, her mouth was dry and felt inflamed. At least it was quiet out here, she thought to herself. Even with her helmet on, which she now removed, the noise in those caverns had been intolerable. From within the helmet she extracted the mic and earpiece she made all her calls with and with her unbloodied hand she wrapped it around her neck and slipped the earpiece over her ear. Having dumped all the pieces of her armour and now her helmet, she spoke into the mouthpiece; though she still had the almost depleted utility belt, hanging over a bruised shoulder.

'Suit, detonate all external panels. Confirm authorisation seven four one four two delta, detonate.'

From behind her, a dozen powerful explosions went off simultaneously, echoing through the hallways of the mountains she stood in.

'Suit, call Zack.'

Her communicator rang for nearly a minute before he picked up.

'Harrow, where have you been? I've been trying to call,' he struggled to hide the genuine concern in his voice.

'Worried about me?' she choked with a smile, still tightly pressing on her bleeding ribs.

'Of course. I wasn't happy about you going in there without comms to me, with the amount of rock blocking your signal, I felt practically blind. I'm just glad you're okay, it would be a shame to have to find a new partner. I was starting to really like you,' he laughed.

'I know the feeling,' she blushed, a tiny butterfly flipped in her stomach.

'Zack, the suit is totalled, I'm coming home for a few days to gear up and see the family before we go get the final two.'

Though Heather had not revealed her identity to Zack or told him any specific details about her, she had begun to be more open with him. More so than she had been with anyone in the world of heroes and vigilantes.

Earlier in the week, they had been talking about their favourite foods and he asked her if she'd ever been to Istanbul before. She told him she hadn't but loved şakşuka and was hoping there would be time to try the authentic version. Zack had it delivered to her hotel room, leaving Heather both pleasantly surprised and perfectly satisfied. She called him after her dinner to thank him and they naturally got onto the topic of families.

That night, what was supposed to be a quick five minute thank you call, turned into a four hour conversation. Zack spoke about his recently deceased mum and how much he missed her. He shared his love of video games and comic books, even unintentionally admitting he enjoyed role playing games and had spent much of his teenage years as the dungeon master for his friends. Heather spoke about her mum too, telling him about her alcohol addiction and though they only lived thirty minutes away, they barely ever spoke. She shared her love for rock climbing and recalled the first time she ever put on the harness and faced that fear of heights. 'You, a fear of heights!?' he had joked over the phone.

Stood looking down at the tree-covered landscape before her, she briefly let her mind wander back to that night and the joy she had felt staying up late with him, like a pair of coy teenagers.

'Good. Your supplies were starting to run low anyway, weren't they? What are you going to tell the family?' asked Zack, after Heather said she was coming home.

'Just that the training courses final module has been delayed.'

'Are they going to be okay with that?'

'Probably not but hey, wouldn't be the first time I've done something to piss them off. I'm going to call home now, see you soon.'

'Good luck!'

Heather hung up, her mind had a twinge of excitement and guilt about talking to Zack like this. It was clear to both of them that there was an energy and spark between them. Heather tried to shove the thought from her mind as she called Kirsty.

It was about nine in the evening in the UK, Heather's wife was probably just settling down to watch some rubbish on TV, and that was if she wasn't working from home.

'Hello, Kirsty speaking. How can I help?' her voice was irritable and short. Definitely working from home, Heather thought to herself.

'Hey hun, it's me,' Heather said brightly, trying to get off on a good foot.

'Hey, how come you're not calling from your phone?'

'Oh, they just asked us to switch them off during presentations today, you know what they're like. So, I'm just using an office one before I go back to the hotel.'

'Fair enough. Everything okay?' Kirsty asked, knowing that this wasn't a routine call. Having not received many during the month Heather had been away.

'Yeah fine, fine thanks. Hey, the team in charge just told us the final module has to be delayed. The tutor has had a death in the family so they're looking for someone to finish the course. They're sending us home for a couple of days and then I'll have to come back out.'

Heather had told Kirsty that her work was putting most of the team in an intensive six-week training course in Japan that would teach them how to operate, develop and repair the new machinery in the factory she supposedly worked at.

'You have to go back out?' Kirsty said, grit in her tone.

'Afraid so, but it shouldn't be for too much longer.'

'There is no point in you coming home for a couple of days just to then go back out again, it's only going to upset Henry more. He is really missing you right now and it's not fair for you to mess him around like this.'

Heather quickly lost her tact and let her temper get the better of her.

'But wouldn't it be better if I come to see my son, even if it is only for a few days. Believe it or not Kirsty but I do miss you both.'

'Then why are you spending so much time away from us!'

At this Heather lost any sense of decorum, she shouted down the mouthpiece. Her voice ricocheted between the vast green mountains around her.

'You think I want to be here?! Doing this! It's shit,

Kirsty. But it's got to be done. If you took a minute to think about someone other than yourself then maybe you'd understand.'

As she shouted her ribs cried out in agony from the strain.

'Well, it certainly looks like you'd rather be there than here. If you cared as much as you said you did, then you'd quit and get a job during the fucking daytime. One that didn't take you away for weeks at a time.'

'I can't do that, Kirst.'

'Yeah, that's what you always say. Bullshit. If you wanted to you could, but you don't want to. Rather than spending your evenings in bed next to me, you'd rather be pressing print of some stupid fucking machine.'

Blood now beginning to drizzle from her open wound, Heather closed down the conversation.

'I'll be home tomorrow to see you and Henry.'

'Whatever.' And with that, the line went dead.

With tears streaming down her face, Heather silently made her way down the mountain to the car she'd stashed at the bottom. On the other side of the world in a sandwiched apartment bedroom, Kirsty was screaming into her pillow.

CHAPTER ELEVEN

Somewhere in a leaf-littered, autumnal university campus, a two-week-old mobile phone rang. Vibrating smoothly on a neat stack of coursework, the phone rang for several seconds before a young, gently moisturised hand picked it up. The young man's hand had been neatly manicured, with not a single bit of dirt hiding obtrusively beneath his nails. He wore a large gold signet ring with the engraving of a crow on the face. It too was pristine and thoroughly polished. Lifting the phone to his ear, he stared out of his bedroom window. Leaves were fluttering to the ground and the sky was a soft pink colour.

'Hello,' he said firmly and without intonation as though he knew who was calling.

'The others, have you heard anything from them?' the voice on the other end of the phone asked darkly.

'No and if they've not been able to enter a new host it must mean the box has been discovered,' he said, still staring out at the gentle autumn scene.

'Yes, I came to the same conclusion. She will be

coming for us next,' said the voice on the phone.

'Do we know who she is?'

'No. I've had my people investigate but they have come up short, there is nothing that gives away her identity.'

'We need to find her pressure points!' the university student shouted.

'You don't think I know that! I am using every resource available to me to find out who she is. What are you doing? Partying and fucking about with humans?'

'I shouldn't need to explain to you why I chose this host, my position here is very profitable. They are at a highly influential phase during this age, something we have capitalised on for centuries,' the young man fought back.

'A discussion for another time. Are you prepared?'

'Yes, if she turns up here she will not be leaving alive,' he said, now pulling his eyes from the view and back into his room.

'See that she doesn't. Oh, and one more thing, if she does come for you next, remember the box is the key. Get it away from her, without it she will be powerless and you can assimilate her as your new host. A human with this much power will be an unquestionable asset to us.'

'Very well. Would it not be beneficial to take less of a defensive position and move with an attack?' he asked the voice on the phone.

'Let me handle that. New London is on a knife edge, as it has been for some time. I am about to tip it over the edge. This will keep Harrow busy and if we're lucky, kill her in the process. You just worry about not dying and getting that accursed box, bring it to me and I will release our imprisoned brothers and sisters back upon this feeble planet.'

It started small. A kid wearing a thick brown hoodie threw a brick through a shop window. Plucking out the small handheld console he'd always wanted. Later that afternoon a group of men were attacked after the sports team they supported beat the New London's Stags. Three went to the hospital, one to the morgue. A large four by four with its wheels scuffed and paintwork peeling, drove into a stock exchange with sixty pounds of C4 in the back rigged to blow. After that, the whole city went to hell and by seven o'clock that night, New London was burning.

Rioting had broken out across the city; violence and brutality covered it like a fog. People were still mistrusting of most, and since Britain's segregation all those years ago, the fear of strangers had only festered. Religious buildings were torn down and decimated. Pubs, bars, clubs and joints were unforgivingly destroyed. But the group that got the most hate on that night, the most mindless and spiteful attacks, were against government bodies.

Number ten was under siege, rioters with flaming bottles of vodka hurled them over armed guards to the windows of the prime minister's house. Across town, tax authorities were being held hostage while numerous angry citizens ransacked their offices. Smashing computers and outdated equipment, tearing through room after room with charged up ferocity and flooding the server rooms, desperately trying to throw the system into disarray.

Some among the people that left their homes that night to join with the riots, were not the expected stereotypes. These were mothers that were just trying to make a little more money, so their kids didn't have to share a bed at night. Husbands who felt they had paid such a large percentage of their wage in tax that year, they had been unable to buy their wife the coffee machine she'd asked for. Even struggling pensioners, who had spent their whole lives working, just to receive the scraps left over once all the other money had been dished out.

Recent times had been difficult for New London's lower classes and that fiery October evening showed the city again, what brutal terrors humanity is capable of. The only saving grace for the city was that its attackers were without leadership and mostly without the serious tools to cause long-lasting harm. That was until the villains arrived.

When superheroes started popping up a few decades ago, so did their counterparts and they were in every way a mirrored parallel of strength and intellect. Admittedly supervillains had become much less prevalent in New London since the arrival of Harrow. However, her absence had been noticed and tonight they crawled out of their secluded holes in greater number than ever before.

While Heather flew back to New London, completely oblivious to the attacks taking place in her city, Kirsty found herself right in the nightmarish centre of it. She and Henry were locked in the canteen of Henry's school, sat on a wobbly plastic chair and surrounded by other kids and their parents. The reports of violence and rioting had come in thick and fast during parents evening, so the headteacher had made the decision to lock the school down. Police had been called but with all that was going on, they were stretched very thinly.

Some of the parents had made the decision to leave with their children but most had thought it wiser to keep off the streets. Henry was sat glued to Kirsty's side, he had not spoken in several minutes. She had asked him a few times if he was okay but only received head nods in response until at last, he asked her a question.

'Mum, is Mummy okay?' he was, of course, asking about Heather.

'Yes sweetie, she's fine. Mummy isn't even in the city at the moment, don't you worry,' she said, looking into Henry's thin, terrified eyes.

'But you said she was coming home today, what if the bad guys got her plane?' His voice was croaking as he spoke.

'Try not to worry, Henry, Mummy is going to be just fine. The police will sort this out really soon and we can go home and see her.'

'Will Paladin and the other heroes save us?' he asked, the glimmer of hope now poking through his fear.

'Someone will sweetie,' she said, hoping herself that it was true.

Kirsty was looking around for the headteacher trying to see if she could find out what was going on out there when a plump woman around Kirsty's age yelled out to the rest of the canteen.

'There's been a shooting on Brownlow road! Three dead!' she said, holding up her phone in the air; displaying the local news update page.

'That's just around the corner!' Worried whispers flickered amongst the parents, and a child in Henry's class broke into floods of tears.

The headteacher had appeared and flitted towards the shouting mother, he tried to calm her down and pleaded with her to remain composed. Kirsty had always had a great deal of respect for the headteacher, Mr Weston, and the few conversations they had had in the past were always pleasant. The woman with the updates sat back down on her chair and continued scrolling through her feed. Mr Weston turned around to see the several dozen parents, teachers and students all looking to him for guidance. With a great deal of pressure building up inside him, and fear twisting and tugging on his every thought, he addressed the room.

'I know this is an extremely scary time for all of us. There are terrible things happening out there tonight and for many of us it is a reminder of Buckingham.' He spoke with authority and confidence, but it was obvious that he was including himself among the group of people that were scared.

'But I must ask you all to remain calm. The police are on their way and all of this will soon be over. The school is completely locked down, you and your children are perfectly safe.'

A moment after these words left his mouth, an enormous crashing noise came from behind him, like an elephant slamming into a sea of brick and glass. The room of parents, children and faculty screamed out in shock, several more of the kids began uncontrollably crying. Terrified parents tried to comfort their children while listening out for further sounds. The noise was too loud to have been anything other than the school building itself.

Anticipation built in the room, Mr Weston quickly made his way over to the canteen doors. But before he could reach them, the handle twisted and the door creaked open.

A thin gangling woman poked her head through the crack, her skin was leathery and coarse and her lifeless eyes were black without a reflection. Before Kirsty could get a good look at her, her head disappeared and the door closed behind her.

'They're all in there,' they could hear the thin woman's tar-like voice from the other side of the door.

As Mr Weston bravely reached out again to open

the door it was blasted off its hinges, sending both the doors and Mr Weston flying across the room. The headteacher hit the floor hard, his head making a horrible cracking noise as it hit the polished concrete. He went very still and the door lay awkwardly over his body. Three people then entered through the splintered frame into the canteen.

On the left was the black-eyed woman. Her hair was long and silky but looked like it hadn't been washed in at least a fortnight. She wore thin dark bandages across her arms and legs and she reminded Kirsty of an Egyptian mummy. On the right, stood a flamboyant man, wearing bright blue robes like a wizard. He held a pulsing white rod in his hand that hummed threateningly.

Between them both was a mountain of a man, whose massive muscles bulged across his body. He was around seven-foot-tall and wore a broad maroon chest plate with a crudely painted R on it. The trio confidently walked into the room surveying its occupants.

'Good evening ladies and gentlemen, boys and girls. We were in the neighbourhood and thought we'd stop by for a little visit. You have probably seen on the news that people are being a bit … well, naughty out there. So, we thought we'd come in here and keep you company. I hope that's okay.'

The huge hulk of a man was walking around groups of parents and kids as he spoke, he stopped in front of a man and his little girl. He bent down onto one knee and almost came nose to nose with the girl.

'Is that okay with you, sweetheart?' he mocked.

The girl, who can't have been much older than six years old responded with a sharp 'No!' her face was defiant and strong.

Letting out a room-filling laugh, the man rolled his

head back briefly but before he could say anything the girl's dad piped up.

'Get away from my daughter you freak.'

Faster than a starved viper, the giant man grabbed her dad tightly around the face, his huge hand covering all his features and hurled him like a ragdoll into the stone walls. Breaking his neck, he was dead before he even left the ground. The little girl ran over to her father in panic and terror and screamed into his chest trying to wake him up.

A parent, who stood along the side of the room holding her daughter's hand, made a break for the exit; but the wizard looking villain held up the strange white rod in his hand. A deep charging sound began and a second later a huge wave of explosive energy slammed into the fleeing pair. They were thrown backwards and collapsed to the ground, their hearts having burst inside them. Screams erupted amongst the crowd, but nobody else got up to run. Most were now off the chairs and on to the floor, trying to make themselves as small of a target as possible.

Getting to his feet the giant man now addressed everyone in a booming voice, hushing most of the room.

'As I was saying, for us to keep you company that means you have to stay here, nobody leaves. Now, let me introduce myself.' He spoke as though he was presenting a theatrical performance for some amateur dramatics society.

'My name is Ravage, I will be your host for this evening. These are my associates, Warlock; who you can all thank for jamming the signal in your phones,' he said gesturing to the man dressed as a wizard. True enough, Kirsty looked down at the display on her phone and she had no connection at all, to anything. 'And The Dom,' pointing at the leech-like woman that had been crawling past the occupants of the room.

The Dom, or Dolores Delamort as she was once known, had been active in New London before and during Buckingham but had since dropped off the grid. It seemed now she had decided to come back out of hiding, and she was relishing it.

Dolores strolled slowly between families, coldly staring at them with her cruel eyes. Her body writhed up and down as she moved, like the hump of a centipede trying to climb something. Then she brushed right next to Kirsty and Henry, she stared at the pair of them for what felt like a lifetime. Her mouth was stretched and thin, her lips were chapped and pale. Raising a cold wrinkled hand towards them, she slowly moved closer and closer. Her nails looked sharp and poisonous, dark veins protruded from her thin bony hand which was now just inches away from Kirsty and Henry's faces, her necrotic breath repulsively spraying over them as she breathed.

'Dom, would you please shut her up,' Ravage whined. The girl whose father he'd just thrown into the wall and killed, would not stop screaming.

Dolores pulled herself away from Kirsty and Henry and scuttled to the other side of the room where the girl lay sprawled across her dad's dead body, screaming for him to come back. Dolores quickly reached out a sharp hand and grabbed the shoulder of the little girl. Immediately she stopped screaming and her body went limp. Dolores now squatted beside the girl; who was still breathing but was completely silent. The only reason the adults in the room knew she wasn't dead was that every now and then her foot would twitch or her head would shake. It just looked as though she was sleeping. The terrifying woman crouched next to her for a minute, stroking the sleeping girl's hair while Ravage spoke again.

'That's better, thank you, Dom. Now, tonight can go very smoothly for you all, or it could not,' he said, carelessly waving a hand towards the dead headteacher.

'The beauty of it is that it's completely up to you how tonight goes. In half an hour, a bus will arrive to take all your children away. They are worth quite a bit to me as I'm sure you can imagine, which is why it's such a shame when they have to misbehave like that,' waving again at the twitching girl still lying on her dad.

'So, we're going to put the kids on the bus, they're going to be sold and make some very rich and deranged people very happy and you get to go home afterwards. Just think of it as a school trip, and hey you don't have to pay for it!'

Warlock stood in the corner of the room, slapping the rod in his gloved hand with a huge smile across his face.

Henry whispered gently to his mum.

'I don't want to go, Mum, please don't let them take me.' His hair was wet with sweat as he pressed his face under her chin.

'I'm not going to let them take you anywhere, Henry.' But she felt inside that her words were empty and hollow. She had never felt more powerless or terrified in her entire life.

CHAPTER TWELVE

Having seen the news updates in the final thirty minutes of the flight, Heather engaged the autopilot on her motorcycle back on the ground and instructed it to drive to the landing strip. Heather hurried from the airport to her closest safe house, just two miles away. There, she wasted no time equipping one of her several spare suits of armour and fully stocked her utility belt. She took the silver cube now filled with the five souls of the Pandarians and locked it inside the suit.

Taking off from her safe house on the great beast of a motorcycle, she soared towards the thick of the action. The further into the centre of New London she rode, the worse it got. She nimbly weaved between abandoned cars that sat trashed and burning in the middle of the road. Their occupants had either been dragged out and beaten or thought an escape on foot was wiser. A few more meters up the road and behind a large delivery van, Heather could see the real reason people had left their vehicles.

A huge flaming roadblock lay stretched across the

entire road. Several battered cars all crunched up next to each other. Heather swerved to the left and detoured down a side alley too narrow for cars. Bulldozing down the alley she focused her foresight, looking to see if this was an ambush. Though she saw nobody waiting for her she did hear the cries for help, coming out of a window a couple of stories above her.

Returning to the present she looked up at the window she'd envisioned the sound coming from. Gracefully bouncing up on to the motorcycle's seat she poised for her moment.

Now! She leapt as high as she could, the hydraulics in her boots gave her incredible height. Up and up she went, her bike now switched back to autopilot. Then at the highest point, she pushed off from the side of the building next to her, sending her flying through the open window on the other side; landing in the shouting woman's apartment lounge without even knocking over the window plant.

Heather stared at the source of the problem. Two men had obviously broken into this woman's apartment to rob her but perhaps didn't bank on her being in that night. They had large hoods on and scarves tightly wrapped around their lower face. When Heather rolled into the room, one of the men was in a heated struggle trying to tear a handbag from the woman's grasp. The other, was in the corner hurriedly attempting to cut through the TV cables with an old pair of pink-handled scissors. All three of them stopped and turned to see Harrow.

'Harrow, help me, please!' the woman cried out.

The man trying to wrestle the handbag from her, let go instantly and ran towards the door. The second man abandoned his task too and sprinted towards the exit; but before he did, he took a wild shot at Harrow, hurling his scissors towards her. Without flinching, she plucked them from the air and sent them flying straight back towards his friend who had reached the door. The sharp blades lightly pierced his shoulder, making the man cry out in pain. He fell towards the closed door, blocking his partner's escape.

'This is gonna hurt,' Heather said as she ran towards the screaming burglars.

The woman, who was tightly squeezing her bag to her chest, took slow steps back into her kitchen, not taking her eyes off Harrow who had just slammed the second man's head into her airing cupboard door.

Wrapping her fingers tightly around the scissor throwing man's leg she dragged him toward her, flipped his body over so he was facing the ceiling rather than the floor, and brought her great heavy boot crashing down on his kneecap. The woman in the kitchen didn't make a sound but Heather could see her body shaking in the kitchen. He, however, made lots of sounds; he yelled out in agony, cupping his knee and then she broke the other.

Heather dropped him and stepped over to the man with the scissors sticking out of his back, he was desperately trying to remove them, but his restricting leather jacket made them difficult to reach. Resisting the urge to punch them in deeper, Heather wrenched them from his body, threw them to the ground and performed the same kneecap shattering operation on this man. One, two.

The pair of them tossed on the floor in complete agony, the apartment was drowning in the sound of their torture. Heather grabbed hold of an ankle of each man and dragged them across the floor towards the open window. But to the right of it saw a large double door that opened to outside, on the other side a metal rail around hip height. Heather stopped for a second and turned her head to look at the shaking woman.

'Is that door unlocked?' her disguised voice just as threatening as it always sounded. The woman didn't say a word and just nodded. The two men didn't need superpowers to know what she was about to do to them.

'Please, please no! Don't do this,' they pleaded. 'I have a family, I was just trying to make a bit of extra money!'

Heather wasn't going to waste her breath on these low lives. She picked the first one from around his torso and lifted him up to the now wide-open door, fluidly picking his feet up behind him she hurled him over the railing. He fell two stories and landed in a crumpled heap on the floor, screaming in even more agony. Heather then turned to retrieve the other man, who had tried crawling away to safety. He cried out to the women he had been trying to rob.

'HELP! Please, Kate! Tell her to stop!' He pulled off his scarf and hood to reveal his young face, crooked broken nose and a full head of curly hair.

'Wait, you know this man?' Heather said, directing her question to the woman still frozen in the corner. Now back pressed against the fridge.

'Yes! I live upstairs, we're neighbours!' Every word he said was drenched in the plea for mercy.

The woman said nothing, but just stared at him on the floor and the warm trail of blood that was spread across her carpet leading to his back.

'Well, that was not very neighbourly.' Heather grabbed him by the ankle again and hurled him out the window too, crashing onto a row of bins below.

'That should stop them taking the stairs, sorry about the mess,' Heather said to the shaking woman. She leapt out the window herself before the shaking woman even got a chance to even thank her.

Moments later she was zooming through the chaotic streets again. Firing tear gas grenades from her bike as she went. All around her there were shops with windows smashed in and looted, people rushing into buildings wielding baseball bats, metal pipes and any other household weapon they could get their hands on. Flames flickered out of windows and indistinguishable bangs and explosions went off sporadically.

Heather had just fired her fourteenth tear gas grenade at a group of teenagers trying to break into a high-end clothing retailer.

'Zack come in.'

A moments silence and then …

'Go, Harrow, I'm here.'

'Are you safe?'

'You're kidding right, nobody even knows I'm here,' he said.

'Good. Listen, I need to call my family but first give me a list of high priority targets.'

'Let's see. In your area you've got; a break-in at Tech Planet, apartment block on fire, large gang and police riot squad engaged in a skirmish, hostage situation at a primary school. Oh, and number ten is under siege, some villain called Kwantron is leading the assault,' said Zack.

'School? What hostages have they got at this time of night?' she questioned.

'I don't know, I just figured it will be some teachers that decided to work late. Err, It's the one on Albion Drive. Saint Lumars.'

Heather's Heart sank to the deepest pits of her body, she slammed on the brake and spun the bike wildly towards the school. From its depths, the heart was pounding faster than the bike would carry her. She felt sick and incredibly light headed.

'Parents evening!' she cried out loud, speeding so fast across the streets that many of the people that saw her that night, just saw a rampaging black blur.

Poorly parked outside the front of the school was a long truck; on the rear, the crest of a cartoon hat-wearing pig. The lights were off and a quick scan through Heather's visor showed her that nobody was on the truck. There was, however, an armed thug stood outside the front door of the school. Slowing down to a snail's pace, Heather switched off her bike's lights and pulled off the road and into the shadows; knowing that stealth was her greatest ally here.

'Harrow, what do you need?' said Zack through her helmet, in a calm collected voice.

'Can you get a video feed of what's going on in there?'

'No, I've already tried, not a single camera on the inside. Makes sense I suppose. I can run the vehicle number plate through the system and see if I can get a match?'

'Don't bother, it's stolen,' said Heather, silently stepping down from her bike. 'I'm going to get closer and do a scan.'

Heather moved through the darkness and hugged the edges of the buildings. Street lamps illuminated much of the road but there were patches of shadow she was able to utilise. Sirens and gunshots wailed through the night's air like a banshee.

Meters away from the armed guard at the door, she pulled out her pistol and inserted a round of tranquilizer darts. Each one filled with five milligrams of inky liquid, which was powerful enough to send a bear into a coma.

For this man, it would probably be much worse.

A single silenced shot later the man dropped to the ground, Heather dashed in and caught his falling body before he could make a sound. Dragging him and the gun she'd just deconstructed and emptied of ammo, she dumped them both in a nearby bush just beneath the Saint Lumars sign.

Moving around the side of the school, Heather crouched down and switched on her hyperspectral imaging to paint a picture of the inside of the building and its inhabitants. But as she turned her head slowly to scan the entirety of the single-story school, she could not see a thing. It reminded her of searching for Ria earlier in the year. There must be people in there, she assumed the problem was more than likely some kind of signal blocker; similar to the ones she used on the Pandarians. The other option was that they too were underground, beneath a foot of lead-lined material and that seemed unlikely. She'd be going in blind again.

Heather surveyed the outside of the school, looking for the most isolated fire exit she could. If there were hostages they would have put them all in one place, she thought to herself. Someplace large enough to fit a hundred or so parents and kids, most likely the canteen. Having been in there before for last year's parents evening, Heather knew there was a skylight on the ceiling.

Climbing to the roof and peaking down through the glass, her hunch paid off. From here she could see clusters of parents and children being pushed and shoved around, separating them from one another. Kids were being grouped in the middle of the room and parents forced to the far wall of the canteen. Several lay dead and scattered about the room, clearly the ones that had tried to put up a fight.

Frantically looking around for signs of Kirsty and Henry she spotted the bright blue jumper she had bought him for his birthday; the one with a large shielded H embroidered on the front. Her son and wife were still glued to each other, but they were one of the last.

Among the hostages, she picked out six people who clearly weren't supposed to be there; three scruffily dressed men, wielding thick shiny blunt weapons and assault rifles slung over their shoulders; and three supervillains. The outfits gave it away. She'd not seen them before but there weren't many active villains left in New London. Or so she thought.

'Get the last few kids in the middle, hurry up!' said Ravage, shouting at one of the goons.

'Well done everyone, you have managed to do this successfully and without wasting too many of the precious kiddies. The grown-ups, we're not too worried about,' he said with a big twisted smile across his face.

'Come on lady, get over there with the rest of them.'

'Get your fucking hands off me!'

Heather instantly recognised the voice of Kirsty and could see one of the thugs trying to tear Henry away from her. Blinking she foresaw him swivel around the gun and fill Kirsty's chest with bullets. Snapping back to the present, Heather didn't delay another second.

Slamming a boot down hard on the glass and with a little persuasion from fate, the skylight shattered and Heather smashed through. The man grabbing her had started to reach for his gun but before he could even touch the grip, Heather had fired her own gun at him while in free fall. One of the tranquillizer darts still loaded, whistled through the air and stabbed into his neck. His hand let go of Kirsty and he fell, paralysed to the floor.

'Get to the wall!' she yelled to Kirsty. This was the first time that Kirsty had ever seen the infamous Harrow in person. The threatening electronic rasp that masked Heather's voice meant the long-kept secret remained one.

Kirsty grabbed Henry around the waist and rushed back as instructed, thinking this woman really was as terrifying as they said. The remaining two goons lifted up their guns to spray her but Heather was feet in front of the circle of children. If they opened fire, some shots would surely miss and catch them instead.

Fiercely concentrating, she imagined the guns jamming and calling on the second part of her power, they did just that. The two men yelled out in frustration and madly started slamming their palms to the side of the gun trying to dislodge whatever it was that was stopping them from working.

Such a profound manipulation of fate always left Heather feeling wearied, momentarily neutering her powers of foresight. Changing fate, after all, did take quite a toll on the mind. This left her vulnerable to the giant concrete-like fist that slammed into her head from behind.

Heather went sliding across the floor, her ears ringing and head fuzzy. She got to her feet quickly, but her vision was blurry and out of focus. 'What the hell is that guy made of,' she thought to herself.

The two goons trying to fix their guns had given up and were running towards her, the three villains were looking for an opening, waiting for the queen to take their pawns.

Steadying herself on a display of year four historical paintings, she shot at the two oncoming men. The first shot hit one in the chest, the bullet's serum seeping instantaneously into his bloodstream. The second dart missed and pinged off a lovingly handmade model of tower bridge. In too much pain to be angry at herself for missing, Heather firmly planted her feet and prepared to spar with the charging attacker.

He leapt forward with a front kick, which she parried and returned with a left hook. He blocked this and sliced his elbow up, narrowly missing the metallic jaw of her helmet. It had been some time since she had fought without her foresight powers and this guy was really trying to even the battlefield. His punches and kicks came thick and fast but cocooned in her armour there was not much his blows could do to her. It was the big guy she was more concerned about.

Blocking another wild swing with her free hand she ducked down to his waist height and sprung back up smashing into his chin with her head. She grabbed a shoulder before he could fall back and shot him point blank in the chest, with the gun she'd somehow managed to hold onto.

Her foresight began to return to her as she envisioned him falling to the ground a moment before he actually did. This returned just in time, as what she envisioned next was truly life-saving.

In her mind, she saw the insect-like woman, who had been making a stealthy approach towards her, dive through the air throwing herself at Heather. Dolores reached out a clawing hand and dug her nails into the thinnest part of Heather's suit. Just under the armpit where there was no armour, but instead a more flexible material; completely necessary for the flexibility she demanded of herself. One of the sharpest fingernails dug in so deep, it pierced the material and the tight lycra beneath. It nipped Heather's skin but that was enough. Heather saw herself collapse just as the girl had done, time seemed to stand still, and she entered a dream-like state.

Stood before her was Heather's mother, she held a flaming black pike in both hands. Her face was stretched and grotesque, screaming a maniacal laugh as she ran towards Heather. Then the scene twisted and sank to pictures of the two men from the night of her rape ... They stood above her, towering like giants looking at an ant. Kyle, whose name she had never forgotten, bent down and opening his mouth he swallowed her whole ... It went pitch black, the place she was in felt warm and wet; her feet were glued to the ground ... A tiny red light popped out of nothing and she could see Henry's face illuminated by the blood coloured light, but he was younger, much younger.

'Help me, Mummy, they're going to hurt me, Mummy. You're not going to let them hurt me, are you?'

More copies of his face began squeezing out of the fleshly walls all around her, there were hundreds of him; bodiless and infant-like. She tried to reach out a hand to him but she was sinking into the ground. Thick bulbs of fleshy sacks popped around her, covering her body and face in warm chunky goo. She sank deeper and deeper, the whole time thrashing about in the gunk trying to get free. The warm paste now had reached her face and was pouring into her screaming mouth.

'Don't let me die, Mummy, try harder! YOU'RE NOT TRYING HARD ENOUGH!' the countless blood-covered faces screamed.

Heather was dragged back into reality and overcome with bewildered terror. She barely leapt out of the way in time. Dolores relentlessly sliced and slashed at Harrow with her claws, cumbersomely Heather dodged and ducked away still horrified by the eternal nightmare she was desperately trying to avoid being put into.

Dolores dived again, her fingers stretched out like

a sabretooth. Heather slid beneath her, two sharpened black fingernails scratched across Heather's visor as she slid, it sounded like nails on a chalkboard. Spinning around on her knees, Heather fired a tranquilizer dart at the horrifying villain. It buried itself deeply in her spine and she crashed face first on the floor.

Before Heather could compose herself, she foresaw Ravage charging at her again. In a panic she opened fire on him, emptying her remaining darts into his neck and face. But he carried on running towards her, brushing the darts off his skin chuckling as he did so.

He slammed his shoulder into Heather's stomach, rushing her against the wall. She felt like she'd just been thrown into a wrecking ball. Howling in pain she started jabbing at his head with her fists but it didn't seem to make a difference. Not a single punch evoked a flinch, he laughed heartily as he pinned her against the wall.

He began grabbing at panels of Heather's armour ripping them off and flinging them behind him. While they fought, the hostages in the room looked on in terror and awe.

'What are you without your fancy toys and protection?' With each piece he ripped off, his brutish fists squeezed her limbs mercilessly. Her left forearm was now completely exposed, and Ravage could see her pale skin. He grabbed onto it tightly, breaking her arm as though it was a chopstick. 'Just some angry little white woman.'

She screamed out in anger and wrapped her other arm around the back of his head, pulling it close to her chest.

'SUIT, SHOCK!' Heather Roared.

Thunderous energy exploded from her chest and out of the parts of her suit that still remained. Using her fate manipulation, she diverted it away from the exposed bits of her body. Ravage shook violently and fell to the ground, his clutch on Heather loosened.

Warlock, who had at this point been circling the outskirts of the fight for some time, now saw his opportunity. But Heather was ready, she flipped over his first blast which knocked over all the school work displays behind her. He fired again, which she dodged by running across the wall as though gravity had no power over her. He charged up the white rod a third time and fired a blast towards Heather, but she was too quick for him.

Heather, now just mere feet away, Warlock swung the concussive blaster towards the group of children.

'I'LL DO IT!' he screamed, aiming the tip of his blaster straight at the quivering children.

Leaping through the air foot outstretched for a flying kick, she calmly responded, having seen what he really would and would not do.

'No, you won't,' said Heather, as she slammed her boot hard into his chest knocking him to the ground.

Mounting him, she grabbed the hand holding the rod and aimed it at Ravage who had just got up, she squeezed Warlock's hand and fired a blast towards the brute. Throwing him off his feet, he spun through the air and into the flat-packed gymnasium. The metal clanged and rang when he hit it. Heather then forced Warlock's hand down to zap himself in the chest, knowing the rod was biometrically activated and wouldn't work for her hand. The invisible blast thundered across his robe covered chest but didn't seem to have any effect. He cockily laughed in her face and spat on her scratched silver visor.

With her exposed and broken arm, she ripped open the torso of his robe. The pain was excruciating but she fought back the tears and jabbed the rod again into his now bare and hairless chest, wiping the smile from his face.

Squeezing his hand again, the charge of energy burst through his chest like a canon, forcing his whole body to convulse. A moment later his writhing had stopped and his bloodshot eyes stared blankly at the ceiling.

Slowly getting up, trying to be gentle with her broken arm, she turned to face the still standing Ravage. The tips of his hair were singed and standing up, his face was sweaty and his breaths quick and heavy. Hunched over near the door he was firmly holding the shoulder of a young boy in Henry's class. Heather recognised him from a birthday party earlier in the year that Henry had been invited to. Ben was his name, he looked to Harrow with both fear and begging eyes that simply said, 'save me.'

'I'm leaving here, Harrow. You're going to let me go and this boy is coming as my insurance. You try and follow me, and he dies,' he spoke between gasps for air.

He stared at her, she was mumbling something under her breath.

'Well! What will it be?'

'Take the boy,' said Heather.

'NO!' the boy's mum screamed out in the group of parents behind her. Heather said it again.

'And get out before I change my mind.'

Not wanting to risk another second with her, Ravage ran through the doorway; hoisting the young boy over his shoulder kicking and screaming.

'You fucking monster!!! That's my son!' his mother yelled at her, lying defeated on the floor.

Heather turned around to look at her and spotted Henry and Kirsty squished together, looking at her in horror. She looked right into his eyes, the pupils all but gone. Showing even more of his soft hazel iris than normal, they were the same hue as hers.

From outside the open school doors and a gaping

hole in the building, they heard the cry of a powerful engine race down the street. Then came the hailstorm of gunfire. It lasted for a couple of seconds and then stopped. There was silence in the room and a panic that more captors were just about to come in and take over, but it was not villains that ran through the open canteen door frame, it was Ben. He ran straight past Heather, stealing a quick close up look and ran right into the outstretched arms of his mum.

Standing outside the school, next to the bullet-ridden supervillain, she rolled his lifeless body over with her foot; Ravage's whole left side was in bloody ribbons. A few feet away was Heather's idle Harley Davidson, its engine purring and the remotely activated machine guns smoking from the barrels.

'Zack, I want a pickup and protection for eighty-two at Saint Lumars.'

'But Harrow, with the rioting the Network has already dispatched-' Heather cut him off.

'I don't care, get them to send someone. Do it now, Zack.'

He went silent for a few moments. Heather stared out at her city, it was on its knees. Smoke swallowed the sky whilst cries of pain and fear filled the gaps in between. Zack returned.

'Network has reassigned fliers to protect the school while they wait for transport. They're two minutes out.'

'Thank you, Zack. Give me the next high priority targets. This night is not over yet.'

Waiting there until the two super-powered vigilantes arrived, she gave them a firm nod and with her torn up armour and badly broken arm, she raced deeper into the chaos.

CHAPTER THIRTEEN

Slumped in her leather wingback chair, wearing her pyjamas and a thick cream dressing gown, Heather stared numbly at her living room television. She was watching the news and felt sicker and more defeated with every word that came out of the reporter's mouth.

'Can you tell us more, Angela? What was the cause of such abhorrent and violent behaviour two nights ago in New London?' A well-dressed and smartly groomed presenter was sat in the news studio interviewing some specialist over a video call.

'Well, I think it's clear to most, Scott, that there was evidence of an organised and synchronised attack on the city rather than just the mindless chaos we thought initially. Let's look at some of the highlighted incidents - two bombs at heavyweight hospitals; the break-in at a key government building which deals in tax collection; and the attempted mass kidnapping that took place at Saint Lumars School. Each of these attacks will have taken considerable prior planning and do not fit the pattern we have seen in the past when rioting breaks out. These, and several other incidents, really stand out for me against the vast number of assaults and theft that took place a few nights ago. People knew this was coming and somehow, they knew that night was the night to do it.'

'And Angela, do you have any inclination on who might be orchestrating these attacks and what their motive might be?' the smartly dressed presenter asked.

'I'm afraid my guess is as good as yours. However, I believe that whoever was behind this has more in store for us. Many of the key incidents were, for the most part, foiled by the police force and unlicensed vigilantes. It was these vigilantes after all, that saved the Prime Minister's life when his home was under siege,' said the specialist.

'Yes, let's talk more about that. The number of unlicensed vigilantes operating in New London has dramatically declined since the registration laws were put in place. But last night there were dozens of sightings of these extraordinary people, putting their lives in danger for us,' he stopped, waiting for a response; though it wasn't really a question.

'I'm sorry, Scott, what are you asking?' There was a slight tang of annoyance in her voice.

'Well, they've suffered a lot of persecution over the last several years, but without them, we may not have made it through. Do you think these individuals are being wrongly accused and should they be allowed to work independently of government bodies?' he fired at her.

'No. No, I do not think they are being wrongly accused. These men and women have made the decision to break the law. Sure, they appear to be helping society but we have seen in the past what happens when these people are left unchecked. Take Skysplitter, in twenty-ten. Operating in the Midlands, there was a man adored by all.

He stood up for the little guy, until tragedy struck in his personal life and he went on to murder hundreds.'

'There have been several cases of unchecked heroes turning bad and using their incredible powers and skills for their own selfish personal gain. Even Harrow, a hero to New London for over a decade, is now the suspect in an ongoing murder investigation. In my opinion, they are as bad as the criminals they seek to stop,' the specialist firmly nodded her head on the final word.

'But Angela, Harrow was spotted on countless occasions during that night, saving people's lives. In fact, there are over a dozen eyewitnesses that said she was at the school you previously mentioned. And saved the lives of nearly fifty school children and their parents. Does that sound like a killer to you?'

Heather stared into the young presenter's face, wondering if she had ever saved his life. He certainly did seem to be a big Harrow supporter.

'Scott, whether we think she is helping or not, nobody knows what her motives are. And for as long as people like this are left unchecked, we will be in serious danger. What she is doing is illegal and we cannot look past that just because she appears to be helping us. I just wish we could get an interview with her.' She finally cracked a smile.

'Don't we all, Angela …' The presenter thanked his guest speaker and continued the news bulletin.

Heather stared at the presenter with blank eyes, now not taking a word of what he said in. She felt hopeless and crushed. Ten years, night after night on the streets of this city protecting its people and now most of whom wished she would stop doing it. Or go and stick on a police uniform and do it for them. What was worse than that, was the feeling that none of her work hunting the Pandarians had made a difference.

She had killed and captured five of them. These beings that drew the worst from people, encouraged sinful and despicable actions, but two nights ago had been one of the darkest she had ever witnessed. Her mind had been in turmoil all day. She couldn't think of anything else. What if everything she did was pointless? Perhaps it would be better if she hung up the cape and had a normal life like everyone else. After all, she didn't owe this screwed up city a thing.

She could hear the key scratching around in the front door lock. Kirsty had arrived from a food shop with Henry, who charged in the second it was open and ran to her.

'Mummy, I got you your favourite!'

In his outstretched hand, he held a large bottle of strawberry milkshake, it was cold and candyfloss pink.

'Oh, you know me so well, thanks, kiddo.' She forced a smile. Though she was grateful, she didn't feel much like smiling.

Henry handed it over to her and ran off to his room.

'That was his idea, not mine,' Kirsty said, now walking into the living room encumbered with shopping bags.

'Yeah, I figured as much,' Heather said.

'When did you get back?' Kirsty nodded to Heather's arm, which was tightly wrapped in a sling.

She had told her wife that she was going to the hospital to get her broken arm seen to, lying that she'd been mugged on the way back from the airport during the riots. The thief broke her arm and left a couple of scars in the process. A believable lie, as Heather looked as though she'd been stamped through a meat grinder. In fact, the riots were a better cover up than how she usually had to explain her crime-fighting injuries. 'I fell off my push bike; Machine malfunction at work; and Sports related, dear. Nothing to worry about,' were just a few of her past excuses.

In truth, Heather had not gone to a hospital at all. But instead flown to a Network controlled medical facility on the edge of Brussels, where they were able to set the bone and apply a chemical compound that Heather didn't understand. This would heal her arm in two weeks instead of ten; the straps were just for show.

'About twenty minutes ago,' Heather said. 'How was it out there?'

'Oh, it's madness, the local is just in pieces so I had to go to the supermarket. It was absolutely packed. I think people are afraid something is going to happen again, they're really stocking up for the winter,' Kirsty called through as she started unloading the shopping in the kitchen.

Heather stood up, so she could talk without Henry hearing in the other room.

'And how is he?' nodding her head towards her son's room.

'How do you think he is? He watched one of his friends and his headteacher die right in front of him, not to mention what that woman did to those assholes, Heather. She blew a man's heart up!' Kirsty was starting to get quite distressed, it was clearly taking its toll on her too.

'I know, you've told me.' Heather tried to stay calm. 'But has he said anything to you?'

'Just that he now thinks Harrow is the coolest superhero ever and he wants to make a costume like hers. Which I promise you now, is not happening!'

The corner of Heather's mouth tilted up in a smirk as Kirsty put the pasta bags into the bottom cupboard.

'You know, she broke her arm in the same place as you that night.'

Heather's smile vanished instantly.

'What do you mean?' Heather asked, trying to sound cool and trivial.

'Well she was trying to hide it but after the humongous one I told you about grabbed her, she stopped using that arm. Must have shattered every bone in it,' said Kirsty.

'Am I supposed to feel glad about that, Kirst?'

'No, I just mean … it's funny isn't it, you and her both get the same injury on the same night,' she said, oblivious to how right she was.

'Yeah Kirsty, it's fricking hilarious.' Heather shot her an eye-rolling glare as Kirsty continued to pack away the shopping.

There was a couple of minutes silence, just the sound of Henry playing on his games console in the other room. Then Kirsty asked another question.

'So how long have work said you can have off?'

'They've not, Kirst. I've got to go back on the course next week.'

'WHAT?!' Kirsty slammed down the carton of almond milk on the side, crushing the bottom.

'Your wife and son have just been victims of a brutal attempted kidnapping and you are going back to work! Please tell me you're joking?' she shouted sharply, the noise of the game in Henry's room had gone silent.

'Yes, I'm going back to work, I need to do my job Kirsty,' Heather was raising her voice now as well.

'No, you don't need to, you want to! Those are two very different things. You need to sort out your goddamn priorities, Heather!'

She wanted to scream it out in her face, 'I'm

Harrow!' more so now than ever, but she'd vowed never to tell Kirsty; it was safer that she didn't have that secret to keep. Everyone knows what happens when the bad guys find out who your loved ones are. Someone, if not everyone, ends up in a body bag. She kept her mouth shut but rage was pouring from her expression.

'Have you got nothing to say, Heather? No more wild excuses?' she baited her.

Heather said nothing, she just returned Kirsty's furious glare.

'Fine! Well if you and your broken arm are well enough to go back to work you can put away the shopping.' She dropped a heavy shopping bag on the floor, fruit went spilling out across the tiles and she stormed past her.

From the hallway, she shouted out again, this time her voice more spiteful and venomous.

'And my mother's apartment block was burnt down in the riots so she's coming to live with us until she can find a new place. Probably be six months, give or take.'

'Fuck that!' Heather bellowed.

But much to Heather's disgust, later that day her mother in law showed up at their door. Her hair was mousy brown and blow dried, she wore a thick cherry pink knitted scarf and carried nothing but a floral handbag.

Heather and Kirsty didn't have a guest room, so Judy got Henry's room and he had a makeshift bed on the floor next to theirs.

Cumbersomely with her arm encased in the sling, Heather spread fresh sheets across the mattress for Judy. She had not so subtly requested something other than the robot sheets Henry usually had - 'If I'm going to be here for a while, I'd like something a little bit less childlike.'

This had happened five minutes into her arrival and Heather was already wishing the apartment fire had started just a few more floors down.

The rest of the night continued in this same way, request after request flew from her mouth. All of which was passed to Heather as Kirsty was still not talking to her. As the night drew on and Heather finished putting Henry to bed she returned to the living room, where Kirsty and her mother quickly stopped whispering to each other. Judy looked over to Heather defiantly, very aware she had just been caught speaking about her behind her back.

'Well if you have you got something to say, you can say it to my face,' Heather had been silently biting back her tongue all night but had finally expended her patience.

Kirsty paused for a moment, inhaling to say something but Judy beat her to it.

'Why were you not at the parent's evening?' she said, her voice shrill and cutting.

'Kirsty already knows that I was on a course with work,' Heather replied defensively.

'Yes well, that's what she told me. It seems to me like you didn't want to be there-' Heather cut her off before she could finish.

'Would you rather I was there to watch those bastards try to kidnap my son too?'

'Well if you had been there, you would have been able to support my daughter and grandson during that dreadful time.'

'What good would that have done!?' Heather felt like walking over to the corner they were huddled in and punching the woman. Judy ignored this question and carried on, Kirsty sat quietly on the sofa looking back and forth between them.

'And now I hear you're leaving again to go back to work. Frankly, I think you're being completely selfish. Again, not thinking about how this would affect my Grandson.'

'He's not your Grandson! There's not a drop of you in him!' Heather's voice now becoming quite loud.

'Heather!' Kirsty stamped. 'Stop, you will wake Henry!'

'Good,' she said. 'I think it's time we told him the truth.'

The pair looked horrified at these words, both of them gasped and fought back.

'How dare you ...' 'He's too young to understand ...' 'Why would you do such a thing to that little boy ...'

Heather did consider that she had taken it too far, but a small part of her truly wanted to tell Henry the truth about his birth. She told so many lies every day and hoped she could just come clean to him about this one.

The room went quiet again, an awkward silence weighed the air down. It was Heather that broke it. She simply said - 'I won't say anything to him,' and she left to go to bed.

Kicking her slippers off quietly in the darkness she crawled into bed, foreseeing that Henry would have already snuck under their duvet so he didn't have to sleep on the floor. Curling up next to him she gave him a light kiss on his messy chestnut coloured hair. Her last thought, before she closed her eyes and drifted into a deep, well-needed sleep; was of the little silver cube hidden beneath her bed, and the five monsters trapped within it. It wasn't a comforting last thought to think that every child's nightmare had, for her, come true.

CHAPTER FOURTEEN

~Then~

With heavy breaths and sweaty brows, Nahmar and his father, crouched silently between two huts. The air was damp and the sky full of scattered black clouds. Nahmar, now entering manhood, peeked around the side of the hut to see if they had lost their pursuer.

'Father, I think we are safe here for now. Do you really think we can make it to the Persuader's hut?' he asked with uncertainty. It had already been a challenge to get this far.

'Yes, my son, I believe we can. More importantly, we must,' said Freon.

Nahmar was referring to the chief they had encountered over a decade ago. In the months that followed their narrow escape, Freon and Nahmar had completely avoided that forest and the tribe within it. However, as the years went by, the size of the tribe and the chief's influence over the land increased. Forcing the father and son to flee in fear for their lives. They did not part, after all, on good terms.

However, it did not take long for the "Persuader's" reach to extend across the land. More and more people left their homes to join his tribe, for the bountiful promises of food and protection he offered. This disturbed Freon greatly, but it only got worse over time.

When the food began to run out and space became an issue, the Persuader's tribe would mercilessly take it from others that refused to join him. Freon and Nahmar had managed to integrate themselves with a tribe near the coast and had been there eighteen months when the slaughter took place. The patriarch of their new community had refused to be led by another and it was his head that was one of the first to be put on a spike. It was only Freon and Nahmar that made it out alive, both using their powers over fate to get to safety.

That had been three weeks ago and the pain for them both was still quite raw. The two of them planned to sneak into the camp and end the life of the man that was corrupting their lands.

Scurrying through the sleepy camp, they approached the largest of all the huts; it was on a small hill, overlooking the others surrounding it. Sliding between two hanging floor-length furs they both entered the hut, drawing their sharp handcrafted daggers.

Lying between three young women, one of whom was very clearly pregnant, was the chief. He was in a deep sleep, gently snoring; but even asleep he was very intimidating, his muscular chest was bare and large trunk-like arms were wrapped around one of the women. His strong hand rested on her soft exposed breast.

Without delaying a moment more, Freon stepped forward, tightly gripping the dagger in his hand. Kneeling down at the head of the sleeping foursome and taking a deep silent breath in, he brought his dagger sharply down across the chief's neck.

The noise that followed woke the entire camp; there was not a single man, woman or child that didn't hear those screams. It took a few moments for the chief to die and Freon didn't envision far enough to see what came a few seconds later; at which point it was already too late.

A thick orange energy burst from the chief's pores, flowing from his skin like concentrated smoke. The cloud of energy soared around the clay splattered walls, it sounded like a hurricane. Spinning around the hut, it blew up bits of warm clinging dirt against Freon and Nahmar's skin.

The father and son followed it with their eyes as the energy spiralled around the hut, both of them transfixed by the unnatural phenomena that illuminated the entire space. Just as the three girls began to startle, the cloudy energy swooped through the air and pummelled into the chest of the pregnant woman. She had sat up in alarm because of the noise and bright light but was hurled back down to the floor while the energy filled her body.

For a moment she was still, her eyes were open but there a vacantness there. The two other women, who had also woken, looked at Nahmar and Freon in alarm and then down to their dead lover; his blood lightly spattered across their naked bodies. It was the noise of their screaming that awoke the entire camp. The pregnant women now conscious and very much alert, had gotten to her feet and in a powerful booming voice yelled out.

'Our chief has been killed! Kill the assassins!'

Nahmar and Freon had darted out of the hut the second that orange mist had disappeared. They were sprinting through the camp, but residents were seconds away from pouring out of their huts. Freon grabbed his son's arms and wrenched him into a particularly grubby looking hut to avoid the enormous search party. Freon had picked this hut using his foresight, not because it was empty (none of them were), but because the only person in here clearly didn't want to be.

Tightly tied to a post, deeply planted in the ground, was a woman with hair like fire. She looked up at the two of them in surprise. Her face bruised and battered, her body covered in scars and fresh cuts. Her gorgeous crimson hair was tangled and matted and she wore loosely fitting rags for clothes. From her appearance, she was probably a few years older than Nahmar, but her blazing defiant eyes looked as though she had witnessed centuries pass by. Light from a smouldering fire outside leaked into the hut, warmly resting on the lower half of the walls.

Nahmar and Freon stared at the beautiful prisoner for a moment, she was unlike anyone they had ever seen before. Snapping back to his senses, Nahmar turned to his dad.

'Father, what on earth happened there? What was that coloured fog that came out of him!?' Nahmar asked, looking both scared and confused.

'I do not know, Nahmar,' he peeled his eyes off the woman and peeked back outside the hut.

Armed with heavy spears and broad bows the men of the tribe canvassed hut after hut. Pulling everyone out so they could inspect inside. Freon could hear shouts and angry cries all around them.

'You killed the one they called chief and saw what lived inside him,' the beautiful prisoner said. Her voice was delicate and melodic, like the sound of a perfectly tuned harp in the hands of a god.

'How did you-' Nahmar began but Freon cut him off.

'Son, we have moments to escape, come.' He put a hand on Nahmar's shoulder who was again looking at the woman.

'There is a reason you killed this man. I can tell you everything you want to know and so much more, just set me free.' Her fierce golden eyes pierced into Nahmar's.

Nahmar pulled his dagger from its sheath and began to slice down the back of her bonds.

'Nahmar we haven't got time for this!'

'Father, for years you have been telling me that the Persuader is an unnatural abomination and cannot exist on this earth. Then after trying to take him from it, we saw ... that!' He pointed with his knife in the rough direction of the chief's hut. 'And now this woman says she has answers. We must take her with us.' He continued cutting the rope, but she was very tightly tied up and the rope had been wrapped around several times.

Freon hesitated for a moment but then leapt to help Nahmar. Gently pushing his son out of the way, he gave one of the knots of rope a gentle tug and the whole thing fell to the ground.

'How did you do that, Father?' Nahmar asked with surprise.

'Son, you still have much to learn about the control over fate that we both possess. Can you run?' he said to the woman as he helped her to her feet.

Before she could reply, a short man holding a crudely made spear stepped into the hut.

'THEY'RE IN HERE!' he screeched, in a voice far too loud for his stature. Nahmar leapt forward and sunk his dagger into the man's chest. But the damage had already been done. Shoving past the short man, dagger still buried in his chest, the three of them ran into the night.

The air was bitter with cold and the grass was glazed in a thin layer of frost, though it didn't feel cold to Nahmar. As he ran between exposed tree roots and the undergrowth, sweat flowed down his face and neck. In front of him, ran the woman they had just freed and behind him was his father, yelling out commands for them to dodge left or right. Arrow after arrow whistled through the air, narrowly missing them and plunging into trees or bushes instead.

They had been running for at least twenty minutes without stopping and it was obvious the red-haired woman was struggling to keep the speed they needed. Their pursuers were hot on their trail. Freon envisioned her tripping over an especially grabby exposed tree root and shouted out to her. 'Jump!'

She did so, but not quite understanding why she had to, it was dark and the full black clouds were blocking any chance of a moonlit guide through the woods.

'So, who are you?!' Nahmar shouted out to the woman as they fled.

'Do you really think now is the best time for introductions?!' she shouted back.

'Well, I just thought … can you at least tell me your name?' he asked, ducking beneath a poison-tipped arrow that bit the dirt several yards in front of him.

'My name is Thaesilia! There, happy now?'

'Well, I wouldn't say happy but it's nice to meet you, I'm Nahmar,' he said coolly.

'Nahmar, focus!' his father snapped.

Another spear slammed through the tree, inches to the right of Nahmar, even he had barely seen that one coming. They needed to change their strategy. Freon thinking the same thing stopped in his tracks and wheeled about to face his attackers.

'Papa!' Nahmar screamed, stopping too when he realised his father had.

'Do not stop running, my son! Get to safety, I will delay them and catch up with you!' And with that, he ran towards the hail of arrows and spears, nimbly darting between every projectile.

'Hurry, your father has given us a chance, do not squander it.' The redheaded woman grabbed hold of Nahmar's sweaty hand and pulled him further into the forest, running deeper and deeper into the black abyss.

The clouds finally burst, drenching everything beneath them. The ground became soggy and water-logged within minutes and Nahmar's brilliant white soaking hair, stuck against his face as they ran.

He looked over his shoulder to try and pick out the silhouette of his Father, through the trees and against the black rainy canvas; but he could not see a thing.

CHAPTER FIFTEEN

~Now~

Gravel filled her bloody knee like sprinkles on an iced cake. Heather was eight and crying inconsolably; having just taken a head-first dive over her scooter handlebars into the road. There was no breeze and the scenery around her was distorted and out of focus. She sat sobbing on the pavement for several minutes before materialising in front of her dad.

He was slouched in that memorable green leather armchair, the edges of which were frayed and peeling. The two of them were in the middle of the elongated living room Heather distantly remembered as her childhood home. The wallpaper was floral and garish, selected by some long deceased relative with archaic taste in decor. Heather's knees bled onto the thick stained carpet; the floor splashed with spillages of red wine from her mother and fallen take-away from her father.

'What are you doing, Heather? You're in the way,' her father grunted between a mouthful of his second burger.

Behind Heather was the enormous television screen, the light seemed to bulge and pop from within it. The sound was muffled and indistinguishable, but it sounded like people were mad at each other.

'Dad, I fell off my scooter and hurt myself,' she sobbed and looked down at her knees. However, to her surprise, she saw there was no blood anymore, in fact, there was no sign that she'd fallen off her scooter at all.

'There's nothing wrong with you, you nasty little liar,' he burped, taking a huge gulp from a mug the size of his face.

'Did I hear someone say LIAR!?' a shrill and venomous screech came from behind Heather, who whipped round to see her mother staring down at her. Her body towered over Heather like a crooked lamppost, her dark eyes were unnaturally round, and her chin was elongated like a hag's. Heather sunk down beneath her giant mother, still clutching the silver scooter in her quaking hands.

'We do not allow liars to live in this house! You are a liar and therefore you will have to go,' she snarled, reaching out an elongated thin arm towards the door that had just fabricated from thin air, but felt as though it had been there the whole time.

'But I'm not lying, please you must believe me,' Heather begged, looking back to her knees in disbelief.

'You filthy little liar, get out now!' Her mum had opened the door which revealed a realm of terrifying darkness. There were spasms of darker black within it and horrifying screams and laughter echoed from the depths. It felt as though the door was sucking her in and no matter how hard she tried to pull away from its grasp, she continued to be dragged towards it.

'Don't ever come back, Heather, we don't want you here anymore,' her dad mumbled, without taking his eyes off the television, not even to select his favourite sweet from a large bucket of them (he knew them all incredibly well by their individual shapes).

Fighting against the current, she screamed back at her parents. 'I'm not lying!' and with that, she tightly gripped her scooter with both hands and swung it around her head to hit her mother.

It sharply collided with her thin angled face and knocked her long spindly body to the ground. Next, Heather swung it towards her father, who had nearly finished demolishing his third burger. The scooter smashed into him, throwing him from the armchair and across the room.

Heather picked the scooter up again and began laying into her mother's crooked body. Breaking bone after bone with unbelievable strength and ferocity. When her mother had gone still and the shrill screech had stopped, she walked over to her father.

'Stop Heather, stop!' the fat man begged, holding a chubby sausage-fingered hand towards his daughter.

'I'm not a liar, Dad,' she said calmly. As she swung the scooter down to silence him too … the scene changed, and she was swinging a small iron golf club. And instead of swinging it at her gluttonous father it was a small bright pink golf ball.

'Holy shit, you've done this before,' a cute blonde woman exclaimed. She was a few inches taller than Heather and wore a tight-fitting white t-shirt and a blue denim jacket.

Heather was twenty-two and on a second date. The mini golf park they were playing at was brightly lit and had a space theme to it, model rockets and large plastic aliens surrounded the two of them. Heather had just scored another hole in one. She did have a bit of an unfair advantage though, fixing fate at every turn. But her date didn't need to know that.

'I've had a little practice,' Heather replied with a cheeky grin, flickering her eyes up to her nameless date.

'I'll say! Look, how many more holes do we have to do? I'm getting kind of hungry.' With that, the scene dissolved and the two of them reappeared in a romantically lit restaurant. Tucked into a round table with thick crimson tablecloths and located in a quiet corner, the two exchanged stories about their families.

'My folks got divorced when I was fourteen,' Heather said. 'No, it wasn't tough really. It was going to happen eventually, so I wasn't really shocked by it. I don't really see my dad anymore but Mum lives in Croydon. How about you?'

Heather tried to listen intently but all she could think about as her date spoke was ripping that t-shirt off and running her hands through that long caramel hair. Her body started to tingle and she stretched a foot out underneath the table to press it lightly against the woman's calf. The blonde woman didn't flinch or pull away and the pair continued to talk about her family, except now a slight twinkle danced in her eye and the corner of her mouth was tilted up showing a smile she was trying to hide.

Conversation flowed freely and the two of them spent hours talking and laughing with each other. Heather finished the final bite of her sticky toffee pudding and got the bill. The scene blurred again and drifted effortlessly to Heather's old apartment. It was right in the centre of the city, she'd all but forgotten what it looked like, but here it felt entirely familiar.

The sound of their kisses chimed through the living

room, their lips smacking against one another. The blonde woman gently ran her hands through Heather's soft dark hair, pulling Heather's face close to hers. Heather's hands gripped tightly around her waist and thigh. They were sat on Heather's couch but she was pushing her date down onto her back, which made her stop kissing and pull her lips away.

'Hey, listen Heather. I really like you but I don't think I'm ready to go that far yet,' she paused looking slightly embarrassed. 'I've never been with a woman before and I'm not ready to go all the way yet.'

'But you've been giving me signals all night? Come on, I really want you,' Heather said, reaching a hand out to stroke her chest, still mostly covered by the tightly fitting t-shirt.

This put her date even more on edge, pushing Heather's eager hand out of the way she went to stand up. But as she did, Heather forcefully pushed her down against the sofa.

'What do you think you're doing, please stop,' stammered the blonde woman.

Heather held her hair tightly and with the other hand, she started peeling off her top.

The room twisted and melted until the two of them were both lying naked on the soft carpet.

Heather knelt above her, forcing pleasure out of her reluctantly. Occasionally she would reach down and squeeze her own breasts firmly as she pressed herself against the woman. Both of them moaned and cried out as Heather took her, their deep breaths echoed across the apartment.

'Please, please stop!' The woman pleaded as Heather came up for air again.

'You're not enjoying it?'

'I am, but I don't want to.'

'Well if you shut the fuck up and stop squirming maybe you'll start wanting to.'

Heather dived in again, digging both her hands into curves of the woman's buttocks. After a moment Heather could hear her deep involuntary moans start up again. The sound of her soft rich voice rippled down Heather's body. And then she felt it … warm breath and the first touch of rhythmic, melodic reciprocation …

Heather woke up after that. For a split second, she was confused, realising she was not in her bedroom. But remembered the argument with Kirsty and her mother in law the night before, hence why she was waking up on the living room couch. She could remember every bit of her dream, she lay there for a few minutes thinking about it before quietly going to the kitchen to get a drink.

It had not been the first time she'd dreamt of raping someone or attacking her parents. Though neither had ever happened, she didn't know how to feel about it. Every time she forced someone in her dream, it gave her this great rush of power and thrill. Sometimes it was a woman, sometimes a man.

Pouring out a glass of strawberry milkshake with her sling-free arm, she wished she could go back to sleep and finish. As for killing her parents, she had mixed feelings about this recurring dream. Relief, revenge and remorse, but at the end of the day, they were only dreams.

Pulling on her jeans and a warm fleece jacket that she had thrown by the couch last night, she grabbed her wallet and phone and left the house.

The path outside her apartment building was buried in leaves, giving the pavement a gentle brownish hue. Sunlight was blazing through the green-less trees, creating sharp tangled shadows on the buildings they rooted closest to.

Heather stomped across the ground and made her way towards the graffiti-riddled BMX park about a mile from her house.

Considering this was the biggest city in Great Britain, it was very quiet for eight in the morning. The attacks and riots earlier in the week had people scared and so the only people Heather saw on foot, were a couple of devoted joggers and a dog walker being dragged by their Springer.

Heather's phone began to buzz in her pocket, but envisioning that it was Kirsty, she let it ring out. She didn't feel much like talking to her wife right now.

On her way to the park, she noticed a handful of shops and buildings that had clearly been damaged in the riots. Windows temporarily sealed up with large tarpaulin sheets. Doors that had been kicked down, now stood propped up inside the hallways. She spotted a completely burnt out convertible and a large digital billboard covered in phalluses and profanity.

As she walked, hands loosely tucked into her jacket pockets, Heather couldn't shake the feelings of guilt and hopelessness that flittered around her mind. She had left New London undefended for a month. The longest she had ever been away from her city since putting on a cape and mask. If she had been here maybe she could have stopped the carnage before it got out of hand. Maybe it wouldn't have happened at all. In her experience, the criminal underworld noticed when she went missing, even for a few days. But she was busy hunting down Pandarians, emotional parasites that brought out the worst in people. The problem was, she'd managed to defeat five of them and things didn't seem to be getting any better. The death toll from this week had still not been publicly announced, but Heather felt responsible for every last one of them. This weight was crippling and with what was going on at home, Heather started to feel that maybe it was time to put all this vigilante nonsense behind her. It would, after all, be easier to just get a normal nine-till-five job and get a crummy pension like everyone else.

Reaching the BMX Park, she approached the half pipe ramp and knelt down at the base of it.

'Access, Harrow. Twenty-four axle spark,' she said, speaking at the grimy graffiti-covered ramp.

A small burst of pressurised gas could be heard from inside it and a panel in the ramp, wide enough to fit her motorcycle through, retracted in on itself. It wasn't her most discreet safe house, but it was the closest to home.

Heather walked down the slope and her hideout switched itself on. Like all her safe houses, it was basic and only stocked the essentials. One of her many suits of armour stood sentinel in the corner. Heather sat down at her heavy steel desk and pulled her chair in close, so she was tucked in comfortably. She then spent a few moments switching on her computer and slipping her arm out of its phantom sling; it was still a bit tender but she could already move her fingers without discomfort.

She would often tinker with her gear when things weren't going so well at home and recently she'd been tinkering a lot more. Heather worked on the projection radius of her smoke grenades, recalculating the pressurisation and smallest possible size of the canisters. After running a few mathematical simulations on her computer, she 3D printed the components she needed and started to build her latest iteration.

Though she enjoyed working in silence and crafting her own gear, the feelings of loneliness and guilt that had been bombarding her all morning were difficult to shift. Heather decided to take a break and give Zack a call, having not spoken to him since the night of the attacks.

'Hey, you,' said Zack as soon as he answered the call.

'Hey,' said Heather, in a rather glum tone.

'I was worried about you. You kind of dropped off the grid midway through the other night, are you okay?' he asked, genuine concern radiating from his voice.

'Honestly? I feel like shit, Zack,' confessed Heather, she then told him how she felt about the work they'd been doing together and that she didn't feel it had made any difference to the behaviours of mankind. 'I just feel like everything is as bad as it was before, worse even. I don't know if I can do this anymore, Zack.'

'What do you mean?' he asked.

'This. Being a superhero, vigilante, whatever I am. Maybe I'm just not cut out for it anymore. Maybe I never was.' Heather stared at her helmet as she spoke, her gloomy reflection stared back at her.

'Are you kidding?! You've done so much good for this city. The whole country! It wouldn't be where it is today without you. As for the Pandarians, I know it's been tough but you're so close to the end now, Harrow. Perhaps you just have to defeat them all before their influence will wear off. Or maybe it lasts for a long time after they're gone? The important thing to remember is because of you, there are five fewer parasites feeding off the innocent now. That must count for something?'

'Yeah, I suppose,' Heather replied, but she didn't sound convinced.

'Let's meet up,' he blurted out.

'What?'

'Now, come on. Let's meet up, and not at the

Catacombs. I've been down here for ages, I need to get some air. Let's get some dinner or something.'

'Or something?' Heather asked curiously.

'Yeah, I don't know. Let's just meet up. Where are you now?'

'I'm just at one of my hideouts. You want to meet now?'

'Yeah, why not?' he asked.

'Well, because it's the middle of the day and going out in my armour draws quite a lot of attention, especially anywhere you can get dinner ... or something.'

There was an awkward pause. Heather didn't need superpowers to know what Zack was thinking.

'Zack, I'm not sure that I'm ready for you to see my face yet,' Heather said slowly like a heartfelt rejection.

'Oh ... yeah. I totally understand. I'm sorry ...'

'Don't be sorry,' she jumped in. 'I'm nearly ready, just not yet.'

There was another drawn-out silence where neither spoke. Heather could hear the scratching of the 3D printer nearly coming to the end of its job.

'But I do want to meet, so how about tonight?'

'Yeah?' Zack said, the joy in his voice sparked up again.

'Yes,' said Heather, with a little smile on her face. She was looking forward to seeing him again. They hadn't actually spoken face to face since Heather stopped the massive arms shipment, with Zack's invaluable help.

There was another silence between them but this time it was gentle and deliberate. It was Zack that broke it.

'So, you've got a kid?'

'How did you ...' she began to ask in shock.

'The other night, you went straight to the school and the way you said the name, it was obvious there was someone important there.'

'You noticed that?'

'Yeah. A little boy or girl?' he asked.

'Boy. My son is ten,' she admitted.

'Wow, ten! So, you must be older than me!' said Zack, triumphantly.

'Zack!' Heather feigned anger but found this quite amusing. Zack laughed a bit before apologising.

'You and your husband must have your hands full, with a ten-year-old boy?'

'My wife,' she gently corrected him. 'And no not really, he's a pretty great kid.'

'Oh, I'm sorry,' he fumbled around with his words for a moment at his careless faux pas. 'I just assumed …'

'It's okay,' she reassured him. 'Everyone's fallen into that bear trap before. I'm actually bi.'

'Ohh!' he said, this time with an interest in his tone rather than embarrassment. Heather had a big grin on her face. She caught a glimpse of her expression in the reflection of the helmet.

'So, I'll see you tonight, Zack?' Heather said softly.

'Definitely.' And Heather closed the call, feeling much better than when she had started it.

For a moment she sat in her chair, gently rocking back and forth. Her mind wandering as it had done this morning after she woke. Her daydream was disturbed by the loud completion beep of the 3D printer.

CHAPTER SIXTEEN

Heather had removed her fake arm sling before heading out that night, her bones still heavy and numb. She tenderly flexed the fingers of her injured arm as she traversed the city skyscrapers with care, launching from one building to another with her magnetised grapnel hook.

Leaping from a particularly tall building she glided down to land gracefully on the roof garden Zack had asked to meet at. The city was alive and sleepless but something about this garden felt like it was shielded from all the noise and light. Tall shadowy plants that were battling the chill, stood steadfast all around her. Their height and width blocked out much of the light from neighbouring buildings giving the whole garden a peaceful and tranquil presence.

Standing on his own, Heather could see Zack peering through the closely-knit branches and leaves at the street below. He was wearing a smart shirt, thick grey woolly jumper and an expensive looking canvas trench coat, like the ones detectives wear in those old police shows. His blonde hair was smoothly brushed back, though it looked more blue from the neon light of a nearby sign.

'You came?' he said, as she crossed the short distance between them and stood next to him against the railing.

'Of course I did, you asked me to.' Heather looked him up and down. She thought he looked simply stunning and had the strong urge to feel the material of his coat. Luckily, she could foresee what it felt like and he'd never need to know.

Heather felt weird standing here, in her full armour. Face covered and thick nightmarish cape draping behind her. She wanted to take it off, she wanted to take all of it off.

'What kept you? Is everything okay?' he asked. She was several minutes later than they'd arranged.

'Oh, there was a couple of police trapped in a gunfight on Dartson Street,' she said, snapping back to the present. 'Six armed thugs firing on two officers. I took out the thugs but then the police tried to arrest me.'

The anger and hopelessness she had been feeling for the last few days was boiling up inside her again.

'What's the fucking point, Zack. If they don't trust me to do what needs to be done, what's the point in doing any of this?'

'That's why I wanted to bring you here tonight.'

He reached down and took her hand, gripping onto the cold graphene of her glove tightly. She couldn't feel the warmth of his hand but imagined what it would feel like to touch his skin. He led her to the edge of the roof garden and the two of them stood next to the hip height glass wall.

'Do you know what that building is?' With his free hand he pointed at an old stone building about twenty yards away, narrowly tucked in between several others of the same sort of style.

'Yes,' she replied, already knowing where he was going with this. Her heart lifted at the thought.

'One of New London's most underfunded women's shelters. That was until two weeks ago when they received an extraordinary anonymous donation. A donation that came from you.'

As he spoke he pointed at the building several times and barely took his eyes away from Heather, who was about an inch shorter than him. He continued to tightly hold her hand as he spoke.

'The money that you took from that third Pandarian and poured back into the city, it's making a real difference, Harrow. It's changing people's lives for the better.' He smiled warmly and she spotted a tiny slither of a tear in his eyes.

'The staff here were able to buy new beds and refurbish some of the older areas of the building. They're opening up two other branches and have been able to take in more women and children than ever before. Just this morning they accepted thirty-seven new women and twenty-eight children into their system whose homes were destroyed or damaged in the attacks. Each one of them has a brand new comfortable bed to sleep on and three delicious meals every day. Maria, twenty-one; Alexis, nineteen and with a new-born; Satwinder, forty-two and widowed. That's the point.' He turned away for a moment and stared out across the city.

'You've done so much for this city; the people here owe you so much but not once have you demanded anything from them, just their trust. It's not been an easy few months I know, and we're not done yet, but I just wanted you to know that you're making this world a better place to live in.'

The two of them stood there in silence for a moment, the city felt serene and peaceful. The usual blunt wail of car horns or loud music spilling out of an apartment window wasn't there. It was clear the city and its people were recovering from the events earlier that week. Heather could faintly hear the tiny footprints of a small bird, pottering about on the branches behind her looking for an evening snack.

'Zack?'

'Yes?' he said, turning back to face his partner.

'Would you do something for me?' she quietly asked, her voice still distorted and amplified through the microphone in her helmet.

'What is it?' He looked at her with curiosity.

'Close your eyes, and keep them closed,' she said, letting go of his hand and reaching both of hers up to her helmet to remove it.

He looked into her mask, where he thought her eyes would be and nodded. Then he closed his eyes.

Twisting the helmet from her head, she rested it on a tall plant vase next to her and stepped in closer to Zack. Looking at him for the first time without her helmet, she could properly see the smooth gentle tone of his flawless skin. Slowly she inched closer to him and allowed her hands to fall down by her side, softly searching for his fingertips. His eyes remained firmly shut as she gently held his hands. Heather pressed her lips against his, now allowing herself to close her eyes. Zack's lips were cold from the outside exposure, but they were smooth and satisfying to kiss.

Heather had intended to give him a meaningful kiss on the lips but as the two of them connected she felt herself giving more. Zack also pressed his body securely against hers, letting go of her hand, he traced the back of his fingers across her cheek and through her hair. Heather's other hand now slid forward and held the lower of his back.

She couldn't tell how long they kissed for, a few seconds, a minute or longer but when they finished, true to his word, Zack kept his eyes closed.

Locking the helmet back in place she told him to open his eyes.

'Thank you, Zack,' she said, smiling broadly beneath her mask.

'No ... thank you,' he flustered, having not quite expected that. He looked at her and awkwardly laughed. 'It's really hard to tell if you're smiling or not.'

Heather laughed too.

'I'm smiling,' she said warmly, and they laughed together like a pair of embarrassed teenagers.

'What do you say we get out of here and go plan how we're going to finish off our next target?' said Zack.

'After you,' and she pointed out to the sheer twenty-story drop off the other side of the glass railing.

'I think I'll take the stairs thanks. I've never really had the desire to leap off the edge of a building!'

Heather and Zack clambered out of the lift that Zack had installed as a route into his underground lair; a small manhole service entrance that was once used to access a section of Old London's plumbing. The two of them walked down the cylindrical tunnel for a few seconds before turning sharply left to face a decrepit and quite inconspicuous maintenance panel. Zack lifted up a discrete lever, entered the series of voice activation codes and completed the retinal scans on both eyes.

The Catacomb's lights switched on as they walked onto the underground train platform and made their way towards the stationary carriage.

'Okay, wait here a second,' Zack said, turning to Heather as he walked into the carriage.

He fiddled around with his computer for a minute or so while Heather stood looking around aimlessly. The place looked the same as it had when she visited a few months ago, except now it had a couple of heating units dotted about the place. It wasn't too cold down there and she couldn't imagine why he would need heaters but within a few moments, Heather had put it out of her mind.

Zack walked out of the carriage and towards Heather, carrying a paper-thin glass tablet. He tapped a couple of buttons and the lights of the station dimmed, filling the platform with shadow. Then without warning, bright vivid blue light shot across the platform in every direction. Like fireflies made of lasers, they fluttered between the tiled walls and ceiling. The light formed together to make a 3D projected screen, plastered with information and data about Heather's next Pandarian. Twenty-year-old Francis Cotton.

'He's a student at Cambridge University and a pretty special one at that,' Zack said, scrolling through his tablet and bringing up photos of Francis.

'Wouldn't be a Pandarian if there wasn't something special about him. Let me guess, he's captain of the football team? said Heather.

'Nearly. He's the captain of the swim team. Won five gold medals at last year's Olympics. He's been on the front cover of Bloom twice and there's talk of him hosting a TV show when he finishes his studies.'

'Impressive,' Heather remarked, looking the floating 3D model of him up and down.

'Cambridge. Well, it'll be nice not to have to travel far for this one. Any indication of where and when the best time to strike might be?'

'He's unlikely to be on his own for much of the day, what with classes, swim practice and the parties. And the fact that he's at a university means we've got to be even more careful. If you're seen killing kids … well, there's no coming back from that, Harrow.'

'So, where's he living, is there going to be anyone else there?' Heather was very aware that there would be no coming back from that.

'Unfortunately, he's living in halls on campus, so it's not going to be easy to get to him. But there's no sign of a girlfriend on his social networking sites, so if you can get to his room hopefully there will be nobody there but him. That's even if he is in his room, it seems like these kids just never sleep!'

Heather paced around the screen, passing through the edges of the lasers sending them shooting off into the tunnel from the reflection of her suit. Thinking about how far she had come and how she just had two left to defeat. Zack silently watched her as she thought.

'Zack, I want you to come with me on this one. I want you out in the field, close by and on hand.'

He looked terrified at the request, he nearly dropped the tablet.

'I don't know if I can do that, Harrow. I'm really not a frontline kind of guy.'

'You don't need to be there by my side pulling the trigger, but I just want you close by. We're in this together now, aren't we?' said Heather. She did feel a bit guilty for putting him in this situation, she was manipulating him, but she couldn't help it. Heather enjoyed being close to him and taking him on this next mission would be comforting.

Zack thought about her proposal for a few moments and then in a slightly stuttered response agreed to it, on the condition that he didn't have to leave the van or hotel room he would work from.

They spent more time going through some logistics together and Heather noted key entrance and exits points to the campus and Francis' halls residence. They also discussed how she would execute the assassination. The campus was expected to have some kind of foot traffic at all times, even at night. Zack suggested planting some sort of controlled explosive device but there was too much risk it would harm other students in the blast. Not to mention the need to capture the Pandarians corporeal form when it no longer had a human host to leech onto. Whatever way she killed him, she had to be very close by.

While Heather looked at a graph of police response times for the area, Zack disappeared for a couple of minutes. He walked across the train tracks and into the north facing tunnel and returned shortly after carrying a shiny black pentagonal case.

'I've made something for you, Harrow,' he called as Heather cycled through a list of names and information about Francis's roommates.

He placed the case on the floor in front of them and opened it up. Inside were six of the drones he had lent her during their first night working together. Except these were flatter and had sharper angles. They were more like chunky frisbees than the spheres from months ago. Each of the six was identical and made of the same metallic material.

'They're for your suit.' He glanced up at Harrow's helmet, really wishing he could see her face and reaction.

'They've got the same features as before and I've added a few new ones. They're a lot stronger and can carry a lot more weight. If you have four of them attached to your suit ...' he pointed at the final item in the case, a backplate for her armour with six sunken dips, '... you'll actually be able to-'

'Fly?!' she finished his sentence for him. 'Zack, this is freaking amazing!'

'You like it? I couldn't tell, with the whole face mask and blank expression syndrome. But you do like it?' his face lit up and a huge smile flashed across it.

'I love it, thank you,' Heather said, taking both his hands and holding them gently in hers. 'Since I was a little girl, I've always wanted to fly.'

CHAPTER SEVENTEEN

Feet sloppily trudged across the neatly mowed lawns of Cambridge University. Students were stumbling back to their rooms after a night of partying and fireworks. It was November the fifth - the night that Britain celebrated the brutal execution of a subversive, who had tried to blow up Parliament - and the sky sparkled with blades of red and blue. The last few stragglers finished off their beers and switched off their e-cigs.

Soaring through the faded imprints of the fireworks, Heather fluidly flew across the sky above campus. Though she was encased in her armour and she couldn't feel the breeze against her skin or through her hair, it was exhilarating. She quietly zoomed several feet above all drunk and oblivious students; all except one.

A photographer, who had finished capturing the dazzling spectacle of lights and explosions was about to get ready to pack up his equipment. He looked through the eyepiece one final time and to his surprise, saw a flash of electric blue rocket by. Whipping his face away from the camera he eagerly stared upwards to search for the source.

'What's your position, Harrow?' came Zack's voice from her helmet earpiece.

'I'm about thirty seconds from Cotton's dormitory. How are you keeping back there?' she smiled, knowing Zack was probably not enjoying it in the van about a mile from where she was.

'It smells like stale fast food in here, and a girl in a V for Vendetta mask has just thrown up in front of the van. So, I'm doing great.' The sarcasm in his last words were transparent.

'I'm glad you came with me, Zack,' said Heather truthfully.

Francis Cotton was the sixth target that Nahmar had given Heather, she expected resistance but even superpowered foresight couldn't help her with what happened next.

Reaching the large archaic dormitory block, home to roughly a hundred and twenty students, Heather hovered down to Francis' window. Zack had pinched his room number and blueprints of the building from the university databases. The drones giving Heather her flight were incredibly responsive and could be controlled by voice and movement. Though Heather felt they may as well be reading her thoughts, because drifting down to the fourth floor was effortless.

She pushed closer to the window, its curtains pulled shut and activated her scanner. But before it could even complete the scan, she knew it was meaningless.

'Zack, there's a bomb! Get fire and rescue crews here, NOW!!!'

She leapt back from the window and could hear Zack on the communications channel yell back, 'What's going-' but the noise of the explosion cut him off.

Hurled backwards by the blast, Heather tumbled through the air and crashed into the leaf-covered lawn, splattering dirt across the back of her suit. She held her mending arm close to her chest to ensure she didn't break it again. Beside her, landed fragments of glass and chunks of crumbled brick, the swarm of clay red dust hovered around her; while an imposing black cloud of smoke protruded from the enormous explosion, like the mushroom of a volcano. The building itself was groaning, as floor after floor toppled down on each other, shooting jets of smoke and dust in every direction.

Leaping from the floor, Heather launched upwards and flew towards the decimated building. The roof and top two floors had entirely vanished, and the rest of the building was moments away from completely caving in.

'Harrow, are you okay?!' Zack shouted over the comms.

'I'm fine, I'm fine! Zack, the whole building went. They knew we were coming.' She hovered above it as smoke and dust licked her suit. Her scanners and the drones were picking up signs of life within the building's collapsing carcass. Heather cursed to herself under her breath.

'There are still people in there, Zack. Tell fire and rescue there are six survivors on the ground floor and three on the first,' she said solemnly.

'Where are you going?' Zack asked in confusion, assuming she'd be diving in to save the people herself.

'He's not here. That blast was triggered remotely, and I know where from.' Heather slowly started to rise higher and higher in the air, her thick black cape billowing in the ash-filled breeze.

'My suit picked up a signal ping to this exact location right before the blast, I've just pulled it up on my display and I've got the coordinates; a manor estate just on the outskirts of Cambridge.'

'Passive vicinity signal tracing? That's some serious tech, Harrow,' he sounded quite impressed.

'It should be, it cost more than every other component of the suit,' Heather said, as she pitched down and eastward. 'Keep me up to speed on the rescue, Zack.'

Heather felt horrible inside for leaving these young people trapped beneath the rubble. But she knew any hasty effort she made to save them would probably end up crushing them and would guarantee Francis' escape. Booming through the sky, she flew towards the signal's point of origin, aching to wrap her hand round the neck of the monster that did this.

But the young photographer, that had just captured every frame of the last few minutes, thought that the monster responsible was the one right in front of him.

It took Heather about a minute to fly across Cambridge towards the signal's point of origin, where she hoped to find her missing Pandarian. But as she passed the summit of trees surrounding the manor estate, she found more than she bargained for.

About a hundred meters away, neatly nestled in the surrounding forests, was a truly stunning manor house. Huge two-story windows reflected the lilac blob of moonlight, tall pillars of stone supported a lavish oak balcony.

Heather didn't have much time to take this in though; as soon as she saw the house over the tips of the trees, a dozen or more bright beams of red light burst through the sky towards her. She swerved like a car about to miss its exit on a motorway, dodging the incoming hail of plasma fire. This sort of weaponry was incredibly rare and extraordinarily expensive, Heather had no doubt she was in the right place.

As she soared towards the house the storm of fire continued, she didn't need foresight to know what a single graze of one of these projectiles would do to her. Spinning wildly to avoid the shots, she wished she had spent more time practising flying using the drones before going after Francis. A long line of red light, hummed past her ear as she flew low to the ground, she could hear the trees behind her taking the brunt of the attack. The sound of plasma bolts bombarding the forest sounded like a whip being slashed against glass.

Continuing to dodge the molten hot beams, she pushed further toward the balcony of the house, which was where Heather could see her attackers. Two figures, barely visible with the blasts of light over-exposing their bodies, stood on the balcony each firing mounted rail-guns. The closer she got along the long stretch of perfectly attended grass, the harder it was to avoid the onslaught. The grass was getting shredded as she rolled and darted out of the way.

Heather blasted upwards; now just meters away from the house, she pulled out a modified smoke grenade and hurled it towards the balcony. Weaving and swirling down at the closest attacker, she dived like a hawk about to seize its prey; a barrage of plasma fire narrowly missing her as she did.

She slammed into the attacker's shoulders at full speed, throwing him hard into the exquisite wooden balcony, a few of the newly varnished planks cracked as his body smashed into it. On the other side of the balcony the second attacker, having seen this, wheeled the turret around to face her and madly opened fire. Springing quickly into the air before he could even squeeze the trigger, Heather leapt towards him; leaving the downed assailant to be completely obliterated, not even having time to scream as his flesh was torn from his bones. Snapping the other man's jaw with her fist, she grabbed hold of the straps on his Kevlar vest and threw him into the balcony railing, but he was heavy and didn't move very far. Spinning round to face her, clutching his now wickedly wonky jaw, he withdrew a thick long serrated knife and launched himself towards Heather. However, she was on the other end of his railgun, pointing it straight towards him. Nothing was left for the police to find but a singed pair of size eleven leather boots.

Within the multi-million-pound house, there were eight more extremely skilled and disciplined mercenaries, all built like stallions and wielding unworldly weapons of death. Heather killed every last one of them, unwilling to take any more chances. Finally, she reached a large coffee coloured double door and after shooting both men stood outside, (with a gun she picked up from one of the mercenaries), she called out down the hallway.

'Francis Cotton, I know what you are!' she bellowed.

There were a couple moments of deadly silence, followed by the sound of six large mechanical locks retracting from the door. It swung open and stood in the doorway was an athletic young man wearing an expensive looking shirt and a pristine tailored suit jacket. His hair was short and neatly styled and he wore a shimmering gold wristwatch, which glimmered gently as he raised his arm. Francis pointed a small white pistol down the hallway at Heather, the chamber glowed the same bright crimson as the other guns.

'Well you have me at a disadvantage it seems, as I know not who you are,' he said, his accent pompous and his words perfectly enunciated. 'Why don't you take off that helmet and we can meet properly?'

Heather didn't say anything but started to walk towards him.

'Ah no thank you, that is quite far enough.' He lifted his other hand to show a small round device about the size of an apple. 'You see I purchased another little toy, as well that lovely gun in your hand,' he smirked, nodding at the looted plasma pistol Heather held.

'Do you know what this is?' He held up the dark metallic orb.

'It's a deadman switch,' Heather replied in a monotone.

'Why yes, it is! My my, you really are as insightful as they say you are,' he said, of course, unaware that she'd used her foresight to see what he would tell her it was.

'And that means, if my heat signature or fingerprints come off the sensors, the three hydrogen bombs I have planted in New London will detonate. I don't think I need to explain what that will do to your beloved city?' he smiled, revealing his brilliant white teeth. 'Now, drop the gun and kick it over to me.'

Heather stood there calmly, fully aware of the gravity of the situation. Carefully she bent down and placed the gun on the floor, focusing deeply on the orb as he spoke.

'So, let me tell you what is going to happen next. You're going to hand over that annoying little box you've been using to capture my brothers and sisters. Do that, and your precious city will live. Have I made myself clear?' he said, still pointing his gun towards her.

'Zack, three bombs in New London. Find them,' Heather whispered, as she took another step over the discarded gun, towards Francis.

He fired a warning shot at the floor in front of her.

'If you take another step forward, the next shot will be at your chest. Do you think that fancy costume of yours will be able to handle it?' he smiled.

Heather continued to focus on the orb in his other hand, squeezing the components inside with her mind.

'Well?!' he yelled out in frustration. A tiny strand of his hair fell out of place as he cried out.

'If you want to see the box, I'll take you to it!' Heather laughed and then sprinted towards him.

'Damn you, bitch,' he said, releasing his grip on the device and looked at it, listening for a tiny beep. Nothing happened. Expecting a sound as confirmation, he pressed his fingers to the device's sensors and released it again; again nothing.

In a flustered panic, he whipped his focus across to Heather to shoot, but she was a blink ahead. A single bullet from her hip holstered gun sailed through the air and shattered through the knuckle of his index finger.

Francis roared out in agony, dropping both the gun and the orb. But still, no signal was sent. Heather had spent the last twenty seconds imagining the complex circuitry inside the device overheating and frying; and so, they did. She bounded across the hallway like a gazelle and leapt into her adversary. Her strong hands wrapped around his throat as the two of them smashed into the floor.

She squeezed tightly, crumpling his shirt collar and crushing his windpipe. His eyes wailed with torment as she suffocated him. He tried to thrash about, slamming his fist into the side of her head but Heather was immovable. Using her sharp knees, she dug in forcefully into his ribs.

His legs wildly flailed about like a fish out of water, trying to reach up and drag her down but she just gripped tighter. After a few moments, the prideful life left his eyes and the struggle stopped. Then just as the five other Pandarians before him, bright coloured light burst from his stolen body, this time a maple gold colour. It swirled above them for a moment, desperately trying to find a new host before being forcibly dragged down into the small silver box in Heather's hand. Heather carefully secured it back in her utility pouch, it hadn't left her sight since Nahmar had entrusted her with it.

She went to stand up, taking a final look at the dead boy, wondering what his life would have been like if it hadn't been taken over by whatever these beings were. But her train of thought was interrupted sharply by the foresight of someone shouting. It was a grand booming voice coming from outside. It seemed the law had finally caught up with her.

'Harrow! I know you're in there, come out. NOW!' the voice thundered.

Minutes later, Heather appeared outside, leaving through a side door to the house to face her summoner. She stared up at the floating man, grey clouds now dotted about the sky above them both.

'How did you find me?' Heather asked, recognising his bright blue and white uniform and straight cut look, it was Paladin.

'You're in the news,' Paladin said in a cruel tone, not hovering down to her level, but instead towering over her.

'What?' said Heather. Paladin explained how some photographer had seen her about twenty minutes ago and caught a picture. He had tagged her at Cambridge University, then it didn't take long for it to go viral; it never did with superheroes.

'I haven't seen the photo, but I was dispatched to investigate,' he said.

This was good, Heather thought to herself. If he hadn't seen the picture, then perhaps he didn't know about her flight. She hoped she could use this to her advantage, she'd need it.

'On my way in, calls came in about a building explosion and I knew it had to be you. Then I saw a plasma blast fly from this direction and knew that also had to be you. A trail of destruction seems to follow you wherever you go, Harrow,' he gestured to the smoking house, torn up lawn and decimated forest at the bottom of the estate, where many of the missed plasma blasts had impacted.

'There are at least ninety dead in that building and I don't know how many more in the one you've just walked out of. I should have brought you in after the prison attack. It's over Harrow, this ends here, tonight.'

He began to hover down angelically to the shredded ground as Heather pleaded with him.

'That building explosion wasn't me, and this-' she nodded to the multi-million-pound house with giant molten holes in it. '-you just have to trust me. There's so much going on right now that you just don't understand,' said Heather imploringly.

'How can I trust you anymore? After California, how can anyone trust you? Your disregard for life is abhorrent, and the way you treat criminals is despicable.'

His white and black boots gently touched down on the ground and he started walking towards Heather.

'You don't show an ounce of mercy and I've allowed this to go on for far too long. You need to come with me,' he said his voice firm and threatening.

Heather told him where he could stick his request.

Paladin took a deep sigh. 'I tried to do this the easy way and give you a chance, damn you, Harrow.' Then he charged towards her like a rhinoceros, Heather drew her sword and pistol.

It took him a single breath to reach her and his flurry of fists began. Precisely firing punch after deadly punch. Each one flew at such speed, even with her foresight, it was incredibly difficult to think that quickly and several bulldozing punches made their way through her guard. Crushing into her armour and ripping her breath away. She parried and stabbed her sword into his abdomen several times. Glanced off his skin like paper, it didn't seem to slow him at all, in fact, it was as though he couldn't even feel it. She hoped to slow him a bit by shooting him and after a graceful dodge backwards opened fire at his face. However, the bullets just seemed to ping off his skin and any visible marks they left cleared up seconds later.

His attacks became less forgiving and more painful for Heather as their fight continued. She managed to get her fair share of kicks, jabs and slices in, but it didn't seem to make a dent. That was until she switched on the electricity in her sword. Bright blue bolts stabbed into him as she sliced across his chest mid-jump. The electricity seemed to slow him down somewhat, and the flinches he made as the fragments of intense energy hit him, made Heather think it must be hurting him. Though he didn't stop his attack.

A particularly large whip of electric energy ricocheted across Paladin's arm, just before it collided with the side of Heather's head. It was practically impossible to foresee at the speed Paladin could move. Paladin let out a cry of anger and pain, clutching onto his shocked arm, as Heather went flying across the grass churning it up as she crashed into it.

The interface display inside her helmet flicked off for a moment but then returned, the suit was holding up. For now.

Paladin shook himself off and charged again at Heather, his steps seemed to boom like heavy drums as he ran towards her. This time Heather was ready for him.

She rapidly dodged his first four attacks and before the fifth, swung the sword over her head pounding it against his temple. He stumbled back in a stupor giving Heather a chance to hurl three smoke grenades at the ground. They burst open, enveloping the pair of them in a thick black fog.

The sound of the spark-spitting sword vanished, and an unordinary silence befell the dense smoke cloud. Quickly, Paladin regained his focus and blasted away the smoke with a giant single puff of air. But Heather was nowhere to be seen.

He spun around to look behind and stared across the lawn, his extraordinary vision peering through the darkness for signs of his foe. Paladin floated up, scouring the entire field but could not see Heather at all. He flew the perimeter of the estate and then surveyed several loops around the Cambridge campus, but there was no sign of Heather anywhere. After nearly an hour, anger dripping from him like a sweat, he gave up and returned to the police department back in New London.

Heather watched all of this from at least fifty feet above him, having silently burst from the smoke using the drones Zack gave her. The problem with people who think they're the biggest and best around, they never think to look above them.

CHAPTER EIGHTEEN

Wearing his favourite crimson top, that flashed the different emblems of well-known superheroes, Henry raced through his home blasting aliens from another planet. He looked through his augmented reality glasses at the hulking slimy beasts that were clawing their way through the hallways. Blasting several of the smaller more globular creatures with the linked laser gun, he screamed with delight and fled the virtual splatter of cartoonish goop. Whistles of laser fire and alien guts splashing played through the device's headphones.

Firing a particularly well-aimed plasma grenade, Henry charged out of harm's way and into his parent's bedroom to take cover. Scampering across his mum's bed he crouched behind the far side, Heather's side.

Two more massive aliens clambered through the doorway, their melon sized eyes staring into Henrys menacingly. He shot at the two of them, proficiently defeating the virtual aliens. He dived underneath the bed to hide and reload the toy gun, but as he did, something small bumped against his head that was dangling from the planks of the bed. Glancing up at whatever it was that he hit, he saw a small black leather pouch. It was hanging by its brown shoelace-like drawstrings.

Reaching up a sweaty hand, Henry pulled it from its hiding place. He pushed the off switch on his glasses and crawled out from under the bed, holding the mysterious black pouch.

Then sat on the floor and leaning against the bed, he opened it.

He beheld the small silver cube, with strange carvings and protrusions coming out of it. The people on it, they looked quite calm and their bodies were relaxed but there was something not quite right about them. There was a tinge of pain on the people's faces like something was subtly gnawing at them. Henry couldn't be certain, but in this light, the box looked like it was glowing. It was incredibly heavy for its size, but Henry didn't put it down. Its dull silver colour was slightly iridescent and seemed to transform colour as he twisted it round in his hands.

'WHAT DO YOU THINK YOU'RE DOING!?' Heather roared.

A split second from walking in to see him she knew before even entering the bedroom, what he had found.

Henry spun round in pre-emptive shock and looked like he leapt a foot off the ground.

'I just …'

'What do you think you're doing!? Heather shouted at him again. 'Give me that now,' she said, shoving her hand towards him.

On the verge of tears, Henry approached his mum.

'I'm s-so sorry M-mum,' he whimpered, passing over the silver cube.

Coming from the hallway, Heather could hear the

sound of Kirsty's rapidly approaching footsteps. She pocketed the cube and turned to face her red-faced wife.

'What on earth is going on in here?' Kirsty demanded, looking back and forth between Heather and her son, who was now sobbing quietly.

'It's nothing Kirsty,' Heather said, not meeting her eyes and attempted to scoot past her. But Kirsty shifted and blocked the doorway.

'Doesn't sound like nothing, you've brought our son to tears. What did he do that warranted a reaction like that?!'

Nobody was used to Heather being the shouty parent, it was just something she never really did. Henry didn't know what to do with himself. He stood close to the bed, gripping onto a tag of the bed sheet aimlessly whilst wiping his eyes with the bottom of his t-shirt.

'Really, Kirsty, it's no big deal. He just shouldn't be messing around in here.'

'You've never had a problem with it before. What the hell is going on with you?' said Kirsty, glaring at Heather with unfamiliarity and disgust.

'I'm fine, can you move please,' Heather said, trying and failing to barge past again.

'You think just because you're in a foul mood, and you won't tell me what's going on, you can just explode at him and walk away?'

'Get out of the way, Kirsty.'

'No. Tell me what's going on!'

Heather rammed past her wife, knocking into her shoulder as she did so, making a beeline for her coat and shoes.

Further along the corridor, Kirsty's mum stood hunched over and crow-like. She had been eavesdropping on the whole fight and upon seeing Heather lurched back into the living room.

'You can't just walk away from this, Heather!' Kirsty shouted as her wife slipped on an old pair of trainers and tugged a large padded navy-blue coat off its peg.

'Watch me,' said Heather, as she slammed the apartment door shut behind her.

The following few days were tense and strained in Heather's house. Kirsty's mum, who was still living with them while her flat was being repaired, was brash and snooty. She had begun acting as though Heather didn't exist and whenever Heather entered the room, she would turn up the TV just loud enough that they couldn't make conversation or would simply walk out.

Kirsty hadn't said more than a handful of words to Heather since their last fight. She was working later than usual too and some nights she didn't come back in time for the swap over at dinner, before Heather went on patrol.

Henry had been keeping to his room mostly, playing quietly and reading his comic books. His usual playful nature had been extinguished by the abnormal telling off. He'd been trying to figure out what the strange silver cube was that he'd found under the bed, but dared not ask his mother.

As for Heather, she was still waiting for the final target confirmation to come through from Nahmar. It seemed that whoever this last Pandarian was hosting, was clearly in a seat of immense power. For now, Heather and Zack had returned their focus and effort to protecting New London.

Pouring herself a large mug of sugar-filled tea, Heather stared out of her kitchen window. She thought about how much this quest had already cost her, what she had been through and been forced to do. Three days ago, she'd killed a man that was barely out of his teens. Her mind wandered as her eyes gazed out across the cityscape, wondering how long that parasite had been in control and how much of Francis' life was actually Francis'.

One sugary cup of tea later, Heather pulled on her jacket and told Judy she was going to work. After the acknowledging grunt she received she paced down the hallway to Henry's room. Gently knocking on his closed door with her bandage free arm, she called out to him.

'Henry, sweetie. I'm going to work now,' she said, pressing the side of her head against the wooden door she listened for a response. But none came. She could hear him shifting in his seat uncomfortably and possibly the sound of a page crisply turning but he didn't say a thing.

Feeling quite downtrodden, Heather stamped into her shoes and briskly left the apartment with her bicycle, making her way to a safe house.

A few minutes later she swung a leg over the seat and pushed off from the pavement, sailing quickly along the gritty tarmac. Bitter cold sliced her cheeks and knuckles as she rode, and icy rain trickled through her hair and down her neck past her hoodless jacket. Riding one handed through the rain and waterlogged streets quickly became an irritation. Her arm was nearly completely healed and the removable sling was just for show around the house. She slid it off and stuffed it into her jacket. Oblivious to the horrified pair of eyes that spied her doing it. Several meters behind her, in a small and quite unextraordinary car, Kirsty sat in the passenger seat, following her wife.

'See! Did you see that?! I told you. I can't believe she would lie about something like that.' Kirsty hissed at the driver.

Neil was a friend from her work, they'd known

each other for the last three years and got on really well. They worked on the same team and swapped and helped each other with more challenging assignments. Kirsty had asked Neil to take her home, so they could follow Heather in a car she wouldn't recognise. Neil had tried to talk her out of it, 'You're panicking for no reason, Heather's probably just stressed with work.' But seeing the distress and hurt in his friend's eyes, begrudgingly he agreed to help her with this - in his words, 'violation of trust.'

'I told you she was lying about something, Neil. Quick she's turning left.' A few moments later Neil turned after the speeding bicycle, splattering a large black puddle across a disused mailbox.

'Kirst, this is nuts. We shouldn't be following your wife. I mean I know things are hard but this isn't going to make it any better. She's just going to work,' he said, trying to calm down his friend.

'How do we know she's going to work? For all I know, she's off to meet some drug dealer by the river or some skanky whore in a multi-storey!' she rasped. 'And what about the arm sling, that's a "violation of trust,"' she said, loosely imitating Neil's voice.

'Yeah, I can't explain the arm thing, but maybe she never broke it and just wanted a bit of sympathy from you. It looks like a cry for help to me, Kirst.'

'It looks like a lie to me,' she said, the annoyance and frustration quite apparent in her voice.

They followed Heather tightly for another three and a half minutes before getting caught on the wrong side of a traffic signal. Heather put on a burst of speed and went through before the lights changed. Stuck behind a small delivery van, Kirsty and Neil lost sight of her.

Neil refused to help her with following Heather ever again, even with the relentless badgering at work he told her to find her own way of stalking Heather. And that is exactly what Kirsty did. Hoping to see where Heather really went every night, she spent the next fortnight in random taxis, awkwardly telling confused drivers to follow that cyclist. Either receiving confused - 'This isn't the movies, darling' responses or the occasional - 'Yeah, why not.'

CHAPTER NINETEEN

~Then~

'I must rest, Nahmar. I tire and cannot keep up with you.'

Nahmar and Thaesilia had been sprinting through the crisp and frosty woodland for what felt like an hour. The sound of their pursuers had died down and the air had gone quiet. The vacant noises of owls hooting or foxes scraping at the dirt left Nahmar feeling nervous and on edge. Besides their heavy panting, it was silent.

Nahmar stopped running too and turned around to see Thaesilia, hunched over trying to catch her breath. Her flame-like hair was sweaty and clung to her face like seaweed. Nahmar's eyes wandered from her hair, all the way down her body. He'd never seen anyone quite so beautiful. But before his thoughts could drift too far, he was snapped back to the present.

'I must go back for my father!' he said, in a frightfully determined voice.

'We cannot,' puffed Thaesilia. 'It is too dangerous, besides, your father can clearly handle himself,' she said, glancing up at him and catching his gaze. 'You saw what he did back there, how he knew where to move and where was safe. He has been touched by magic, yes?'

Nahmar had never heard this word before, but that wasn't his first question.

'Who are you, really? Why were you their prisoner?'

Thaesilia had managed to catch her breath and moved to sit on a large fallen oak, frost sprinkled between the recesses of the wood. The heavy black clouds above them were groaning and close to bursting point.

'You want to know who I am?' Thaesilia asked and Nahmar impatiently nodded.

She pressed her hands to her grazed and scuffed knees, fighting with herself trying to decide what to tell this man. She knew the information would change his life forever.

'Very well. But I warn you, it is not a pleasant tale,' she whispered.

'I'm sure I can stomach it,' said Nahmar, taking a seat next to her on the fallen tree.

Thaesilia leant back and looked up into the sky. The black clouds were tightly clustered but between a very narrow opening, she could see the sky glittering.

'I am from a land, many stars away. Up there, there are many worlds, Nahmar; quite like this one. One day your people will discover, just as mine once did, that you are not alone.'

Nahmar's expression was perplexed but he continued to focus on what Thaesilia said.

'My people are quite similar to yours, in spirit, temperament and ambition, we even look the same.'

Nahmar did not think they looked the same at all.

'Seventeen cycles ago, a great spellcaster on my

planet created a new way to collect sustainable energy. The energy harnessed would power our machines, bring warmth to our homes and grow our food. There was even potential that the energy could create life!' she cried, her eyes lighting up intensely as she spoke.

'A revered spellcaster created eight entities. They could feed off the variety of emotions that we emitted and transform that essence into fuel. He called them Pandarians.'

Creaking deeply, the clouds ached under the heavy weight of the rain about to burst free.

'For a short time the Pandarians fulfilled their purpose; living among us harmoniously, collecting the embers of all our emotions. But as time went on their goal began to stray from their original purpose. They started to develop a preference for certain emotions and behaviours more than others. No longer did they feed on our happiness, passion and generosity but rather our anger, selfishness and darkest desires. They hungered for the worst in us, it developed into an addiction. And worse, was that they became unwilling to give us the energy that they created from that. Their unquenchable hunger swelled, and they grew more powerful with every passing day. Before we realised the severity of what had happened, it was too late. Shedding the forms the spellcaster had given them, they hid among us. Invading and taking control of our leader's bodies.'

'The time that passed was the gravest in our planets recorded history. War began. For the first time, brothers and sisters fought and killed one another. All while the Pandarians hid among us, feasting on our rage.'

The sky had now given up and the heavens flooded the earth, pouring icy sharp rain onto the two of them where they sat.

'Many of my people died in the conflict, some of them close friends.' Her head dropped and she stared at the ground.

Nahmar didn't know what to do with himself. He wanted to scoot along the log to comfort her but felt confounded and unsure. Much of what she had said did not make much sense. He was still trying to wrap his head around that she was from the stars. After a few moments of rain filled quiet, Nahmar spoke up.

'I still do not understand why it is that you are here?'

She turned her face gently to look at him, her bright eyes pierced into his.

'Some of us realised what had happened. Several of our most warm-hearted and charitable leaders had become tyrannical dictators overnight. I and a handful of others worked together to create instruments that would allow us to track the Pandarians and see through their disguise. We sought the guidance of the spellcaster that created them but we never found him. We assumed that they found him first, eradicating the knowledge of their weaknesses with his death. Therefore, the process of creating such devices took many years, and our world continued to fall to ruin.'

'We needed two things to save our world and return it to peace; a way to find a Pandarian and see through the hosts they hid behind, for this we crafted talismans; and a way to capture or destroy them. Other spellcasters and I created prisons for our enemy, they are called Serathiums. Small enchanted containers built to encase their corporeal forms. If you could sever the connection from the host, they would be exposed and drawn into the box. Otherwise just killing the host would not be enough, they would simply find a new one.'

Nahmar now understood what had happened back in the Persuader's hut. Killing him had revealed the Pandarian inside but not having a way of capturing it, it only needed another host to leech onto.

'Once we had both the talisman to see the Pandarians and the Serathium to capture them, a small band of spellcasters and I took the fight to them. By this time their influence over my people was tremendous. My brothers, sisters and I were labelled usurpers and agents of terror and our assault came at a great price.'

'We managed to reach one of the Pandarians, who at this point had started to spread across our world, feeding on all the lands. It was my mother who landed the final blow. Swinging her weapon down with such ferocity she cleaved through the body of a prophet, who inside hid one of the eight. Absorbing the being into a Serathium we left that place with fewer spellcasters but wiser to our cause than before.'

Thaesilia continued, shivering slightly as the cold rainwater gushed down her skin.

'After that day, word spread of the disease that our people had succumbed to. But that there was hope, hope that these terrible monsters could be stopped. Before we could re-group and capture the seven remaining Pandarians, they fled our planet. Escaping on our explorative vessels and finding another planet to feed on.'

'That is why I am here. I and a few others were sent here to capture these parasites and stop them before they can bring another civilisation crashing down to its knees. I was looking for the one you call the Persuader when I was captured by his followers. I was forced to hide the Serathium nearby, but we must find it and return to capture the Pandarian!' Her eyes were now menacing and angry, her expression one of torment.

'You want to go back there?!' Nahmar yelled. 'Are you mad, we will surely be killed!'

'Have you listened to nothing of my story? Your world will decay and fall to ruin if we do not stop them!' shouted Thaesilia.

'We?! I can't-' Nahmar's sentence was interrupted by the distinct sound of men yelling. He spun around on the soaking wet log and could see dozens of bright flaming orange dots, charging towards them.

'Hurry!' Nahmar, grabbed Thaesilia's wrist and the two of them sprinted again through the downpour.

Tearing through the undergrowth, Nahmar and Thaesilia fled again from their hunters. Their legs getting sliced and shredded as they ran through a large patch of thorny bushes and brambles. The sky was still dark, and the rain beat down on them unforgivingly. Several times they splashed through inky black puddles, cracking through the thin layer of ice on top. Spiteful cold bit their ankles as they were plunged into the shallow water. Several yards behind them a large group followed. Their torches illuminated the trees around them and created a halo of heat. Low hanging branches clawed at their hair as it bounced behind them. A pointy, leafless twig scratched across Nahmar's cheek. But neither of them let the terrain slow them, that was until Thaesilia sprung a trap.

Moments before it happened, Nahmar could foresee it. In a panicked voice, he yelled to Thaesillia, who was running alongside him several feet to his right. He shouted out a warning, telling her to jump or move out the way but through the heavy downpour of the rain and the sound of them thrashing through the dense undergrowth, she couldn't hear him properly. Completely powerless, he watched the red-haired woman violently tumble into a hidden spike pit. Designed to catch bears or other large animals, it had a blanket of thin sticks and large walnut coloured leaves resting on top to hide the deadly sharpened stakes inside the dug-out pit. Thaesilia crashed out of view and let out an eye-watering scream of agony.

Nahmar skidded to a halt and raced back to the pit. Four feet beneath him lay Thaesilia, twisted and impaled on several of the wooden stakes. Her screams filled the air and burrowed through Nahmar's ears like shattered glass. He could see at least three of the spikes that had pierced into her but the worst of which was a thick blood splattered one through her thigh. Hot red blood flowed down her leg, dripping into the murky puddle beneath her.

'I'm going to get you out of there, Thaesilia, just hang on!' Nahmar shouted, trying to foresee the safest route to get down into the pit with her.

'No, Nahmar! There's no time,' she winced. 'Even if you could get me out I can't run like this, and one of us has to get away.'

Helplessly he stared at her as she tried to pull her eyes away from the dirt to look up at him. Her bruised and battered face, now drenched in water and agony still retained a tiny hint of her delicacy.

'Give me your hand,' she said, reaching up her own. He knelt down and thrust out his hand urgently, thinking she'd changed her mind.

Taking Nahmar's outstretched coarse hand in her own, she closed her eyes and whispered a few illegible words under her breath. Suddenly Nahmar felt a mighty surge of warmth spread from his hand holding hers, all the way up his arm, across his chest and then to every inch of his body. His heart rate, which was pounding like the beat of a drum, began to slow. It continued to slow until he could feel the bulging pulse in his neck steady to an abnormally slow pace.

'What have you done to me?' Nahmar asked, with a mixture of fear and intense wonderment.

Thaesilia's grip of his hand fell and dropped back into the dirt. She tried to use it to steady herself as the downpour of rain had not stopped for them. Looking back at him with eyes that now appeared duller and less vibrant than before she smiled weakly.

'I have given you my life, Nahmar. Use it well.'

The sound of their pursuers was getting much clearer and Nahmar could almost make out their faces.

'Find the container, Nahmar. You must find the Serathium.' She reached a hand behind her sodden hair, wiping dirt and blood in her thick red curls as she routed round in it.

From the depths of her hair, she pulled out a small amulet, which dangled from a frayed bit of string. She held it up for Nahmar to take, her grip on the pit slid a bit as she did so, and the spikes dug an inch deeper into her body. She let out a howl of pain but didn't let go of the amulet.

'You must t-take this. Wear it and think of the Pandarians, think about what they r-really are and the amulet will guide your thoughts to t-them.' Handing it over, she was now shaking from the excruciating pain and bone splitting cold.

The group of men and women hunting them were now just seconds away. Nahmar could hear what they were shouting now.

'Find the Serathium by the lake, kill the h-host and the Pandarian will be absorbed! Now GO!' she shouted.

Arrows were now flying through the air, digging into the wet ground as they narrowly missed.

'GO!!!' she roared again, Nahmar couldn't tell if it was rain or tears that ran down her face.

'I'm so sorry,' Nahmar mumbled, feeling

bewildered, terrified and exhausted as he whirled round to run for his life one final time that night.

Arrows and deadly sharp spears whistled through the air, landing all around him as he ran. He clutched the amulet from Thaesilia tightly in his wet hand. He just had time enough to hear her scream out in anger one final time before she went eerily silent. A scream that would haunt his dreams for millennia to come.

CHAPTER TWENTY

~Now~

Zooming across the cool light speckled river, Heather flew inches from the surface of the water. The Thames reflected New London's dazzling assortment of multicoloured lights back at her, making her armour glow with a mix of greens, blues and pinks. The river was gentle and flowed like an old garden hose pipe with no pressure.

Christmas lights were up, and their vibrancy leaked into the river too. Bright white stars the size of car wheels were draped across the sides of bridges like checkpoints in a video game.

'Have you got any plans for Christmas, Zack?' Heather asked, as she silently flashed past an ancient looking, but well-loved sailboat.

'Hmm, I'm not sure. Don't really see my parents much these days, I might go and see my brother in Glasgow though,' said Zack, on the other end of the comms channel.

'How come you don't see your folks much?' asked

Heather, soaring underneath another light littered bridge.

'Ah they went travelling a few years back, but after Buckingham decided not to come back, "England's time is over," they said. So sometimes we vid-chat, but to be honest, we were never that close,' said Zack.

'And your brother?' asked Heather curiously. She was now meters away from her target.

Heather and Zack had finally managed to track down Neuro Calvins and the Duke Brothers. On that night there was going to be an auction and rumour was that Neuro had something remarkable to sell. However, unlike an ordinary auction, this one was to bid for girls; young ones. And since the government was more actively monitoring human trafficking sites on the web, selling these girls in person seemed to be the safest way for them to operate. Or so they thought.

Deploying two of the drones she wasn't using for flight, Heather hovered like a dragonfly above the water next to the lavish multi-million-pound yacht. It was docked in a particularly affluent area of New London. The pair of drones hustled above the ship, scanning crew members and guests to relay the data back to Heather and Zack.

'Well my brother and I have a pretty good relationship, I even told him about me doing this stuff. But then he had to go and tell his wife and well … I'm sure you can imagine how that went.'

'I'm betting not well?' Heather surmised, thinking as she had so many times before, what would happen if Kirsty ever found out about her being Harrow. A thought that had plagued her mind for years.

'No, not well at all. She won't let me see my niece or nephews at all and I barely get to see Joshua. But a couple of times a year the two of us meet up for a bit.

Maybe we'll go for a drink together around Christmas or New Year but that's it,' said Zack glumly.

The two drones returned, attaching themselves back to the rear plates on Heather's armour. Two narrow numbers flicked up on Heather's head-up display on the inside of her helmet, twenty-eight and thirty-four; the numbers of hostiles and unarmed guests on this yacht. Switching the display to her hyperspectral imaging she floated up from the surface to land lightly on the deck.

There were half a dozen armed guards wearing pristine black suits on the deck of the ship and many more spread throughout. Heather quietly sprinted along the edge of the ship on the riverside, two men were guarding a door that would take her down into the bowels of the ship.

'Zack, that's terrible,' whispered Heather, as she ran towards to two men with her long black bladed sword drawn. 'What's he like? Joshua.'

Pouncing towards the guards she slashed her sword sharply through the air, it cut through the first guard's jugular before they'd even realised she was there. Her suit blended into the shadows and against the black of the river, making it difficult to see. Smoothly twirling the sword around for a second attack, she killed the next man before his hand could reach for his gun. Driving the blade through his torso and holding her icy cold hand over his terrified mouth.

'Oh, I guess how you imagine every older brother would be. Patronising, big-headed, self-absorbed but he'd do anything for you if you were in trouble. Joshua is an amazing brother and I honestly don't know if I would have made it this far without him.'

'What do you mean?' asked Heather, as she discreetly lowered the two bodies into the water to hide the obvious trace of her being here.

'Well, Mum and Dad weren't around much growing up. They both had full-time jobs and had pretty elaborate social lives. They wanted kids, but I think out of not wanting their money to go to waste, rather than actually wanting to be a family. I acted out a lot during school, hacking into teacher's computers, changing all the kid's grades from passes to fails and fails to passes. Mum and Dad were mad but not willing to actually spend any time with me or be involved. I was an absolute brat, but I was also just lonely and wanted some recognition.'

Zack confessed all of this as Heather sleuthed her way through the quietest parts of the ship to get to the onboard master bedroom. It felt odd to be talking about personal things during a mission but it made a nice change from the silence Heather had become accustomed to since becoming Harrow ten years ago. And besides, she loved the sound of Zack's voice, so she had no desire at all to ask him to stop talking.

'Anyway, my brother had noticed I was acting out on purpose, trying to get someone's attention no matter what. He started spending more time with me, taking me to the cinema or to museums we liked the sound of, he even took me to Comic-Con every year which I knew he hated doing. I think the reason it meant even more, was because of his age, there's a six-year gap between us. So, when he was getting offers to go to elaborate parties in Oxford or go on dates with beautiful young women, he always made sure I was okay first. Which often meant missing out on the party or several dates with a hot girl. Yeah, he's a pretty good brother.'

He had said this just as Heather jabbed her fist into another suited guard's throat, sending him into a flailing stupor, grasping at his neck trying to find a breath. A second fist followed, thudding into his temple which knocked him out cold. She dragged his dead weight body down a narrow hallway and into a generously sized bathroom. Dumping him next to the toilet she left quickly and locked the door from the outside. 'He sounds like an amazing brother,' she said, listening to Zack wholeheartedly.

'Harrow, I've been meaning to ask you something,' Zack said slowly.

'Shoot,' she said, as she snuck behind another man and snapped his neck.

'Do you like Greek food?'

Heather stopped. 'You've been meaning to ask me if I like Greek food?' she laughed quietly. 'Do tell me, Zack, how long has this been a desire of yours to discover?'

'Well?' said Zack. She could tell in the way he said it, he was smiling.

'Yes, I do have the appetite for it.'

Heather had now reached the master bedroom. Stealthily darting in and closing the door, she began planting a series of tiny explosives in a circle on the delicately varnished mahogany floor. Heather knew from the designs of this ship, that Zack had managed to steal from somewhere, that the master bedroom sat directly above the main lounge. Which was where all of tonight's auctions were taking place.

She Looked through the floor with her hyper-spectral imaging, and though she couldn't identify faces with the tech, she could see the few dozen guests all adorned in expensive gowns and tailored suits. From the information Zack had gathered before tonight's mission Heather learnt the people here tonight included some of the world's most rich and powerful. Actors, celebrity chefs and athletes were among some of the buyers. And if their intel was correct, Neuro Calvins, Warren and Neil Duke were here too.

'Why do want to know if I like Greek food, Zack?' she asked with a grin, already knowing the answer as she usually did.

'I … well, I was hoping that you would …' he flustered. Heather decided to let him bumble his own way through this, broadly grinning under her helmet but keeping quiet.

Meanwhile a floor below, the auctions were well underway and nearly at a close. The room was mostly shrouded in darkness except for thin blue light strips that lined the rim of the walls and the spotlights that pointed down to a raised platform. On the platform stood a large bellied middle-aged man with expensive hair implants and pearl-like white teeth. By his side stood a young girl wearing a long black see-through dress and nothing underneath. She wore an inordinate amount of makeup, but even that struggled to hide the fact that this girl had not slept properly in weeks. The chunky auctioneer waved a flabby hand towards the crowd, several gold rings squeezed onto his sausage fingers.

'Sold! To the gentleman at the back with the mustard yellow tie!' the auctioneer shouted across the room. Heather, of course, listening to all of this with her in-built parabolic microphone.

'Perhaps we could …' Zack continued. Desperately trying to ask without sounding like a fool.

'Perhaps we could what, Zack?' teased Heather.

'Maybe after you finish up there ... tonight ... you'd like to have dinner with me? Greek?' he concluded, sounding exasperated but pleased he'd managed to finally have the balls to ask.

The auctioneer had sent off the young girl in the

black silk and two new girls took her place. They were a couple of years older but still only teenagers. Each girl had bouncy curly brown hair that must have taken hours to style, and wore elegant floral-patterned material, like a prom dress; one bronze, one silver.

Before Heather responded, the auctioneer began his introduction to the sale.

'Now, I know these are the items many of you have been waiting so patiently for.' His wide smile was clumpy and unpleasant to look at, even with perfect white teeth.

'These two sisters not only offer a beautiful and unspoilt opportunity …' he said in a loud and slimy voice. '… but they also come with one other gift. Extraordinary metahuman abilities!'

The crowd hushed, and subconsciously edged closer to the platform that the girls and the obese man stood on, he continued.

'Our first exquisite young lady has the power to inspire the growth of living organisms! Please allow me to demonstrate.'

An assistant wearing a knee length, backless, cherry red dress, appeared holding a small silver plant pot. Innocently sprouting from the soil within, was a tiny green shoot, barely visible from the back of the lounge. She stood at the foot of the platform, next to the two girls and placed it on a tall table that had been set up for it. The auctioneer gave the girl in the bronze dress an intimidating stare.

Reaching out a single tender finger the young girl tapped the tip of the plant. In an instant, it grew to the size of a pencil and then a moment later, the size of a large spatula. Bold white flowers rapidly bloomed from the plant. The audience let out a unified gasp of amazement. The girl that had touched the plant seemed like she'd just run up and down a large set of stairs, a warm bead of sweat dripped down her brow.

'And our second young lady has the power of decay! Watch and witness how deadly a woman's touch can be.' He winked at the crowd and a ripple of cordial laughter waved across the room.

The second sister scowled defiantly at her captor, but he glared back, fondling something in his pocket and gesturing towards it. A wince of pain flickered across her face and she obediently stretched out a gloved hand. Removing it with the other she stroked a finger across the blossomed white petals of the flower. As quickly as it had grown to its grand size, the flower began to wilt and die. The bright green and white now a dusty grey, a moment later it was nothing but ash. Seeing this the crowd took a very conscious step backwards.

'Let's start the bidding for both at ten million!' his voice boomed across the room and a sea of raised paddles followed it.

Heather, having seen most of this through the distorted view of her scanners, could see a figure matching Neuro's height and weight move closer to the platform, facing out towards the crowd rather than the girls.

'Greek. Tonight. Your place?' Heather said, standing on the bed and holding her finger over the detonate button on her wrist, her pistol in the other hand.

'Well, if you want to? I just figured we could celebrate after you bring down Neuro and the Dukes,' said Zack.

'You mean after we bring down Neuro and the Dukes,' said Heather, pressing the button.

Several controlled blasts went off across the floor and Heather leapt off the bed and into the centre of it. The floor crashed down beneath her, and she fell to the crowded lounge below. Slamming into the floor her cape swished behind her as she landed, all six drones burst from her suit and raced through the air to block the exits. The guests let out screams of terror and scattered away from her instantly. The first girl in the bronze dress screamed too but her sister grabbed her, now wearing both gloves again, they ran off the platform.

'But, Zack, what will I wear?'

Most of the guests were wearing masks to hide their faces from each other but Heather had planned for this. Her pistol was loaded with the tranquiliser darts she'd used on the supervillains earlier in the year, and she had brought enough for everyone. It was extremely likely that the men and woman in this room had their own child prisoners hidden away at their homes. Heather could stop Neuro and the Dukes but if she kept the rest of the guests alive, she could find a lot of missing kids tonight. As much as she wanted to kill these people, there was far more at stake.

Diving through the air she shot at the guests and the guards, each dart deeply embedding itself into their skin to release the chemicals within. She foresaw the auctioneer draw his own gun but flippantly shot him before his hand even reached his jacket pocket. Many had bolted for the exits on seeing her but were met with the drones. Loaded with the same poisonous coma-inducing darts.

'Well, I was hoping to get you out of that suit,' said Zack, before realising how that might sound.

'Oh, were you now?' said Heather slyly.

'Wait! I just meant … It would be nice to have dinner with you, not … Harrow you.'

Heather laughed at this as she skidded across the now empty platform towards Neuro.

'Is that really what you meant?' she said, in a slightly huskier voice. 'I was thinking the same thing. It would be nice to spend time with you, armour free.'

She had switched off her suits voice projection, so only Zack could hear her speaking above the sounds of screaming millionaires.

Bullets pinged off her armour as she approached Neuro, who was wilding firing at her. Slamming her forearm into his collar she backhanded the gun from his hand and tore off his mask, it was him. Pulling back slightly beforehand, she hammered into his chin with a headbutt, feeling his jaw snap from the impact.

'Do you want me to bring anything with me?' she asked as Neuro's towering figure collapsed on the ground, writhing on the floor in unparalleled agony.

'Just some wine maybe? Wait, you're okay with not wearing your disguise in front of me?' said Zack, anticipation in his voice.

Heather had spun round to face several more attackers, battering each one with a flurry of fists and well-aimed shots from her gun.

'Hmm yes, maybe I could use a drink.' Heather decided, thinking that perhaps a night without constantly peering into the possible was exactly what she needed.

'And there's a lot of fancy masks here,' she said, shattering one on a man's face with her fist. 'Perhaps I'll bring one with me.'

'Sure, whatever you want. So, see you soon?' said Zack.

'Very soon,' said Heather, now looking around the body filled room.

'Zack, send a Network clean-up crew. We'll also need interrogation when this lot wakes up. There's a lot a missing person cases that I think can get solved tonight. Call the police if we need, I don't care if this other scum gets processed through the normal system but I want

Neuro, Warren and Neil locked up in Terminus. I don't ever want to see their faces in my city again,' said Heather, retracting the drones back to her suit and nodding at the two girls cowering in the corner.

'And Zack, make sure these girls get home safe.'

'You got it, partner,' said Zack.

CHAPTER TWENTY-ONE

Arriving at Zack's deserted underground lair thirty minutes later, Heather waited for Zack to let her in. She was holding a masquerade eye mask she'd picked up at the auction and a large bottle of wine she had also pinched.

A small electronic beep sounded at the entrance and the secret door swung open. Instantly Heather could hear music; melodic gentle violins echoed through the tunnels and across the station platform. The lights were dimmed, and Heather could smell spiced cinnamon, it smelt like Christmas.

Approaching the platform that Zack's tube carriage was permanently parked at, she saw a large area of the platform was covered in dozens of thick woolly blankets and plump round pillows and pouffes. In the centre lay a sizable picnic basket; two large wine glasses, the spiced cinnamon candles, a delicious selection of Greek dishes and of course, Zack. He sat on one of the pouffes and instead of his usual casual attire, (a fleecy jumper and cheap grey jeans), he wore striking navy-blue suit trousers and a crisp white shirt with the top few buttons undone. His hair was smoothly brushed back as it usually was but somewhat neater.

'You brought the wine,' he smiled, holding up the two glasses.

'I did. You could have told me about the dress code! You look ...' she paused, as she approached the nest of pillows and blankets. '... You look amazing,' she beamed.

He smiled bashfully and nodded to the carriage.

'I got you something. You don't have to if you don't want to, but I just thought it might be nice to let your hair down. I mean it can't be too comfortable wrapped up in that helmet,' he joked, gesturing again to the tube carriage.

Heather walked through the doors and looked around for Zack's gift. Neatly folded on one of the counters Zack had installed, was a simply charming royal-blue dress.

'I hope you like the colour,' came Zack's honey-like voice from the platform.

Heather stared at it, for what felt like an age. Picking it up gently and running her gloves across the material. Her mind was conflicted with two very distinct choices. Take off her armour, slide into this dress and enjoy a delicious, much-needed dinner with Zack. Something she so desperately wanted to do. Or put down the gift, walk out of there and go home. But thinking of home she thought about the months of fighting with Kirsty, the constant interrogation and the countless nights where Heather felt worthless and unwanted. She put down the dress and started unfastening her suit.

Minutes later Heather appeared at the exit to the carriage, her hair hung lightly over her shoulder and across the edge of the masquerade mask, which she had decided to put on too. The dress flowed weightlessly to the tops of her knees and fluttered as she walked towards Zack, her bare feet pattered against the concrete. She expected it to be cold, but her exposed shoulders and legs were warmed by the inviting heaters Zack had placed around the platform. He looked up from the floor to watch her walk towards him, unable to take his eyes off her.

'So, do you like it?' he asked apprehensively.

Heather knelt down next to him on the soft warm blankets, her knee brushed against his. Leaning in close, she kissed him on the cheek. 'I do, thank you.'

'Well, I hope you're hungry. I didn't know what kind of Greek food you liked, so I got us a selection,' he said, as he extracted two plates from the picnic basket and handed one to her.

'What do you want to try first?'

The pair of them ate, drank and laughed with each other for hours, quickly losing track of time. They shared stories from growing up, what it was like starting out as a crime fighter and what they wanted to do when they were older. Zack told her more about his Mum and Dad and what it was like to work for Captain Mega-stone. Heather told him about her troubles with Paladin and how she longed to put him in his place.

'He's a smug self-righteous bastard and he needs to wake up. Every single thing he does is an order from the government and it's only a matter of time before they send him on a dedicated manhunt for me,' Heather complained, starting to get a bit tipsy from the overpriced wine.

'You think they'll send him after you?' Zack asked.

'Well yeah, after Cambridge I expect they're already doubling their efforts to bring me in. And they'll send their favourite dog Paladin of course,' Heather scoffed.

'Are you not tempted to just finish him off?' said Zack, taking another large helping of tomato fritters.

'I have been in the past, but if I killed Paladin they'd send the whole United Nations army after me. I'll tell you what though. It wouldn't be hard,' she hinted.

'He's incredibly susceptible to concentrated electric current, that's one of the reasons I made my sword the way it is. Pump enough volts through him and his regenerative abilities slow down, after that it would be easy.'

He looked both worried and impressed at the same time. 'Rather you than me!'

Later, Zack poured them both a third helping of wine and dripped the bottle dry. He hurried over to the carriage to get more and Heather quickly snuck the last almond cookie while his back was turned.

When he returned, they both filled their glasses back to the top and drank deeply. Drinking alcohol was one of the few ways that Heather could subdue her abilities. Not something she did often when out of her home and Zack picked up on her eagerness to drink.

'I'm not that boring to be around, am I?' he joked, nodding to the glass as she drank.

'Oh no,' she spluttered. 'It's just … this is the only way I can stop my powers.'

'Why would you want to do that?' Zack asked. 'If I had superpowers I wouldn't want to switch them off.'

'Well, it can get pretty tiring always seeing what's about to happen, constantly being five seconds ahead of everyone else … It's just nice to turn off the preview function every now and then,' Heather laughed.

'I knew it had to be something like that! You always seem to know what's about to happen. And …' he rounded on her with excitement, '... you are always guessing what I'm going to say before I say it!'

'Maybe that's just because you're so damn predictable,' she winked, absent-mindedly biting her lip.

'Is that so?' Zack chuckled. 'Then did you know I was going to do this?' He smoothly pressed his body closer to hers and planted a slow kiss on her supple lips.

After a brief moment, Heather could feel Zack start to pull away but she grabbed the back of his neck and held him firmly, passionately kissing him back. With one hand on Heather's arm and the other placed softly on the side of her face, Zack pressed himself against her body. Heather's hair dangled over her shoulder and across the sleeve of Zack's shirt. Urgently she pulled her fingers from out of his soft golden hair and reached down to his shirt to unbutton it, while Zack caressed the bottom of her jaw with his hand. She was still wearing the masquerade mask she had stolen from the auction. But as they kissed it was starting to get in the way.

'Zack, can we turn the lights down? I want to take this off,' she lightly stroked a finger across the cheek of her mask but carried on stroking down, past her chin and neck to her dress.

He looked at her with hunger and desire in his eyes. 'Lights, dim to five percent,' he said and then dived back to kiss her, reaching his hand round to her lower back and unzipping her dress slightly. All at once the platform lights dimmed and plunged them into near darkness, leaving a gentle amber glow so they could still see each other's outlines. Heather pulled off the mask and dropped it near the discarded wine glasses

Slipping her tongue out of his mouth she started nibbling his neck, pulling apart his shirt as she sucked. Zack fumbled with the last buttons of his shirt as they knelt on the thick fluffy blankets. Heather's hands raced down his bare chest and stomach, thinking to herself for someone that spent much of the day sitting in front of computer screens, he was quite well toned. She pushed him onto his back, cushions and pouffes softening his fall and swung a leg over his to straddle him. Her heart was racing with excitement and longing, she had wanted to take him for so long. Pushing her hips down on him she could feel him hardening already. Reaching a hand back behind her she began rubbing him profusely.

His grip of her hips tightened as she did this, squirming beneath her with pleasure. When his anticipation had built too much, he shot a hand out, grabbed her wrist and in one fluid movement, rolled the pair of them over so she was on her back. The warm sea of pillows again cushioning everything.

Sliding down her body he removed his shirt and lifted up the bottom of Heather's dress. She carried on pulling it up and somewhat cumbersomely dragged it over her head. Now wearing nothing but thin black underwear, she squeezed her breasts firmly as Zack sunk his head down between her legs, parting the lace with a couple of fingers. Heather moaned loudly with bliss as his tongue danced on her, one of his hands tightly squeezed her buttocks. Heather's deep cries of pleasure filled the platform and echoed down the tunnels.

After a little while, Zack unbuttoned his trousers and ripped off Heather's underwear. Completely enticed in that moment with Zack, Heather's anticipation had built to unequalled heights. Without warning, Zack took her, making Heather gasp with shock and delight. The two of them pounded against one another forcefully, the echoed noise of their skin slapping against each other was like an acoustic drug.

Though she couldn't see his face or expression in the darkness, Heather could hear and feel how much he was enjoying himself. He throbbed with every thrust, so Heather stopped before both of them were forced unintentionally into an early conclusion; she was enjoying herself far too much to finish now. Rolling Heather onto her front, Zack pressed himself against her and kicked off the trousers that still hung around his ankles.

Stroking his smooth hands across her, Zack revelled in her pleasure. He lent forward to breath in the honey-like smell of Heather's hair. She writhed her hips rhythmically in time with the quiet background music, her body bouncing lightly as she moved. Zack's smooth hands reached underneath to cup her breasts while he pushed against her body, his thumb and finger plucking at her rosy nipples.

'I've wanted you for so long,' Zack breathed to her, barely audible over the heavy sound of the skin-pounding against skin.

'And now you have me, so tell me …' she stopped, lifting her hips up to just tease him. 'What are you going to do now you have?'

Her whispered bait was irresistible to him and she got just the reaction she wanted. Grabbing her waist firmly he lifted her off the floor and the two of them got to their feet, her muscular thighs glistened against the dim orange light. Taking her hand, he led her to the train, then pressed her back against the side of it so she was facing him. The train's surface felt cool against the warmth of Heather's skin but it quickly warmed up. Lifting her up against the glass and pressing his body to hers, Zack continued to thrust deeply. Heather wrapped her arms tightly around his neck and leant her head back, her smooth legs wrapped around his hips. Her cries of pleasure and his groans of bliss continued to fill the expanse of the platform and echo down the lightless tunnels. They carried on like this until it became nearly unbearable, each thrust brought Heather so much closer to her climax. Zack must have been fighting his own back for a while, sweat dripped down his chest and neck.

She could feel her body tensing up, her heart booming in her chest, the tips of her fingers and toes felt electric and the tingling surge was rocketing towards her core. All she could think about was his body, his hands holding her legs up and the impending explosion of euphoria. The mind-numbing sensation built and built, pleasure flowed from the back of her head all the way down to the tip of her spine and then ... the release. Zack was pulsating and throbbing within, she could feel his body tighten and his grip stiffen, then he too gave in. The two of them moaned deeply as they rode the waves together, slowing down their pace and pressing closer to kiss each other. Her lips were wet, and she brushed them tenderly against his while running her hands through his Midas-touched hair.

As the tide of pleasure began to slowly sweep away, the clouds of guilt appeared. She felt twisted and warped inside like something had gnawed through her belly and was burning her heart from the inside. But even with that feeling, Heather couldn't help but want to do it all over again.

CHAPTER TWENTY-TWO

The smell of frying bacon and pancakes woke Heather up, but it took her a moment to realise where she was. She couldn't quite understand why there were yellow handrails running across the ceiling, then she remembered last night.

Heather still ached from last night's activities, but the good kind of ache. On the other side of the carriage, Zack stood at the oven he'd installed, wearing green checked pyjama bottoms and an un-fastened fleecy grey dressing gown.

'Good morning,' he smiled, noticing her stir.

'Good morning,' she replied sleepily, but then her hand shot up to her face.

'You put that back on when we got into bed last night,' Zack chuckled, referring to the eye mask on Heather's face. 'Don't worry, your secret identity is still secret from me.'

'Sorry, Zack, old habits and all that,' she shrugged awkwardly, sitting up in bed to watch him.

'It's okay, I get it. You've got a family you've got

to keep safe, I understand,' he said, flipping a pancake over as though he'd been rehearsing.

Then the feeling of guilt flooded back to her. What time was it? She needed to get back before Kirsty started to get suspicious.

'Zack, I'm sorry I have to go.' Heather climbed out of bed and began scouring around for her abandoned underwear. Feeling unfairly exposed as Zack stood in bottoms and his dressing gown.

'If you hang on for a little while, Nahmar just sent us a message saying he wants to talk. He's got your final target and wants to brief you. So, you may as well have some breakfast while we wait for his call.' Zack placed three hearty sized pancakes and several strips of dripping bacon next to them on a plate and handed it to Heather.

'I ... thank you,' she said gratefully, as she took the plate.

Zack had dragged most of the pouffes and blankets inside, after pulling on the underlayer of her armour she sat down and tucked in to breakfast. Sitting on a pouffe opposite her, Zack told Heather about this amazing all you can eat dessert place he went to a few years back and their extraordinary pancakes. He loved the taste so much he hacked into their database and stole the recipe. This made Heather laugh so hard, orange juice squirted out of her nose.

'Oh my god it stings so much!' Heather cried. Zack was in pieces, laughing with a mouthful of the stolen pancakes.

'You can literally steal any file you want, in the world almost ... and you steal a pancake recipe?' she yelled in hysterics.

'Well they're good, aren't they?' Zack chuckled. Heather did have to admit, they were excellent.

The conversation turned to the task at hand, defeating and capturing the final Pandarian. They had come so far together and now just one remained before this hugely demanding quest would be over. Heather quietly wondered to herself whether the two of them would continue working together after this was done. She had begun to hope so.

In the middle of eating her fourth pancake, one of the monitors of Zack's computers lit up and an old-fashioned telephone ringing sounded through the carriage. Heather stood up and picked up her helmet from a side counter. Zack rushed over to the computer and with his back turned to Heather she swapped the mask for her helmet.

The screen flickered, and they could see one of the many Nahmar's, one Heather had not seen before, appear on the screen. Dangling from his neck was the familiar amulet he always wore. The video feed was one way, but Heather wanted to wear her helmet nonetheless.

'Harrow,' he said in his usual calm slow monotone.

'I'm here, Nahmar, and I've got Zack with me too.'

'Ah yes, I'm very glad to see your partnership is working out. I heard about what you did last night, congratulations.' Heather's heart shot right up into her throat, for some reason thinking he was referring to the sex. 'I know you've been trying to bring down Neuro and the Duke brothers for some time.' Her heart settled back down.

'Congratulations to you as well, Zack. It can't have been easy to gather the amount of intel required for a mission like that,' said Nahmar.

'Really sir, Harrow did all the heavy lifting. I just enjoyed the show,' he smiled coyly at her.

'Very good. Now to business. I have considered

this for a great deal of time and have found your final target, Harrow.' The three of them paused with baited breath, Nahmar didn't seem to want to say who it was.

'I'm sorry, Harrow, both of you. Your final target is the President of The Republic of China,' he said solemnly.

Easily one of the three most powerful people on the planet. Tão Jũn ruled over all of China and his grasp expanded over much of Asia.

'My informants throughout the Network tell me that President Jũn will be attending his son's orchestral recital thirty-six hours from now, this will be the opportune moment to strike. He will be more exposed here than anywhere else you could possibly reach him.'

'I will send you all the relevant details the Network has gathered, Zack. Harrow ...' he paused thoughtfully, 'you have done so much for me, and I will not forget it. Soon I will give you what you have desired for so long. But know that should you fail this mission or be seen assassinating Tão Jũn, it won't just be The Republic of China coming after you, the entire world will want to see you dead and will not rest until you are.'

'I must go, we are so close now, Harrow. You have no idea how long I have waited for the day when that scourge is wiped from the face of this planet.' Then the screen went black.

Heather and Zack stood quietly for a moment staring at the blank screen, then Heather broke away and quickly gathered up the rest of her armour.

'I've got to go home, Zack, collect some things and then I'll get on the first flight to China you can get me. I'll just tell my wife I've got to go on another training course or something,' she said while pressing the breastplate of her armour into place, the locks engaged and she felt power and unearthly confidence surging through her again.

'Sure thing, partner, I'll get something arranged now. What did he mean "I'll give you what you have desired for so long"?' Zack asked, unable to hide his curiosity.

Clipping the final shoulder plate of her armour into place she turned back to Zack.

'He's going to tell me who he is,' she grinned.

Bursting through the front door of her apartment as quickly as subtly possible, Heather raced into her bedroom to grab a few of her things. It was a Saturday morning and she could hear Henry watching cartoons in the living room while eating his cereal. Having briefly visited a safe house to get changed, she pulled off her long chocolate coloured coat and hung it up by the front door.

Kirsty wasn't in the bedroom, she must be busy in the kitchen or something but no sooner than Heather wrenched a travel bag out from the top shelf of her wardrobe, Kirsty's voice called out to her.

'Good morning, Heather, how was work?' said Kirsty, her voice trailing from the hallway sounding delightfully upbeat.

'Yeah, you know, same old stuff. We met our target for November though and probably the year,' Heather lied. 'I think they're going to give us Christmas bonuses.'

'Oh really? That's great news,' said Kirsty, trying to sound more interested but she was busy rooting through the pockets of Heather's coat. She was trying to be as quiet as possible, so she didn't disturb the keys or give any kind of clue as to what she was doing. Meanwhile, Heather was throwing a couple of changes of clothes into her bag and grabbing a towel and toiletries from the en-suite.

'Are you going somewhere?' Kirsty called out, hearing the rapid packing.

Heather responded with some previously expended excuse about going on another training course, something that Kirsty didn't believe a word of. Reaching the final inside pocket, Kirsty felt a small packet of tablets and pulled them out to see.

Thirteen small circular red pills still lay tucked into their plastic beds, but one was missing. Turning the packet over hesitantly, Kirsty read the clear clinical label and confirmed her own fears. Commonly referred to ask Negate, the latest in post-intercourse contraception pills. Kirsty's hands began to shake with rage and betrayal, her body felt like it was glued in place.

'... do you want me to pick you anything up?' asked Heather from the other room.

Kirsty stood there, frozen, unable to speak, just staring at the packet of cherry red pills.

'Kirsty?' Heather called, grabbing her bag and making her way quickly back to the front door. 'I'm going to the airport, do you want anything from the duty-free?' she asked again, now back in the hallway looking at her stiff wife.

Kirsty had put the pills back in the inside pocket moments ago, but her legs still felt like they were encased in concrete.

'No, nothing for me.' Kirsty stared into her wife's face, Heather looked cool and relaxed. No different than she usually did, Kirsty thought to herself. If she was lying about this and clearly, she had just cheated on her, what else could she be lying about?

'Okay then.' Heather reached forward and grabbed her coat from the peg where she left it. 'I've got to go now

I'm afraid, they want us out on the first flight possible. Hey, are you okay?'

Kirsty flicked her hair and smiled. 'Of course. Now quick, you don't want to miss your flight.'

'Oh, I was just going to say goodbye to Henry before I go.' Heather made a nod towards the living room.

'Maybe it's best if you don't, he doesn't cope well when you have to leave at the last moment. I'll tell him later,' said Kirsty, stretching her face into the most forced smile she had ever constructed.

Heather considered if for a moment and then agreed. 'Are you sure you're okay?'

In agony, Kirsty forced herself to meet Heather's gaze, then replied as gently as she could muster. 'Yeah, I'm fine, hun, just a bit tired that's all,' Kirsty said, faking a yawn.

Not entirely convinced but very aware she was running out of time, Heather gave her a quick guilt-ridden kiss on the cheek and left. Telling her to call if she changed her mind about the duty-free.

Heather closed the front door behind herself, leaving Kirsty awkwardly posed in the hallway. Then not entirely realising how she got there, Kirsty quietly closed the door to her bedroom, clambered into the middle of the bed, brought a pillow to her face and screamed. She howled so loud and so ferociously, the back of her throat felt as though it was being rubbed with a cheese grater. For minutes she lay there, screaming horribly into the pillow. Her body felt like it was in a cold sweat and her hands and feet trembled as she howled into the gentle white polyester.

CHAPTER TWENTY-THREE

Frigid snowy wind bombarded the tall walls of Beijing's grand theatre. The roof was covered in a thinning blanket of snow, which with every hour, melted away slightly due to the heat inside. The bitter air outside was filled with the shouts and car horns of frustration as drivers tried to get to their destinations through the chaotic white sludge. All of this noise however, could not be heard at all from inside the theatre, where President Jũn's eleven-year-old son and the rest of the orchestra were performing their second symphony of the night.

Inside the multi-tiered auditorium itself, over a thousand classical music enthusiasts sat transfixed, gazing at the musicians on the stage. Li Jũn, the President's son, performed cello amongst a patch of other musicians his age, however many of the musicians were much older. His father often told others with great enthusiasm that this was a testament to Li Jũn's clear talent. The President himself was sat among his security detail on one of the highest platforms in the hall. He was completely focused on his son and the harmony of the orchestra, whilst his security constantly scoured the hall for signs of danger.

Several platforms away, keeping pressed to the shadows behind an oblivious dignitary and his wife, stood Heather. She wore her glistening midnight blue armour, but her cape was draped over the majority of her body, to avoid any possible reflections from the lights in its shiny surface. The last thing she needed was for some eagle-eyed security guard or the wandering eyes of an audience member to spot her. Using her powers and a great deal of luck, she had managed to get to this point without needing to attack or neutralise a single member of the security detail. Zack's help had, as usual, been invaluable. Collecting exact details of the building that Heather could use to her advantage and exploitable facts about the President's security.

The music from the orchestra was powerful and booming. Their awe-inspiring harmony penetrated every inch of the room and it may have been that or her un-paralleled nerves, that were making the hairs on the back of Heather's neck stand on end. After all, this was easily the most insane thing Heather had ever attempted to do. She was about to kill the President of the Republic of China. She would have to get close, a ranged attack might give the Pandarian the chance to escape and invade a new host and if Heather wasn't right next to the President with the silver cube from Nahmar, this would be a certainty. As with the six Pandarians before, she would need to be practically on top of him.

Drawing a large smoke grenade from her utility belt, Heather took a long quiet breath before stepping alongside the seated dignitary and hurling the canister through the air onto the President's platform. She heard a single shout of warning in Chinese before the canister exploded and thick black smoke plumed out. The orchestra was so loud most of the audience remained blissfully ignorant. That was until a flautist towards the front of the stage, that was waiting for her cue, spotted the smoke and the phantom-like figure gliding across the ceiling towards it. She stood up and waved in panic at the audience.

Trying not to be distracted by this wild outburst, the conductor glared at the flautist menacingly but when he saw the genuine fear in her eyes, he also turned around to see the large black cloud spreading across the ceiling. Just then, the smoke alarms went off, sending the whole room into a tumultuous panic.

Heather was hovering above the cloud, propelled by the drones latched to her suit. Using her scanners, she located the President and drew her blade, holding the box in her other hand. This was it, the final Pandarian, she thought to herself. But then something happened that she had never considered a possibility.

Envisioning herself plummeting to the surface of the platform and striking her sword through the President, she held out the tiny silver prison, but nothing happened. She did not foresee the familiar wisps of energy pulsing around the President's lifeless body. No tornado-like effect as the coloured smoke was dragged into the box. She just saw herself ... standing over Tão Jũn's lifeless body. Nahmar was wrong, the President was not the final Pandarian, but then who was?

Dragging her mind back to the present, Heather backed away in shock. Her eyes darted around the grand theatre, brushing across the hundreds of people fleeing in panic. Stewards lit the way to fire exits and the orchestra had all abandoned their instruments, everyone looked frightened or confused. All except one face.

On the other side of the room from Heather,

standing next to an overturned cello and staring right back at her was Li Jūn, the President's son. His expression was not one of fear or bewilderment but of anger and hatred. For a moment the two of them stared at each other, Heather was floating just outside the black ball of smoke but it lapped at her feet as she hovered. The boy, barely older than Henry, looked at her venomously and then turned his back and ran into the wings of the stage. Heather didn't understand how but she was almost certain that the final Pandarian was inside this boy and that, in fact, this had all been a trap.

Heather rolled forward and hurtled across the auditorium, cape billowing behind her. A hailstorm of gunfire rained onto Heather from several directions, the security detail now recognising her as the President's attacker. Her suit was peppered with bullets as she zoomed towards the stage, a couple managing to find a slither of her body that wasn't protected fully, but she couldn't afford to waste time dodging and risk losing the boy. If the Pandarian had somehow managed to switch hosts without Nahmar knowing, it could probably do it again and they may lose the trail.

The fire alarm was screeching and gnawing at Heather, amplified by the acoustics of the room to a nauseating level. A particularly well-aimed shot from one of the upper platforms pierced through her cape and into one of the drone's extraction valves, sending Heather plummeting to the ground and into a row of chairs.

Splinters of wood and plastic flew through the air as Heather landed in a crumpled heap, the box went flying out of her hand and landed further along the aisle she crashed into. Heather's lower back stung and itched with pain where the drone had exploded, and she could feel a heavy ache just above her hips where a bullet had hit. Tiny shards of her armour felt like they were nipping at her skin. Pulling herself up quickly and looking back to the stage, she just caught sight of the foot of the boy as he rushed off stage behind the curtains.

A short-bearded man in the President's security detail was charging towards her from above, he positioned himself at the edge of the aisle and began shooting at her. Expensive armour piercing bullets thudded into her mask, deeply scratching the glass on impact.

Heather withdrew her grapnel gun and fired it at the box, mere feet away from the agent shooting. The magnetic headed cable whizzed across the aisle and gripped onto the tiny box. Rapidly retracting it and plucking the box from the gun's grip, Heather vaulted the chairs in front and used her drones to leap onto the stage at least thirty feet away. The jets of the remaining drones rumbled fiercely as she flew towards the stage, bright blue and red sparks spat from the damaged drone thruster.

Heavily she slammed into the wooden floor of the stage, crushing the planks beneath her feet. Then she bolted across the stage in the direction the boy had run off. Another agent appeared in the wings of the stage, unloading an entire magazine into Heather before she could slam a sharp armour-plated shoulder into his chest. This sent him tumbling down the steps backwards to the lower levels.

Tearing through the backstage alleyways, Heather's mind flittered with apprehension on what she was going to do when she caught up with this kid. Skidding around a bend with a large fake cardboard blossom tree propped against the corner, Heather spotted the boy charging towards the fire exit at the end of the corridor. The path between them was clear and uninterrupted.

'STOP!!!' Heather shouted. 'Don't make me kill

this boy!'

But he did not stop, now inches away from the glowing fire exit Heather drew her pistol and aimed it at the back of his head.

Blinking painfully, Heather foresaw herself pulling the trigger and a single fatal bullet ripping into the boy's spine. He fell through the fire doors, having opened them a moment before, and tumbled down the steps below, leaving a bloody crimson trail behind him. His gentle angelic skin scraping against the harsh concrete. Just before her mind was dragged back to the present, Heather could see the orange energy swirling above his lifeless body.

Her mind flipping back to the now, she held the gun up to shoot but couldn't bring herself to do it. She didn't want to begin to contemplate the person she would have become after crossing that line. Feeling like her heart was made of dense heavy lead, she raced after the boy who had just run out into the snowy streets of Beijing. Heather zoomed after him and could hear the sounds of encroaching agents, hurling through the backstage maze. Crossing through the open door out into the street, she grabbed a grenade from her belt and hurled it back into the building to block her exit. A ground shaking explosion followed and the fire exit she had just left crumbled and collapsed, giving her the seconds she needed.

Hundreds of startled faces looked up in the direction of the explosion. Busy shoppers, eager vendors in the market and impatient taxi drivers, all froze in shock for a moment to look at the explosion; except the fleeing boy. Heather easily pinpointed him running through a winter dressed crowd, past a tall iron statue in the middle of the market.

Launching through the air using the remaining

working drones, Heather soared over the busy crowd of onlookers and landed in front of the boy, who slipped on the icy path as his pursuer hit the ground. Sat in the snow, crying out for help in Chinese, the boy tried to scoot backwards away from Heather. A large crowd started to gather around the two of them, all captivated but too terrified of the renown of Harrow to help the boy. At the top of the market, the President and his staff attempted to battle their way through the hoard of onlookers to get to Li Jūn.

'Stop! I know what you are, it's over. Just let the boy go,' Heather bellowed, towering above the child.

His feigned expression of fear and horror suddenly transformed into a twisted sinister grin. 'You know I'm not going to do that. If you want to capture me, the child will die too,' said the President's son, now speaking in English to her.

'That ridiculous box my creators built to contain me will not hold me forever, you have no idea how powerful we have become. Millennia of feeding on you weak and feeble humans has made us strong, the Pandarians will rise again,' the boy said darkly, in a tone that felt unsuitable for the soft face it belonged to.

Snowflakes dropped gently onto Heather's armour, lightly collecting across her shoulders and on the top of her helmet. The President's staff were barging their way through the dense crowd on the other side of the market, desperately trying to get to Heather and Li Jūn.

'Your control over us has finished, let the boy go and I'll at least put you somewhere with a nice view,' spat Heather.

Lying in the freezing cold snow, the Pandarian glanced across the crowd. Looking into the terrified eyes of the people surrounding him, not one of whom was running to his rescue. Then he turned back to look up at Heather.

'Control ... Control. What an interesting word,' he mused.

'For thousands of years, your type has always sought to stop me and failed. Priests, warriors, soldiers and now you ... a superhero. Since I first arrived here on this planet doomed to die, your type has always thought it was we that were controlling you. Forcing you to make bad choices and give in to your most primal and evil desires. Well, I'll tell you the same thing I told the others before I killed them.'

The President and his staff were now close enough they were yelling at people to get out of the way. Firing their guns into the air to clear a pathway through the mass of people.

'Humans are the problem, not us. All we did was feed on your sins and my my it has been a feast. But my kin and I never forced you to do anything, aside from inhabiting a few of these repugnant forms,' he hissed, slamming a hand on his chest. Heather watched his hand as he did this and her mind raced with a spark.

'It's so easy to find the worst in you all. Humans are addicted to making bad choices and wanting what is undoubtedly worst for them. And your bad choices are so delicious.' His eyes flashed and a hand slowly started reaching for his pocket.

'What was that human phrase? Oh yes – like stealing candy from a baby!'

Just then several agents that had battled their way through the crowd shouted a command to Heather, each with guns drawn and aimed at her. The Pandarian whipped out a concealed plasma pistol and blasted it straight at Heather's chest and the Chinese President cried out in horror.

Heather spun out of the way and pulling her fist back, brought it smashing down into the boy's chest; a punch that could have easily shattered brick. Li Jūn dropped the gun and his cruel eyes went lifeless.

The President's guard went to open fire on Heather, but the President shoved between the wall of bodyguards and tried to run to his fallen son, who now lay in a crumpled heap on the cold snowy cobbled street.

A moment afterwards the thick orange cloud-like energy burst from the pours of Li Jūn's body, its violent cyclonic form whirled around Heather and the surrounding crowd. The snow getting mixed in with the orange energy reflected a warm hazy glow around her. The crowd stared with pure wonder at this unearthly phenomenon. The President had managed to push his way to the front of the crowd, with a most puzzling expression on his face. His eyes bounced back and forth between the orange whirlwind, his son and Heather, who now stood in the centre of the storm holding out the Serathium. Like the others before, the energy began to gravitate towards the cube and get dragged into it. It shook powerfully as Heather held it until every last spec of the orange cloud had vanished into the cube.

The swirl of energy stopped and the snow on the ground that had been hastily blown away, slowly started to pile up again. The crowd was silent and speechless, but a few continued to hold out handheld devices, having recorded the last few minutes of action. Even the President stood motionless and quiet on the side-lines, though some could see his knees shaking and not because of the cold.

Heather secured the cube in her belt and quickly knelt down above Li Jūn's body, snow now littering his coarse black hair. She held out both hands over his chest and stared into his lifeless eyes. Thinking of Henry back home, her throat had gone as dry as a desert, but her eyes were quite the opposite. Several tears flowed down her face as she spoke.

'Suit, divert full shock power to hands,' Heather barked.

Pressing her hands onto the boy's chest she could see the President fall to his knees out of her peripheral. His own hands clasped against his mouth, tears flooding down his cold face.

'Suit, Shock!' Heather yelled.

A great surge of electricity boomed across the boy's body. It lurched upwards slightly but fell back to the floor unsuccessfully.

'SUIT, SHOCK!' Heather roared again, pressing her hands forcefully against his chest for the second powerful blast of electricity.

The boy let out a wheezy gasp and his eyes flickered several times before opening fully, snow had built up on his face and he couldn't see properly. However, he could just about make out the tall black figure leaning over him.

Heather stood up slowly and took a few steps away from the young boy, raising her hands to show she meant no harm. Without waiting for permission, President Tão Jũn launched himself towards his son, feet and hands scraping through the snow and dirt.

The crowd was completely dumbfounded, staring back and forth between Heather and the President of their country. The security detail moved in and surrounded the President and his son. Heather could see the young boy rapidly whispering to his father in Chinese in between pained breaths. A single agent had begun stalking towards Heather from behind, preparing to attempt an arrest.

Heather, foreseeing this, casually turned around to look down at him as he aimed his gun at her.

'Don't even think about it, tough guy,' she breathed, her fear-inspiring voice transcending any language barrier there may have been between them.

'My son says you saved him from the demon,' said Tão Jǔn, still crouched down next to his boy, tightly gripping his hand and stroking his hair.

'Thank you. The Republic of China will remember this day. How may we honour you?' he asked.

Heather activated the remaining drones, quickly bursting to life she hovered a few inches from the ground. Snow whirled away from beneath her and the hole-riddled cape flickered behind her in tatters.

'Just get your son into the warmth and take care of him. The pair of you have earnt a break,' Heather answered.

The President nodded thankfully as Heather rose heroically higher and higher, then once she was far enough above the crowd, she launched upwards into the clouds above the dazzled onlookers.

Snow hammered against her suit and dribbled through the shattered panel on her back as she flew. A few minutes away from the theatre she pulled up the feed from her phone to her visor display, there were twelve missed calls from Kirsty.

CHAPTER TWENTY-FOUR

'In a tragic turn of events this evening in New London, the superhero, Paladin, has been killed,' proclaimed a young and ambitiously dressed newsreader.

'It appears that the much-loved hero was engaged in a deadly conflict above the Charters arena, with the supervillain known as Jackal. Earlier in the night, we know that Jackal had attempted to unleash a deadly toxin into the stadium. One that threatened to infect everyone within the arena and potentially more. His maniacal plan was foiled by Paladin but had come at a great cost. We have a clip of the conflict but please be warned, the footage is graphic which some viewers may find disturbing.'

The shot of the well-dressed newsreader cut to shaky footage of bright emerald green turf and then whizzed up to the cloudless sky, focusing on two blurry dots above. After a second, the camera zoomed in, and the two tiny dots became more clear and distinguishable.

First was Paladin, the white of his uniform was torn and bloody. It was impossible to make out his face with the distance and the speed that he moved but it was clearly him. He threw a barrage of punches at the second blur, Jackal. The villain spun a large bow staff expertly round his body, deflecting Paladins strikes. Both of them floated meters above the open roof of the stadium trading attacks. The person filming was shouting to his friend throughout the video, commentating on the fight above. 'He's just smashed Jackal in the face, damn that had to hurt! Wait look, Jackal is doing something, there's some sort of blue glow! Can you see …'

But before the man filming could finish his sentence, a huge electric ball of white and blue energy burst from them and rippled across the entire stadium. It made a tremendous bang similar to a sonic boom, and terrified screams from the hoards within the stadium followed. The screen flashed pure white and as the light dissipated and the image began to re-focus, two bodies tumbled from the sky and came crashing down onto the pitch heavily. Paladin lay grotesquely crumpled at the edge of the grassy field and Jackal a few feet away, face buried in the dirt. The video stopped and the news reporter reappeared on the screen.

'There has been no statement from New London Police yet, but armed officers were seen collecting Paladin's body moments after the attack.'

'In other related news, the vigilante Harrow was spotted in Beijing this afternoon. In what appeared to be an assassination attempt on the Chinese President's life, turned out to be some sort of exorcism of his son.'

A still image of Harrow stood above Li Jūn's body, surrounded by the bright misty energy of the Pandarian, lingered on the screen; the newsreader continued.

'It is unclear what took place here or what Harrow's intentions were. Experts remain baffled and theories across the globe are varied and speculative. The President of the Republic of China had this to say at his press conference hours after the event.'

The report cut to the image of the exhausted and frail looking President, his short hair looked damp and his suit jacket slightly ruffled but his eyes sparkled with determination. He spoke in Chinese but subtitles and a British voice-over dictated what he said.

'Many are already aware of what happened to my son earlier today. Before I say anything else, I must say this. The hero, Harrow, saved my son's life. That is a fact.'

He starred out fiercely at the reporters, nobody dared interrupt him.

'Science, religion and everything in between, will try to explain what it was that possessed my son. I have no more answers for you than they do, except that whatever it was is gone, and that is thanks to Harrow.'

The reporters in the press conference hurled their flurry of questions - 'How do you know Harrow can be trusted?' 'Do you think anyone else close to you is being possessed?' and other pointed questions.

Taking a long slow breath out, he collected his thoughts, the room's noise and the interrogation from the reporters died down as quickly as it began. Gripping hold of the edges of the podium in front of him, he leant closer to the microphones.

'Let me ask you this? How do you decide who you can trust? Is it by the way they look? Perhaps it is by where they are from or what sort of education they received. I once knew a man who distrusted others simply based on how they walked. A little too much bounce in their stride and he instantly felt he could not trust them. I trust through actions and my heart.'

He paused dramatically, his knuckles flexing

tightly as he gripped the podium.

'Harrow has been in the news a lot recently, most of it paints a very sinister picture of the vigilante. However, from what I have seen, I do not think she is the beast many say she is. I see a woman who is trying her hardest to make a difference in this world, I do not condone her methods but my heart tells me I can trust her, we can all trust her. Thank you.'

He steped away from the podium and the reporters burst into another flurry of questions, then the news channel cut back to the reporter to finish the story.

Henry was quietly sobbing to himself, wrapped up in a fleecy white blanket watching the television. He'd just seen the news broadcast and was mourning the death of his beloved hero, Paladin. Tears trickled down his face and he dabbed at them with the edge of his blanket. He felt cold and his chest was heavy, as though large bags of sand had been tied to it, dragging him to the earth.

He carried on watching through the Harrow report. It was way past his bedtime, but routines had become very brittle lately. As a result, Henry was awake, and in the front room watching something that was certainly not suitable. The video of Paladin slamming into the ground after his battle with Jackal, caused Henry to twist awkwardly in his seat. Pain and heartbreak prickling his face.

The news story concluded, and the loud news outro tune played, Kirty's mum heard this from her room and came through to see her grandson curled up, red-eyed and sniffling.

'Henry, what's the matter? Why aren't you in bed sweetie?' Judy asked softly.

'Grandma, it's Paladin … he's dead.' Henry's eyes filled with tears again, moments away from leaking over the edge.

'Who is Paladin my dear?' she whispered, stepping forward and holding his hand in her own.

'He's a superhero, Grandma,' he mumbled, trying to fight back the tears.

'Oh, my poor boy, I'm sorry,' she said and pressed herself to him to hug him awkwardly while he sat on the chair wrapped in his blanket. 'Come on, Henry, let's get you to bed.'

Meekly he rose from the chair and followed his Grandmother through to his mum's room, where he had been sleeping since Judy moved in with them. Judy pulled back his duvet to tuck him into bed.

'Would you like me to make you a hot chocolate, my sweet?' she whispered gently, smiling with maternal warmth as she helped him into his makeshift bed.

'Yes please-' he had started to say before a quiet but firm knock on the front door interrupted.

'Who on earth could that be at this time of night,' Judy muttered, pulling herself up from Henry's side and making her way to the front door. Once she had left the room, Henry scrambled out of bed to peer around the edge of the door frame, watching his Grandma to see who it was.

Peeping through the glass hole in the door, Judy eyed up the stranger. He had gently angled features and vivid blue eyes behind his glasses. She couldn't see his whole body, but he wore a thick brown leather jacket and a maroon diamond checked jumper.

Henry watched his grandmother slide the security chain into place and slowly crack the door open. She stared through the slot at the smartly dressed stranger.

'Can I help you?' she grumbled with a slightly sharp and unwelcoming tone.

'No, you can't,' he said and lifting a hand out of his pocket, sprayed inky black liquid at her face.

The effects where instantaneous. Judy let out a high-pitched scream of pain and terror, falling down away from the door. Her hands darted up to her face and clawed at her disintegrating skin in agony. Henry stood in the doorway shaking with fear.

The front door burst open, the latch flung back, looking as though it had been melted off and the man stepped into the apartment. He walked past Judy who had stopped screaming and had gone eerily still, her entire body an ashy grey colour, her face looked sunken in. He glanced down at her body and made a tutting noise while he shook his head, his styled blonde hair flicking sharply as he did.

'Oh dear, I had rather hoped she would do that quietly. That was quite the racket she made wouldn't you say, young man?' He turned slyly to face Henry.

Henry was shaking profusely in the corner, he had dropped his blanket and his knees clattered against each other. They could both hear the sound of the shower stuttering off in the bathroom down the hallway. Henry's traumatised eyes flickered back and forth between the man and Judy's rapidly decaying body.

'Though I must say, I have never used a pepper spray quite like this one,' he chuckled, looking at the canister in his hand before pocketing it.

'W-who are y-you?' Henry whimpered, trying desperately to move but unable to lift a toe.

'I'm a very good friend of your mums, you can call me Zack, if you like,' Zack smiled. 'I just thought I'd drop by before she got home. I hope that's okay, Henry?'

'How … how do you know my name?' Henry cried, his voice croaking.

'I know lots about you,' he smiled again, his toothy grin felt unsettlingly twisted.

Just then, the door to the bathroom flew open and Kirsty, stood wrapped in a thick cream coloured bathrobe, darted out.

'Mum, I heard …' Kirsty started but then she saw Zack standing in the hallway, her terrified son shivering a foot away from him and the remains of her faceless mother speckled across the floor.

'Good evening, Kirsty. I've been waiting for so long to meet you and I must tell you …' Zack paused, glazing his eyes across her body from top to bottom. 'You haven't disappointed.'

Kirsty screamed which such force and pitch, it felt as though every inch of glass in their home would shatter.

CHAPTER TWENTY-FIVE

Carollers chimed in unison, their voices harmonising and singing into the cold night air. At the edge of a bustling seasonal market, Nahmar sat underneath the tall glowing hulk of a Christmas tree. The thousands of lights within it buzzed like carefree insects. The market was full of life and excitable shoppers, classic Christmas songs played jovially through discrete speakers scattered across the market. Where Nahmar sat, there were practically no shoppers and the cold wooden bench he had sat on had a good view of the rest of the busy square.

Heather approached his bench, carrying two large cups of smouldering hot chocolate. She wore a thick black coat with the hood pulled up, a heavy woollen scarf and a few prosthetic facial features for good measure. She sat down next to Nahmar and handed him the steaming hot drink. It was the same Nahmar that she had spoken to at the comic-con earlier in the year.

'Still don't trust me?' Nahmar asked, nodding towards her hood while he gratefully sipped at the hot chocolate.

'Hey that's my line,' Heather joked, sipping her own drink. The warmth of it filled her belly, running down to the tips of her fingers and making the bitter cold much more tolerable.

'Oh, merry Christmas,' she said, pulling the little silver cube, filled with the seven Pandarians out of her coat pocket and handing it to Nahmar.

As she handed it to Nahmar he received it with an exhausted expression, one that radiated relief. The quest he had set out to complete millennia ago, was finally over and literally in his grasp. His hands shook as he took it from Heather.

'What will you do with it?' Heather asked.

Nahmar couldn't speak, he just stared at the engravings across the box and seeing for the first time how they had changed.

'Nahmar?' Heather nudged him.

'What will I do with it?' he stirred, repeating her question. 'The woman who gave me this box told me the beings I would capture inside it could never be destroyed, only captured. I'm ashamed that after all this time it was someone else who hunted and captured these monsters, I never had the courage to do the dirty work myself.' Heather listened quietly, not wanting to interrupt him.

'Harrow, I told you why we needed to capture these beings but I didn't tell you everything,' Nahmar said. Heather couldn't help but interrupt now.

'You said the Pandarians had been here for over four thousand years,' said Heather. 'You're ... you're older than you look, aren't you?'

Nahmar smiled, still tightly gripping the silver cube in his hand.

'I certainly am, considerably.'

'Harrow, I'm going to tell you everything, from the beginning, but please do not think less of me ...' His smile twisted painfully as though he was pleading with her.

'Why would I think less of you?' Heather asked.

'Well when you realise how old I really am, I expect it will anger you as to why it has taken so long for me to fulfil my duty,' said Nahmar, his head dropped shamefully.

'If I had shown a bit of courage and resilience, many of the tragedies throughout history could have been averted.' His usual calm and soothing voice had gone horse and croaked.

Heather, scooted up closer to him and put an arm over his shoulders. He could definitely see her face now, but she no longer cared. Foreseeing what he was about to tell her, she couldn't see any reason to hide her identity from Nahmar anymore.

'Firstly, I am Nahmar. The real Nahmar. I know that nothing I say can surprise you because you see fate moments before it transpires. You are a Fateweaver, just like myself. Which may interest you to know, that in some distant way you and I will be related.' His eyes twinkled brightly as he said this. Heather was speechless.

'My father was the first that I knew. He was an extraordinary man that bent fate to his will as though it were blades of grass. When I was a boy he told me that our kind lived in the earth, deep under the surface of the world. Similar to humans in many ways but with subtle differences - "We can see the path of fate before it is trodden and change it if we do not like the track." That was something he always used to say to me growing up,' recalled Nahmar, his mind wandering distantly through time.

'I was too young when we left our tribe to

remember my ancestors, but my father told me they were a cautious people, terrified of venturing into the outside world. For years he sought an escape, longed to live on the surface but my mother refused. My Father told me our leaders had meditated into the depths of fate and saw only death and misery above, but once my mother passed away there was nothing but superstition keeping my father trapped below. Abandoning his home, friends and family, he left with me and sought a new life on the surface.'

Nahmar then went on to tell Heather of their discovery of the first Pandarian when he was a boy, their trials and hardships as the Persuaders power spread and the night he and his father found Thaesilia in that hut and how she had given him her everlasting life. Heather felt overwhelmed by the story, but she somehow knew that it was the truth. Nahmar stopped for several moments after telling her about the fear he had felt that dreadful night.

'What happened to your Father and Thaesilia?' Heather asked with awe. Christmas shoppers continued browsing, completely oblivious to the extraordinary tale the two were sharing.

'Alas, I do not know. I imagine the Pandarian got to them both, but I never found either of their bodies. It haunted me for centuries and to be truthful, it still does. You never really get over the death of a parent, even if you have lived as long as I have,' whispered Nahmar.

The pair of them sat quietly on the bench for a few moments, drinking in the lights and sounds of the market. They could hear a large band and group of carollers finishing another song and the muffled glove covered applause that followed.

'Did you ever find any of the others like her? Like Thaesilia?' asked Heather.

'Yes. I searched for so long. Travelled to every

conceivable corner of the world looking for them, when at last I found another from her world. A young man, strong and handsome but in his eyes, I saw the pain and desperation that millennia alone can do to a person. I saw the same look in the mirror every day,' he confessed

'I confronted him, told him everything just as I have just told you. I begged him to help me. Help me find a Serathium and capture the Pandarians. But time has a way of eroding one's hope. He had long since given up on any effort to stop the Pandarians, having discarded his amulet and own Serathium, he tried to live amongst humans and forget his past. I asked him about the others from his world and if he knew where they were, but he claimed to have not seen them in centuries. I searched again but after a short time knew my efforts would be fruitless. He expected the others from his world to either have died trying soon after their arrival, or have hidden away as he had, living out their immortal lives on earth in the hope that they would one day be able to return home.'

Heather asked the question that had been squirming through her mind since Nahmar had mentioned it - 'How have you been able to live this long?'

'This man from her world told me about their spell of immortality. It was a perfect solution to two problems his world faced. One, living in repetitive cycles of learning and teaching. As you became wise enough and experienced enough to do great things, your life began to wane and your ageing body would ultimately betray you. Fuelling a need to produce offspring and teach them all you knew, a problem not too dissimilar from our own. The second was a growing population. More and more children were born and the magic and science of his world allowed his race to live far beyond the ages of their ancestors. Again, not unlike our own world's problems.'

'The spellcasters, as he called them, had discovered a way to grant eternal life. An energy that would live inside you until it was passed on or your body became too badly damaged to go on; allowing their people to live forever. But this came with a concrete condition. Should they wish to reproduce, then they must pass on that eternal life to their offspring, or their child's life would be short and meaningless. He told me that most of his people embraced the new way of life and any who didn't were able to continue their lives as the temporary fleeting moments as we know. Soon, nearly every sentient being in his world lived eternally until they were ready to pass on and give their life to their lineage. Quite an eloquent way of handling things if you ask me,' Nahmar smiled.

'And Thaesilia, she gave you her life?' continued Heather.

'She did, yes.' Nahmar said, nodding solemnly.

'This why you have so many proxies?' said Heather, beginning to piece together all the parts that had puzzled her for as long as she knew Nahmar.

'It is, I must shroud my identity this way. If others truly knew what I was, and the power given to me, they would surely attempt to steal it from me. There are men and women that are now able to harness and extract metahuman abilities, perhaps they could do the same with my life. Imagine the damage that some of these madmen would be able to do with eternal life. It is dreadful to contemplate.'

Nahmar turned to look at Heather. Her expression was grave and clearly quite terrified at the thought. Noticing this, Nahmar tried to reassure her – 'And besides, I'm not quite done with living yet!'

She grinned and took several hearty gulps of her hot chocolate. Nahmar looked out onto the Christmas market, his eyes jovially following the trails of lights.

'Can I talk to you about the Pandarians?' Heather asked, genuinely asking permission after he had been so forthright and honest with her.

'Of course, and if I can explain, I will,' replied Nahmar.

'You told Zack and me that Tão Jūn was a Pandarian, but it was actually his son. What happened?'

His face transformed apologetically and bowed with regret.

'Yes, that was a most unfortunate mistake. As I said, using the amulet from Thaesilia, I have been able to focus my thoughts on locating the Pandarians. I have tracked them across millennia, watching from a distance. The final Pandarian, the very same one that my father and I attempted to destroy, had occupied the body of the Chinese President for nearly forty years. But something happened, something I have never seen before. It left before its host was dead.'

'When a Pandarian feels that its host has outlived its usefulness, they destroy the host and move to another. This one didn't, I believe this was so it could still lure you in and avoid being captured. But thanks to your adaptability, this diversion was ineffective,' chuckled Nahmar, with a proud grin on his face.

They sat in silence for a few more moments, Heather's legs beginning to feel numb from the cold wood. A couple of young police cadets patrolled past them with their chests puffed out and a dog that had escaped its owner was sniffing for a good place to relieve itself. The tinkle of Christmas bells chimed through the market and the warm delicious smell of minced pies wafted towards Heather and Nahmar. The police cadets walkie-talkies sparked up and some voice on the other end gave them a series of muffled instructions. In unison, the two of them bolted in the other direction.

'Even after all of this it feels like nothing has changed, people are still bad. I thought stopping the Pandarians would make things better,' Heather laughed, in a sarcastic downtrodden kind of way.

'But you have made things better, my dear. Seven horrifyingly powerful beings are no longer influencing and manipulating our society. Yes, people are still bad, and perhaps they always will be. However, I think people have great potential, I do not believe we are too far gone to be saved from our own sins and mistakes. Humans have been called lots of things, but I truly believe we all have the potential to be good. Give it time and you will see,' said Nahmar, looking into the faces of the crowd of busy shoppers. He turned to look at Heather.

'Something still troubles you?'

'Yes, it's Paladin. I feel … I feel regret, guilt. I should have been there to save him,' choked Heather, her voice breaking slightly on the last two words.

'What could you have done, my dear? Paladin's battle with that villain was over nearly as quickly as it began. There was nothing you could have done to save him,' said Nahmar.

'I should have been here, in New London. If I had been here I could have stopped Jackal before things got out of hand.'

'Then it would have been you lying in the dirt and not Paladin.'

Heather pondered this for a second and then replied solemnly. 'Maybe it should have been me instead.'

Nahmar spun round in his seat to face her completely now, putting a firm hand on her shoulder.

'Listen to me, Harrow. You must let go of this guilt

and anger inside you, it will eat away at your mind like rot if you let it continue. Paladin made his decision to fight monsters like Jackal. He knew the risks and accepted them, just as we all have. Paladin did not die in vain, his sacrifice saved thousands if not millions of lives. We can only hope our deaths will be as meaningful. You need to show yourself mercy. And forgive me for being so bold, but you also need to show that mercy to others. The ones you believe deserve none.'

Heather looked up at him aghast, twisting her shoulder slightly so his hand fell.

'You mean the criminals that show no mercy to others? Beasts that would rather shoot a child than risk ever being recognised by a ten-year-old!' she yelled.

A few passers-by had turned their heads to look at the sudden outburst. Nahmar pulled his hand back but kept his focus on Heather. There was a tense pause between them until Nahmar spoke again.

'There is a quote that I can never really remember ...' said Nahmar, trying to diffuse the situation. '... over four thousand years old I'm sure it's no surprise I forget things. I met the man that came up with it, but it speaks about changing the world and that that change starts from within.'

'These murderers, thieves and rapists ... their actions do not warrant mercy, nevertheless, we must show it to them. Else we are just as bad as they are, cold-hearted and unforgiving. Showing them mercy is being the change that you want to see.'

Heather gazed into Nahmar's face, carefully calculating every sentence. Finally, she sighed and nodded.

'I know you're right, Nahmar. It's just difficult,' said Heather, sighing again.

They spoke together for a few more minutes, Nahmar gratefully thanked her for her sacrifices and all she had done over the last several months. Then picking up her now empty cup, Heather stood up.

'You never told me what you were going to do with the box?' Heather asked, pulling her coat tightly around her to fend off the cutting cold.

'Well I've had a few ideas but the one that stands out to me at the moment is taking it back to its home.' A sincere little smile formed across Nahmar's face.

'You're joking! To another world, Thaesilia's world?' Heather exclaimed.

'I am serious. I've pondered on it for a great deal of time and it seems the most fitting place. This kind of power doesn't belong here on our planet,' said Nahmar.

'But you don't even know where this world is! It could be trillions of lightyears away,' said Heather in near disbelief. 'It's impossible.'

'Harrow, my friend, I have seen countless men and women say that something was impossible and somehow …' He stood up, with the same warm radiant smile he often wore. '… the human race always manages to find a way to make it so.'

'See you soon.' Nahmar winked and walked away from her into the crowd of bustling shoppers, leaving Heather underneath the massive glowing tree and for the first time in a long time, she felt closure.

CHAPTER TWENTY-SIX

Cascading across town on a hyper bus, Heather made her way to Zack's hideout. Still wearing her civilian clothes, she was eager to get to the warmth of Zack's underground station. She had tried to return Kirsty's missed calls again but there was still no response.

Climbing through the discrete entrance to Knights Bridge station, which opened automatically for her, Heather quickly walked towards Zack's platform; carrying a warm bottle of mulled wine in one hand and a bag of ginger biscuits in the other. Walking onto the platform, the steps of her steel-heeled boots echoing across the station, she looked for Zack. But other than the familiar hum of the heaters, it was silent. No sound of fingers clattering on the keys of a keyboard, no gentle violin music, it was abnormally quiet.

'Zack?' Heather called out, walking into the stationary carriage.

The carriage looked as it always did, books neatly stacked on some makeshift shelves, dishes washed up and resting on the draining board and everything else neatly tidied and clean.

Heather went to call out again, but as she began calling out his name, Zack's voice boomed through the speakers of his computer.

'Harrow, I'm glad you finally made it. I trust everything went well?' His calm voice resonated clearly through the carriage.

'Yeah, all good, Nahmar is going to get rid of the box. It's over, Zack, we did it,' Heather smiled with relief again, being able to say it out loud. 'Where are you by the way?'

'Oh, just out at the moment, but I've got something to show you. I think you'll find it quite interesting.'

'New gear?' Heather asked.

'No no no, something much more interesting than that. I'll take you there.' Something about Zack's voice had shifted slightly, it was more erratic and sharp than usual. Before Heather could ask if there was something going on, the doors of the carriage slammed shut.

'Zack, what …?' Heather stuttered, she hadn't foreseen the doors slamming shut. And in fact, couldn't foresee anything. Everything Zack said over the computer, she was hearing for the first time. The mulled wine and biscuits fell to the floor, shattering and spilling everywhere. The carriage gave a sudden lurch forwards and began etching itself away from the station along the tracks into the darkness.

'Zack, what the fuck is going on? I can't-'

'See what's about to happen?' he interrupted. 'No, I thought it would be best that way, wouldn't want to ruin the surprise now would we.'

The Carriage plunged into the blackness of the tunnel, picking up a hearty pace. Mundane orange light filled the carriage Heather was in, but she couldn't see a thing outside the windows and the light of the platform behind her was shrinking rapidly.

Heather darted to the doors and tried to prise them open, but they didn't budge an inch. She slammed a hammer-like elbow into the glass but she may as well have flicked it because it had no effect at all.

'I have a confession to make, Harrow. Well a few actually,' he laughed coldly. 'Firstly, I know that your name is Heather, Heather Green-Woods. What an ordinary name for such an extraordinary person. Lovely name if you ask me. It wasn't my first guess, but I think it suits you nicely. Did you double barrel it when you got married? I never bothered to check.'

Panic seeping in, Heather was looking for something to prise open the door but there was nothing in here more useful than a wooden spatula. She tried to will the mechanisms to malfunction and release with her powers but to no avail.

'My next confession is that I'm a collector. I love collecting, bit of an obsession to be entirely honest with you. Been doing it for most of my life but in the last few years I've discovered my true calling and you are just going to die for it.'

'What have you done to me?' Heather yelled, still desperately trying to use her powers.

'Oh, well I've taken away your powers for now. And actually, you have yourself to thank for that one. Telling me that alcohol negates your abilities was one of your more spectacular blunders.'

'But I haven't-' Heather began, but Zack interrupted her again.

'No, you haven't had any alcohol but I synthesised a gaseous substance that would replicate the same effects and I've been pumping it into the station profusely since you arrived. Now would you like to see why I call this place the Catacombs?'

The train carriage came to a controlled but sudden halt and the doors violently sprang open. Ominous pale blue light leaked across the walls of the tunnel and reflected off clouds of sparse vapour that drifted past the windows.

'Now, I've never shown my collection to anyone else ever, but I'm making an exception for you Heather. After all, you really are quite extraordinary and I felt it would be fitting to share this with you. Especially as you're going to help me add two very integral parts to my collection.'

Heather stood on the carriage peering through the front window, it was difficult to see but she could make out two adjacent rows of blue lights, blossoming from metallic canisters, each one at least two meters tall. The smoke gently billowed from behind each canister and floated down towards the carriage.

'Well, what are you just standing there for Heather? We're not all immortal.'

Cautiously stepping down from the carriage and dropping onto the tracks feet below, she was sure of two things; Zack knew more about Nahmar than he had originally made out and she had seriously fucked up.

'Welcome to the main exhibition! As I said, nobody else has seen this yet, Heather, so please keep your spoilers to yourself.' Zack's voice now spoke from several small but effective speakers stuck against the tunnel walls.

Cold air hit Heather like a crashing wave, the pale blue smoke stung her eyes as she stepped away from the carriage and towards the tunnel of huge canisters. Several dozens of these pods lined the edge of the tracks, leaning against the tunnel walls. Hundreds of pipes and thin trails of tubbing lead away from the track and towards a noisy whirring sound.

As Heather walked along the abandoned tracks the canisters became clearer, they looked like incubation chambers from old science fiction movies, but Heather knew exactly what they were, cryogenics pods. Slowly she approached the first one, the large glass panel at the front was covered with a thin layer of ice. But for Heather there was no mistaking the face inside, it was Captain Megastone, still wearing his distinctive costume and iron shaded eye mask.

'Ah yes, my partner before you and as you said, shit names, you end up dead.' said Zack, speaking as though he could see Heather's every movement.

'You killed him because of his name?!' Heather roared, anger boiled inside her.

'No, don't be ridiculous. I killed him because he outlived his usefulness and was better suited here keeping the rest of my trophies company.'

Heather now rushed across to peer into the rest of the pods, there were almost forty that had been turned on and were filled with the bodies of dead heroes. Most of whom Heather recognised throughout her years of crime fighting, some of whom she did not. The vast number of frozen mutilated bodies was haunting. Further along the tunnel, now running between the icy coffins while Zack whistled carelessly through the speakers, Heather spotted a number of large crates supposedly with more canisters inside. Even with the cold, she was sweating profusely. She found the bodies of the twin sisters she'd rescued on the yacht, their tiny bodies pressed awkwardly against each other in a singular canister, sections of their arms and torso looked as though they had been scooped out and poorly sewn back together. Heather's stomach felt constricted and her shoulders felt inhumanly heavy, but it was only magnified when she looked into one of the last pods.

Barely fitting in because of his broad shoulders and expansive chest, was Paladin. His skin was burnt and scarred badly, and his costume was covered in cuts and slices from the blast that killed him. The bitter ice inside the pod appeared to have thinly covered all of his exposed skin. The ghost of his last pained expression still scratched across his face.

'Why show me all this?' Heather demanded, staring painfully at the body of her old friend. 'What the hell do you want?'

'Do you like it? I can't take credit for killing all of them myself but I just like the way they look. The cryogenics pods mean I can keep the bodies fresh and intact. You haven't said what you think of it yet, Heather?' said Zack mockingly. 'There's even a space for you.'

And sure enough, one more pod along from Paladin's was an empty one that had been switched on.

'I'm getting it nice and cool and ready for you,' growled Zack. Heather could hear in his voice that he was grinning wickedly.

'WHAT DO YOU WANT FROM ME!?' screamed Heather, her voice thundered down the tunnels and screamed back at her again and again.

Zack laughed once more, the same cold sharp laugh as before.

'Oh, there's that Harrow rage we all know and love. There is one more person that I want to procure for my collection, and it is vital that I have them. I've been trying to figure out how to get to them for so long but just couldn't crack it. It seems that has been the most closely guarded piece of information there is, no way to obtain it. That was until you came along, Heather Green-Woods!'

'You see, Nahmar is viewed as one of the most influential and powerful people among the hero community but not many people realise that he is one of the most influential and powerful people in time. Present at some of the most pivotal moments in our world history, and you know his true identity.'

'I knew from the moment I met you that he had some strange preference for you. The way he looked at you when you entered the Network meeting, he looked at you unlike anyone else. I knew that if I wanted to get to him, I'd have to get to you and it seems my patience has finally paid off,' said Zack, excitement in his voice building to bursting point.

'He didn't tell me anything Zack,' Heather lied. 'Just took the box, thanked me and left.'

There was a long pause and then Zack let out a huge sigh, 'Don't lie to me, Heather.'

'I'm not lying, I don't know anything more about Nahmar than you do.'

'I don't believe you,' Zack hissed, his frustrated voice also echoing through the tunnels.

'I don't care what you believe, you sick twisted fuck. I'm done.' Heather quickly started walking away from the corridor of frozen bodies in the other direction.

'Maybe you'll care if I start to cut Kirsty into little pieces.' Heather stopped dead still. 'Or if I start to burn your son, one inch at a time until there's nothing left but ash. Little Henry will be able to fit in a shoe box or neat little Christmas jar.'

'YOU MOTHER FUCKING! ... IF YOU GO ANYWHERE NEAR THEM, I'LL-' Heather roared, her head throbbed with unbridled rage, but Zack cut her off, shouting quite loudly himself.

'I've already gone near them, in fact, I've got them both here with me right now! At the same dirty and dingy hotel this all began at for you. I read the police reports from the rape, I'm quite sentimental like that. It must have been so traumatic for you, nineteen and forced to do such terrible things. It's no wonder you're such an angry person, I imagine you wanted nothing more than to get the revenge you deserved and give them both the punishment they deserved.'

Heather's hands were squeezed so tightly into fists, her short nails dug into her palms painfully. Her knuckles were white, and her teeth crushed against each other as she clenched her jaw.

'How unfortunate that someone beat you to the mark and killed them both before you could. From what I've read, it seems that this pair managed to do what they did to you, to quite a few women. Reading it and all about you was quite the superhero origin story!' said Zack.

'When I get my hands on you, I will tear your head from your neck, you bastard,' Heather said, in almost a whisper.

'You know where the hotel is, you have thirty minutes to get here and show me who Nahmar is. Room nine-one-four, I even managed to get the same room! Now, whoever said romance is dead?' Zack chuckled to himself.

Heather raced past the carriage in a sprint and charged back up the tracks towards the station platform.

'And don't think about suiting up or bringing any weapons. Not only will the drones I gave you explode on my command, but I have also obtained three hydrogen bombs, courtesy of the trigger-happy Pandarian, Francis Cotton. I've moved them to other locations across the country, so any attempted heroics and the rest of England can enjoy an early Christmas present.'

Sprinting like a lioness, Heather bounded through the tunnel towards the dim orange light of the platform. Her mind racing and her heart pounding furiously, still unable to glimpse even a moment into fate.

'Oh, and Heather, don't keep me waiting. You were delicious but this wife of yours looks even more appetising.'

CHAPTER TWENTY-SEVEN

Soaring through the wintery streets of New London on her summoned Harley, Heather did not care who saw her riding Harrow's motorcycle. When she got to the hotel she could not remember how exactly she got there, her mind was fragmented and blurry. The gas Zack had poured into the Catacombs was still flowing thickly through her bloodstream and mixed with the violent rage she felt for Zack, it was a miracle she made it there in one piece. Several times she nearly collided with oncoming traffic and about four hundred yards away from the hotel, she was inches away from maiming a small group of tourists crossing the road.

Leaping from the bike in the hotel's meagre car park, Heather launched herself up the stairs and through the hotel lobby. It was deadly silent, not a single guest in sight. A quivering receptionist stood behind the counter, ran towards her the moment she came through the front door.

'He told me to give you this! Please, he's going to

kill my dad,' the young man said, holding out the key card for room nine-one-four with sweaty and unsteady hands.

'He's not going to kill anyone,' growled Heather, snatching the room card and racing towards the lifts. She slammed a fist against the button of the lift, not noticing that the ugly salmon pink carpet the lobby used to have, had been swapped with a regal crimson colour. Her mind was simply hell-bent on wrapping her hands around Zack's neck and squeezing until it snapped.

Arriving outside the room, Heather swiped the plastic card across the reader. A monotone beep sounded, and Heather shoved open the door.

Inside the room, Henry and Kirsty sat tied to chairs with pillowcases tightly wrapped around their mouth as makeshift gags. Both looked utterly terrified and Kirsty looked as though she'd been beaten; large cuts littered her face and her left eye was swollen and bleeding, Henry appeared unharmed. In each corner of the room, one of Zack's drones hovered menacingly and stood casually behind the terrified pair, pressing a large jagged blade to Henry's neck, was Zack.

Heather removed her wig and prosthetic disguise immediately and both Henry and Kirsty started inaudibly shouting through their gags. The door swung shut behind Heather, and Zack looked up to face his partner.

'It really bugs me that hotel rooms only give you one chair. I mean what if there's a couple of you and you both want to sit at the desk at the same time? I had to go and pinch this one from next door.' He flicked his head to the left and shook the back of Henry's chair. Henry stared up at his mum with a look of fear that would break any parent's heart, tears streamed down his face.

'Let them go, Zack, now,' Heather commanded.

'So soon? But I thought we could give little Henry

here a bedtime story first,' said Zack, tapping Henry on the shoulder with his knife-free hand.

'Did you know, young man, that this was the very room that you were conceived?'

Kirsty let out another muffled scream, not wanting her son to hear the story Zack was about to tell. Heather yelled out and stomped forward a step, but Zack pressed the knife to Henry's throat more firmly, drawing blood slightly.

'Take one more step forward, Heather, and Henry dies. And in case your son's life isn't incentive enough, one command from me and the hydrogen bombs will go off. You try to take me out and my drones will fill you with lead before you can take another step.' Zack was breathing heavily, not taking his eyes off Heather who remained frozen on the spot as instructed.

'As I was saying, this room has quite a lot of significance for you and your mum over there,' Zack said, now addressing Henry.

'Ten years ago, your mum made the mistake of trusting someone she shouldn't and it got herself into quite the tricky situation. Isn't it interesting how history so often repeats itself?'

'Do you know how frustrating it is to be as good as I am at what I do, and not being able to show anyone my true potential?' Zack asked Heather, looking quite calm and collected as he spoke, though a single thin strand of hair had fallen out of its slicked back place.

'It's infuriating, being so goddamn good at everything you touch but nobody realises how impressive you really are. Though I imagine you do understand to some degree. Being Harrow, saving all those innocent lives every day, beating up the bad guys. You must just want to shout from the tallest buildings in the city "It's me, everyone, I'm Harrow!" ...'

Heather's eyes flicked down to Kirsty's, who was crying and stared back painfully.

'Oh, don't worry, I already told them who you really are. I was going to wait until you arrived, but I couldn't wait any longer! Kirsty here didn't believe me at first but I'm afraid the evidence is stacked against you. However, you'll be happy to know I didn't tell her you and I have been having sex, she figured that one out all by herself,' Zack smiled cruelly, flippantly waving his hand.

Kirsty looked up at her wife in emotional agony. Heather's head dipped shamefully as she caught Kirsty's glance.

'Now to business!' Zack slapped a hand roughly on Henry's shoulder. 'Tell me-'

'How did you know who I was?' Heather interrupted, desperately trying to buy time to come up with a plan, her powers were still completely absent and all of her gadgets in safe houses across New London.

Zack looked insulted that she had interrupted him, however, it was clear his desire to prove his brilliance was greater; an exploitable flaw among numerous supervillains she had fought in the past.

'If you really must know, it was during the riots in October. I gave you a list of high priority targets, one of them the school.'

Heather knew as he spoke what it was she had done to so royally fuck up.

'The way you shouted, "parents evening!" I knew you must have a child there. Then when you told me you were married to a woman, well it was too easy. There you were, the only married female parents at the school that had an appointment that night. I had everything I needed and more.'

'But why go to all this trouble for the bodies of a couple of superheroes? Are coins not fun enough to collect anymore?' Heather asked, focusing intensely on one of the drones hovering to her right but unable to alter a single thing.

'You still don't see it?' Zack demanded. 'Money means nothing to me, I could be the richest man in the world if I desired. But there's no fun in that, no originality.' It was like he was performing, clearly happy to monologue so someone could finally see his true brilliance.

'Supers, now they are the ultimate prize, the perfect trophies; but more exciting than that is the powers that lie within them. Some are plain regular people, extraordinary but powerless. They still make wonderful items in my collection though. The ones that truly interest me are like you, Heather, somehow imbued with incredible abilities. Abilities that I am learning to harness and extract. I've already been able to take minor elements of my trophies' powers and utilise them. Your mother-in-law was able to feel the touch of decay that I took from that little girl on the yacht, quite extraordinary,' Zack reminisced, looking first into space and then back into Heather's bloodthirsty eyes.

'But the most extraordinary of them all is Nahmar, a man that has been alive for millennia. His immortality isn't a secret as closely guarded as his identity. Since I discovered there was a man who had lived a thousand lifetimes, he has been my only goal. After all, think of all the things you could do with eternal life.'

'Why are you telling me all this?' Heather asked through gritted teeth.

'Because once you've told me which Nahmar is the real one and help me lure him into my trap, I will end your insufferable life and add you to my collection. And as I said before, it's no fun being the smartest kid in school if nobody knows about it,' Zack said, pressing the tip of his tongue against his brilliant white teeth.

'You're fucking crazy,' snarled Heather, glaring across the room at him with venom in her eyes.

'So, what's it going to be, Harrow?' replied Zack, ignoring her last comment. 'Are you going to help me, or do you want to watch your family die?'

Heather was paralysed with indecision; her powers were still missing and no amount of concentration let her glimpse into fate or alter the situation. She felt hopeless and knew she couldn't give up Nahmar, if this monster managed to extract his gift of life then there would be no end to Zack's plague-like schemes. Fury quivered throughout her body, she ached to launch herself across the room and slam every sharp and hard part of her body into Zack's smug looking face.

'Is the decision really that hard?' groaned Zack. He lifted the knife up to Henry's eye and brought it deeply slashing down. The tip of the knife sliced horribly into her son's eye and down through his cheekbone. Heather roared with cyclonic rage, Kirsty screamed through the tightly bound gag and Henry whimpered and wailed like a dog that knows it's about to be put down.

'TELL ME WHICH ONE IS THE REAL NAHMAR!' Zack hissed, spit flying towards Heather's outstretched hands. The drones had all shifted forwards on Zack's outburst, tracking Heather's every movement ready to fire should she move too close.

'Fine …' Heather whispered, the sense of defeat washing over her like an icy shower. 'I'll tell you what you want to know, just let my family go afterwards.'

'Of course,' Zack flashed a gritty twisted smile. Stooping down so his head was at the same level as

Henry's.

'He's-' Heather began but before she said another word, Henry had pushed off the floor hard, slamming the back of his head into Zack's perfect chin. The four drones made a faltered buzzing sound, as though something inside them all had malfunctioned. Still clutching the knife, Zack stumbled back an inch, holding his jaw gingerly as Heather sprang across the room and hurled herself into Zack.

The impact sent the two of them soaring into the floor against the window. Heather lifted her white-knuckled fist high into the air and brought it hurtling down into Zack's temple. The drones remained frozen in place, hovering lightly on the spot. Relentlessly, Heather battered into Zack, strike after strike crushing against his skull. His arms and legs flailed around trying to claw at her or drag her from his body, but she didn't falter. Her knuckles were bloody and aching; again and again, she smashed her fists into him mercilessly. The knife lay in the corner, dripping with Henry's blood.

'Don't let him speak!' Henry cried out from behind his mother, having gotten to his feet, free from his bonds.

Zack had started to say 'Detona-' before Heather rammed her hand over his bloodied and crumbled mouth. Heather quickly darted across his body looking for the device that would receive his voice-activated request.

'It's his watch!' Henry shouted out again. Heather not hesitating to question her son, wrenched up one of Zack's arms and slapped it next to his head, pinning it down with her spare hand.

Zack didn't stop squirming, he wriggled like a fish out of water, eyes screaming with hate at Heather.

'GET HIS WATCH OFF!' Heather shouted. Kirsty, who Henry had just untied from her chair, rushed over to unclip the watch and wrench it from his wrist.

Heather let go of the watch-free arm and slammed her fist into the side of his head again, still holding her other hand forcefully across his sweaty mouth, while Zack's free arm clawed and slashed at her face.

Behind her came the sound of glass being crushed under Kirsty's foot, as she stomped relentlessly on the watch.

Heaving Zack by the collar of his coat, Heather stood up and slammed him against the tall window pane. Unforgivingly she bashed his head into the glass, more times than anyone could count. The glass had begun to crack and thin streaks burst across the entire pane. Dragging Zack away for a moment, who now looked as though he'd been hit by a series of heavy mallets, Heather forcefully kicked at the crack in the glass. It only took a couple of heavy thuds before it gave way and shattered into hundreds of tiny shards, tumbling to the concrete below.

Spinning Zack so that his back now faced the cold open air of the exposed hole, Heather glared into his brutalised face with tears flowing down her own. She had nothing to say to him that could convey the true hatred she felt for him. Her breathing was quick and his blood was splattered across her hair and face. Then she pulled him towards her to hurl him out of the shattered window.

'HEATHER STOP!' Kirsty cried out.

A breath away from launching him out of the window to a fall that would undoubtedly finish him off, Heather stopped and turned to Kirsty, speechless.

'Don't do this, Heather. Not in front of our son,' Kirsty pleaded, looking to Henry who was quietly stood next to Kirsty. Pure horror was etched across his expression, his eye gruesomely dripping with blood and other fluids.

'Don't be the monster they say you are!'

Heather turned back to Zack, who was nearly unrecognisable. His face grotesquely distorted from her attacks, his jaw was shattered and gums toothless. The irritating smug smile had entirely vanished, and his breathing had slowed to sporadic flickering. Heather's chest and throat felt as though it had been squeezed through an unnaturally small space, her head throbbed painfully and felt like it was about to explode.

Stepping away from the deadly hole in the glass, Heather dropped Zack to the floor of the room and slumped against the bed. Then she screamed like she had never screamed before. Every inch of her body felt like it was screaming with her. Her throat stung with the volume and sheer force of it. Only when she stopped could she hear the sirens.

CHAPTER TWENTY-EIGHT

The weeks that followed that night were easily the worst of Heather's life. After stopping Zack and rescuing her family, the police showed up at the hotel. Zack was arrested for kidnapping and Heather was arrested for grievous bodily harm. After a night in a grimy police cell and a phone call to the Network, Heather was released and her record expunged. Zack was released on bail a few days later too but quickly intercepted moments after leaving the police station. Several members of the Network clean-up crew dragged him into the back of a delivery van to take him to Terminus, the Network controlled prison facility. There Zack would rot for the real crimes he committed, far away from government officials looking for information about vigilantes.

Immediately after getting out of the police station, Heather rushed back home but on arriving there discovered both Kirsty and Henry were gone. She called out to them, searched every room of their apartment but she was alone. Hours later she received a message from Kirsty saying that she and Henry were staying with her friend Neil and that Heather should not come looking for them.

Once Zack's poisonous gas had left her system, Heather's powers had begun to return. However, it only made her pain worse. Time seemed to be twice as slow, every moment seeing the mundane nothingness that was about to transpire; it was torturous. It didn't take long for Heather to drain her supply of whisky and go to the shops to collect more.

It was then that she realised it was Christmas day. Her local was shut and she had to walk to several other stores until she could find somewhere that was open just find something to blur the pain.

For weeks she stayed in the house, watching cheesy television and old Christmas movies, easily drinking a bottle a day. She had had to dip into her Harrow accounts, as her own money had quickly dried up with the added expenses. She tried calling Kirsty every day, desperate to speak to her and Henry but it went to voicemail instantly.

A week after New Year's eve, Heather received a lengthy message from Kirsty, saying that she and Henry were going to move into a new apartment; Neil would be coming by later that week to collect their stuff and that her mum's funeral was last week. Heather sent back a series of responses, asking to meet up to talk about things, needing to explain what had happened and begging to speak to Henry. But got nothing in return except for a single soul-crushing text – "Henry doesn't want to speak to you."

Between a glass of whisky and the next, Heather called Nahmar and briefly explained what had happened to her. Telling him of Zack's maniacal plot and how he had intended to kill Nahmar. She also told him of the Catacombs and the dozens of heroes' bodies that were on ice beneath the streets of New London. Nahmar sent teams to collect but, as Heather later found out, every single body had been mysteriously removed before the teams arrived.

Heather's multiple suits of armour lay in her safe houses collecting dust. She hadn't suited up since Beijing over a month ago and New London had started to notice. News magazines printed articles with titles like: "Vigilante taking extended Christmas break" or "Harrow: missing or early retirement?"

It seemed that the criminals had noticed too as crime rates shot through the roof, now that neither Paladin nor Harrow was around to save the day. Heather caught a few stories in-between television programmes but quickly changed the channel when anything like that came on.

The one thing that Heather couldn't push from her mind, no matter how hard she tried, was Zack. She shook with hate every time she thought about him; hate for him and for herself. How had she allowed someone like this to get so close to her, she thought. And the more she thought about it the more she hated herself. Heather had genuinely grown to care for Zack, she loved the way he spoke and how easy he was to talk to. She loved his gentle demeanour and the way he looked at her. A few times, her thoughts escaped her and she thought back to the night they had had sex. He had made her feel like the most cherished woman in the world, something no one, not even her wife, had ever made her feel.

She thought back to the journey to the police station, handcuffed in the back of the van staring at his bloody and toothless face. The imprint of his ruined smile was immovable from her thoughts. As much as her entire being loathed him, she still felt a morsel of something there for him, though she refused to admit it.

Slowly the temperature outside began to warm up

and by late February, the biting winds that had been attacking every dog walker and paperboy had ceased. Heather left the house for the first time in over a month. Her diet of fast food and whiskey had already taken a serious toll, her nightmares were more twisted and horrific than ever.

Returning to the apartment carrying a couple of bags of shopping and a satchel full of alcohol, she thought about what she might watch this evening. Turning the corner of the grey hallway, her front door in sight, Heather stopped abruptly as if she had been turned to stone.

Stood outside the apartment, knocking below the number with delicate hands was Kirsty. She stopped knocking the moment Heather came into view and awkwardly picked up the box she'd rested on the floor.

'Hi,' Kirsty called out from across the corridor. She wore a long black coat and she'd dyed her hair a punchy red colour. Heather stood still not knowing what to say.

'I've got some stuff for you that got mixed in with mine,' said Kirsty, gently shaking the box.

'Oh right, thanks,' said Heather, wrenching her cemented legs forward and towards Kirsty. The corridor to her apartment felt like a mile long, guiltily walking toward her wife. She was only now aware of how appalling she must look to Kirsty, having not washed in at least a week and wearing an uncoordinated mix match of smelly pyjamas and a frumpy brown coat. Kirsty, on the other hand, looked better than ever, her hair neatly straightened, and her tall boots shone as though recently polished.

'What did you get?' Kirsty asked, nodding to the bags of shopping.

'Oh, just food,' replied Heather.

With a fragment of a smile, Kirsty shook her head. 'You know, you're far worse at lying than you used to be.

I can smell the whisky on you from here,' she said.

Again, Heather didn't know what to say and instead sheepishly stared at the floor.

'It's just clothing bits and a couple of books,' said Kirsty, holding up the box.

'Thank you. So umm ... do you want to come inside?' Heather mumbled, trying not to breathe on Kirsty.

'No,' she replied sharply. 'Listen, Heather, I don't think I will ever be able to forgive you for what you've done. I still struggle to even believe it myself!' she let out a fake disbelieving laugh.

'I mean to keep that secret from me, for all the time we've been together. Then to put our son in danger the way you did, I mean it's insanity it really is. Most women that find out their spouse has cheated, don't also have to deal with nearly being killed and seeing their own mother murdered in front of them. It's not exactly something you can ever come back from, you know?'

'Kirsty, I'm just so sorry, for everything,' whispered Heather. Now Kirsty didn't know what to say. She stood on the welcome mat, nervously jabbing it with the toe of her boot.

'How is Henry doing?' Heather asked, desperate for news of her son.

'The doctors say he'll never see out of that eye again, but it's healing well and it doesn't hurt as much as it used to. He doesn't want to see you, Heather. I asked him if he wanted to come today but he was adamant against it.' Kirsty's expression was puzzling to behold, while she almost looked sad for Heather, there was still betrayal and anger etched into her face.

'Sometimes he talks about that night, says that he imagined getting out of the restraints and it happened. He imagined that the drones would break, and they did. He's been acting strange, Heather. And I mean who wouldn't after all this but it's like there's something else, I can't explain it. He looks to me for answers but I don't understand any more than he does. He needs you, Heather.' This looked especially hard for her to say.

Tears were dribbling down Heather's cheeks, she longed to see her son's face and hold him tightly to her chest.

'Maybe give it some time and he will want to see you again,' said Kirsty, forming a very brief but genuine smile.

She handed Heather the box of mixed belongings and pulled out a magazine from the side, gently placing it on top. It was a thick glossy covered comic book and across the top, in large striking capitals letters was the name Harrow. Below was an illustration of Harrow rescuing the Chinese President's son from the clutches of a demon.

'It became so popular in the Republic of China that they started printing copies in English, I thought you might like it. Apparently, there's going to be a series.'

Heather stared at the comic book in disbelief, taking the box from Kirsty.

'I don't know if you've been watching the news at the moment, but things are pretty bad out there. People are going missing, there are shootings every other week and another apartment block went up in flames.'

'For years I hated the idea of Harrow, a lawless, unchecked, merciless vigilante. But strangely, I've started to see why you did it. The police aren't able to do what you do, even the super ones,' said Kirsty heavily.

'Henry might not be ready for his mum, but New London needs its Harrow. But not the Harrow you once were. It needs a hero the people can look up to, who does what's right even if it's not the easiest way, who sacrifices every piece of herself for the betterment of those she protects. They need you back Heather, we all do.'

Kirsty smiled gently and turned away from Heather without another word. Heather stood by the front door for several minutes, once Kirsty had walked out of sight her gaze slid to the front of the comic book. Where Harrow stood in an over exaggerated dynamic and powerful stance, hot orange particles drifted in front of her and a vicious red sky filled the background.

Gathering all her shopping and the box, Heather bustled into the apartment. She discarded the satchel full of booze in the shoe cupboard and heaved the shopping and box onto the cluttered dining room table. She flung her coat onto the back of the chair and hunched forward gripping her hands onto her thighs tightly. She stared at her shoes, her mind raced uncontrollably.

Her breathing was short and sharp, her greasy hair dangled down across her face as she bent over in the living room trying to decide. Picking herself up and taking a huge deliberate breath in and out, she stood up straight and went to get dressed.

*Harrow Will Return
In Fateweaver Volume 2*

Robin

I dedicate my first book to you
Imagination is your greatest tool
Share yours with the world and know
that you are my greatest creation

Special thanks

To Vince, Rebecca, Richard, Peter and Cathryne ... for being my treasured guinea pigs

To Jo ... for your keen eyes

To Polly ... for your voice

To Jack and Emily ... for showing me it's possible to do it all

To Kate ... for your talented hands and channelling my vision

To Mum and Dad ... for always saying, 'you can, Cam!'

To Robin ... for going to sleep when I needed you to

To Becky ... for your patience, love and astounding encouragement

And you ... for taking the chance on me

29251146R00169

Printed in Great Britain
by Amazon